Red

The Watchmaker

Printed in the United States of America

Publishers Cataloging-in-Publication Data

Witt, Amanda Beth.
　The Watchmaker / Amanda Witt.
　pages cm.
　Series : The Red Series.
　ISBN 978-0-9965761-2-3

1. Totalitarianism--Fiction. 2. Dystopias. 3. Dystopian fiction. 4. Science fiction. I. Series. II. Title.

PS3623.I8765 W38 2015
813.4 --dc23   2015945737

Cover Image Pixabay, MysticsArtDesign

River Jude Press
www.riverjudepress.com

For Lian

and Ellie, Lili, Molly, Talia, Guille, Jennai, Isaac

The Watchmaker

Book Three in *The Red Series*

Amanda Witt

River Jude Press

Chapter 1

I awoke to a heavy feeling of dread, shaking off dreams in which I ran through a huge house full of windows, turning frantically from one to another, seeing Tristan smirking at me through every one.

Though it was a cloudy day, the room seemed too bright, and when I sat up everything went round in circles. I held still until the dizziness passed. I kept intending to stand up, but the effort seemed beyond me. I couldn't be sick—not now—we didn't have time. Sheer frustration made tears come to my eyes.

Fiona peeked in, looking fresh and pretty and wide awake. "Oh, you're up," she said, coming the rest of the way into the room and studying me critically. "You look awful."

"Thanks." It came out as a sort of croak.

Fiona's face grew alarmed. She hurried to my side and laid a cool hand against my forehead.

"You're feverish," she said. "And you look like you're about to fall over. Lie back down."

I let myself fall back down against the pillows.

"Did you sleep restfully, or did you have nightmares about Tristan all night?" Fiona said.

"Nightmares."

She nodded knowingly. "And before last night, how long

1

has it been since you got a full night's sleep? A refreshing night, not one when you were worrying about something?"

I shrugged. It wasn't a very good shrug, since I was lying down, but I didn't care.

Fiona shook her head at me. "You haven't had a good night's sleep since you arrived on this island. And before you came—you had, what, two nights in that boat?"

I nodded. It might have been three nights, but what was the point of sorting that out? She was right, I was tired.

"And before that you were wandering around in the dark woods with wild men and Guardians and wardens all chasing after you?"

I nodded again.

"And before that you were being terrorized by city meetings?"

This time I didn't bother to nod. Was she going to ask me questions until I begged for mercy?

Fiona frowned. "No wonder you're exhausted. And being exhausted lowers your resistance. You've probably got a virus that will wear itself out soon enough, but I'll send Angus after the doctor just to be sure."

My eyes were heavy. It was all I could do to keep them open. Mostly open.

Occasionally open.

"Stay here," Fiona said, sounding very far away.

Maybe I slept some more, or maybe I was in that twilight world of half-sleep. Sometimes I heard noises, voices, but they seemed very far away. Once I felt a hand on my forehead and heard a man's voice. Someone raised me up and put a glass against my lips, and I came awake feeling panicked, trying to turn my face away, but Fiona urged me to swallow and I did, or dreamed I did.

Then a door shut and everything was quiet.

***

The next time I awoke, the house was dark and silent. It felt very late.

I put my hand out—Fiona wasn't in bed with me. She must have been sleeping in another room. I hoped I hadn't given her whatever illness I had.

When I swung my legs over the side of the bed the room spun. I waited, and the dizziness passed. Quietly, carefully, I made my way to the door and out into the hallway, holding on to the wall for balance. I could hear the clock ticking in the main room. Somewhere someone was snoring gently. I felt weak and unsteady, and I didn't want to fall and wake anyone up.

I made it to the bathroom and then stood leaning against the sink, drinking water from the faucet. I was very thirsty.

Though I felt wide awake, when I finally made it back to Fiona's room and lay down, I fell asleep immediately.

Distantly I heard someone I knew, someone from home.

"No, you may not," Fiona said. "The last thing she needs is for you to catch it, too."

"Just let me see her," he said. "That's all I ask. I won't even go into the room."

My sister's voice grew gentle. "She'll be all right. I promise. But she wouldn't want you to see her in such a state. Wait until she's feeling better and can sit up and brush her hair and put on a fresh nightgown."

But I didn't care about any of that. If he were here, he wouldn't let Tristan find me, or the wardens, or—I couldn't remember who else frightened me. That was bad. It was dangerous not to know the enemy. He could be watching me and I'd never know it, not if I didn't know he was the enemy.

I tried to call out for Farrell Dean and tried to sit up, but the air in the room was so heavy, pressing down on me like water, pushing me back under into sleep that felt more like drowning.

Then it was dark, and then it was daylight again, or maybe I dreamed the changing shadows in the room.

"The watchmaker watches all the time," Angel said. "That's what watchmakers do. He watches the watch."

I sat bolt upright in bed. The room reeled, and I shut my eyes tight until I thought maybe it had stopped moving. Then, cautiously, I opened them again. The first thing I saw was a note on the bedside table.

"Ring for me!" it said. It was propped against a little silver bell. Fiona, of course—I couldn't see my father dotting his i with a heart.

But summoning my sister with a bell felt way too bossy, and besides I didn't want to call attention to myself. Instead I got out of bed and promptly lost my balance, knocking noisily into the nightstand and a chair.

Fiona came running. She took my arm and helped me back into bed. Then, going to the dresser, she poured a glass of water from a pitcher there.

"This is the first time you've been awake in ages," she said, handing the glass to me. "You're bound to be dehydrated." She looked bright-eyed and healthy, and the cut on her cheek was healing well. How long had I slept?

Before I could ask, Fiona was pressing a hand against my forehead. "No fever. That's good. You haven't had any for about twelve hours now. How do you feel?"

"I'm lightheaded," I admitted. There was no point in pretending otherwise, when I was clutching the bedcovers to stay upright. "But I think I'm better." I didn't feel sick any more, just weak.

"Do you want something to eat? I've been baking."

As if a switch had been flipped, I suddenly smelled sweet pastry. My mouth filled with saliva and my stomach growled ominously.

Fiona smiled. "Is that a yes?"

I nodded, swallowing. "And a bath," I said. My hair felt lank and my nightgown was crumpled and sticking to me in places, as if I'd sweated heavily in it and then it had dried.

"You truly must be feeling better," Fiona said. "Think you can bathe without drowning while I make you some breakfast?"

She supported me down the hall to the bathroom, insisting all the while that she would bring me breakfast in bed. I let her talk, but it wasn't going to happen. I wasn't going back to bed. The ominous dreams that had been pursuing me hadn't left now that I was fully awake, wouldn't leave even when I splashed my face with cold water. Even after I bathed and washed my hair, the dreams hovered just outside my field of vision.

Once I was clean and dressed in a fresh nightgown, I unlatched the bathroom window and managed to shove it open a crack, my arms trembling. I leaned my head against the cold glass, breathed in the crisp fresh air. It made me shiver, but it cleared my head. Leaning there, feeling the chilly autumn breeze against my damp skin, I listened to the sounds of the house. Pans clattered in the kitchen; a man's voice—Rory maybe, or Mick—said something unintelligible and Fiona laughed. Everything seemed normal, but I still didn't feel safe. I was certain something bad had happened while I slept.

Shoving the window shut, I took care to latch it. Then I turned and caught sight of myself in the mirror, white night-gown, pale face, wet hair still a shade too dark.

Of course something bad had happened, though not

while I slept. I'd been kidnapped by Tristan, my deceased mother's childhood boyfriend, and very nearly drowned by him. Maybe that's all it was. Bad memories, bad dreams, and illness, all of which would fade away soon enough.

By the time I'd finished bathing I didn't have much choice; I had to lie down again. It felt good to be clean, and Fiona had changed the sheets and fluffed the pillows and featherbed as well.

Once I was settled she brought me a breakfast tray holding two fried eggs, two pieces of wholemeal toast, five slices of bacon, an apple, some cheese, a piece of peach pie, a mug of mint tea, and a glass of milk. It was stupid, but the sight of that tray of food—and of my sister's friendly face—made my eyes tear up.

"What's wrong?" Fiona said anxiously, pushing my hair back from my forehead.

I didn't even try to answer.

"You'll feel better after you eat," she said, picking up the fork and putting it in my hand. "And then when Farrell Dean gets back from helping with the milking, I'll let him come see you. He's been hounding me non-stop since you fell ill. And Angus and Rory and Papa have been keeping watch around the place, taking turns patrolling, just in case more trouble shows up. Not that Mama has any more scorned lovers lurking around. So you're perfectly safe, and you can rest for as long as you need to without worrying about a thing."

That wasn't true. Even if I wasn't in imminent danger, my friends and old people over in Optica were threatened on all sides, starving, waiting to be killed off. And Meritt was hanging around with Angel, with no idea that his father was sufficiently cold-blooded to have stolen me from my family when I was a newborn.

Fiona chatted while I ate my eggs. When I moved on to the toast and bacon, she went to her dressing table and came back with two photographs. "I found these while you were sleeping," she said, climbing onto the bed to sit beside me. "Our grandparents, when they were young."

The first picture was of our mother's parents. Grandfather was tall and thin, and had been caught gesturing with his pipe as if he'd been in the middle of saying something. Nana was a good deal more trim as well, and in her youthful face I saw elements of my own, the delicate bone structure that weight and age had obscured. She also looked bright-eyed and humorous; it made me sad, to think I'd never know her that way. She was still sweet, but so vague and confused.

At least I'd met this set of grandparents. The other picture was of Eric Alleyn's parents, complete strangers who were my own flesh and blood. I'd never met them and never would, because they'd both died years before. If it hadn't been for Angel, I'd at least have gotten to know Granny Rose.

For some reason I'd assumed that Eric Alleyn looked like his father, but it was his mother he favored. His strong features were softened a little in her face, though, and she was smiling in a way he never did, her dark eyes warm and bright, her expression open and untroubled. The photograph was black-and-white, so I couldn't tell what shade of red her hair had been, but it was very curly, cut to just below her earlobes. Maybe mine would curl that much, too, if I cut it short.

Fiona was smiling fondly at the photograph.

"You can tell she's not a worrier, can't you?" she said. "After she came to live with us, anytime Papa got all wound up Granny would tell him, 'It's nothing until it's something. Don't chase trouble. Let it escape whenever it wants to.' I think Angus takes after her a bit. And maybe Mick—although he does chase trouble, come to think of it, just for fun."

"And Papa was their only child?" I was thinking about missing twins, and Fiona understood.

"Yes, he was the only one," she said. "He was an ordinary single baby, and they never had any others. It was a late marriage—Granny was almost forty when she had Papa. I'm not sure how old Grandpa was. I never met him, of course. He died before we were born. He doesn't look like Papa at all, does he?"

I studied my grandfather's face.

"No. But he looks familiar, somehow."

We leaned together, turning the picture this way and that, trying to trace Eric Alleyn's features in his father's. Eric Alleyn's father was broad-shoulder and smiling, but not with his eyes. Or maybe I was reading into his expression the things others had told me—that he was often sad and troubled, that he sometimes vanished for days.

"Maybe it's only his expression," I said finally.

"Or maybe it isn't Papa we're seeing in him," Fiona said. "Maybe it's Mick." She smiled. "Grandpa was quite good looking, wasn't he?"

I hadn't thought about that, but she was right. Mick did resemble him, at least vaguely, and they both were strikingly handsome men. Rory was good-looking too, but Rory—

"Rory's handsome in a completely different way," Fiona said. "The Drewblood way. Genetics is a funny thing."

So was the way my sister could sometimes finish my thoughts.

"Fiona?" I said, leaning back against the headboard. "When I was in Optica, did you ever have funny dreams?"

She pulled her knees up and wrapped her arms around them, turning her face toward the window and the gray drizzly day.

"I never had dreams like Uncle Gabriel had about Rafe," she said, "But sometimes I dreamed that I was cold and couldn't get warm, or hungry and couldn't get full, and that didn't make sense. I've always had everything I needed, warm clothes, a warm house, food whenever I wanted it." Her eyes met mine. "But you didn't."

"Not always," I said, and took another bite of apple.

"What about you?"

I finished chewing and swallowed. "I dreamed about the sea all the time," I said. "But as far as I knew I'd never seen it. Usually in my dream I would be standing on the sand looking across the sea. Sometimes light would be dancing on the water, and sometimes the sky would be so gray that I'd look at the horizon and couldn't tell where it ended and the sea began."

Fiona smiled and touched my hand. "All those mornings when I went to check the beach," she said. "And finally, there you were."

Eric Alleyn appeared in the doorway.

"It's clearly too late to tell you to go easy," he said, nodding at my almost-empty tray.

My mouth was full, but I smiled at him. He smiled back at me, the corners of his eyes crinkling. He really was an attractive man when he smiled, I thought, even if in a more workaday sort of way than his poor unhappy father. And he was solid and real, a force to be reckoned with despite his bad leg. He had swept in on his horse and saved my life. Though my bad dreams hadn't completely faded, I felt a bit safer, seeing my father standing there.

"I'm glad you're better," he said, studying me as if to make sure I really had improved. "Let me know if you need anything."

"I will. Thank you."

He stepped forward and smoothed my hair back from my forehead, leaving his hand there for a moment, warm and strong and reassuring. "Fiona's a good nurse," he said, and when he turned to smile at her, he caught sight of the photographs on the bed. "She takes after my father in that respect.

He was quite a healer. Unlike him, however, Fiona chatters. Don't let her wear you out."

"I'm being careful," Fiona said demurely.

Eric Alleyn winked at me, then turned and stumped out of the room. The sudden absence where a large male figure had been reminded me of something.

"Who else has been here?" I asked Fiona, vaguely remembering hearing a voice I hadn't recognized.

"Just the boys," she said. "And Gabriel, off and on. Did they disturb you?"

"No, I meant who has been right here, in this room?"

"Only Papa and me, and one time the doctor. He didn't come as soon as I wanted, but he finally got here." As she spoke a reserved expression crossed her face, and panic rose in my throat.

"What is it?" I said. "Is it Ezzie? Is he all right?"

Fiona looked startled at my tone. "He's improving," she said. "And you only had a regular old virus, just as I thought. Not what Ezzie has."

That possibility hadn't crossed my mind. Now that it had, I felt the need to verify. "I don't have what Ezzie has," I repeated.

"No. You were exhausted and that made your immune system weak, but you'll make a full recovery."

"Good." I sat up straighter and thought about getting out of bed. "I need to get moving. I have to figure out how we can get back to Optica."

"Not today," Fiona said. "It'll take a few days before you're completely well again."

"I don't have a few days." And besides I felt too vulnerable, lying there in a nightgown. I had to get up.

Fiona's expression was stern. "Rushing things won't do any good," she said. "You'll only give yourself a relapse."

Feeling rebellious, I turned my face away from her,

toward the window. Through the drizzle I could see the little white gazebo where we'd sat the first day I came to this place. That day felt like a million years ago. Anything could have happened in Optica while I was gone; all my friends could be dead, and Meritt, too.

All the same, frustratingly, the thought of being out in the rain made me want to pull the covers over my head and go back to sleep. I felt better, now that the food was hitting my bloodstream, but I was still so tired.

Fiona saw the direction of my gaze. Getting up, she pulled the curtains shut, closing out the dreary cold day.

"I have to get up," I said stubbornly, arguing with my own body as much as with my sister. "I have to talk to Farrell Dean. We have to figure out what to do."

Fiona crossed her arms over her chest. "Farrell Dean isn't here right now."

"But I have to do something." My chin wobbled as if I might suddenly burst into tears, and I had to stop and get myself under control before I went on. "Our friends could be dying over there."

Fiona's expression softened. "Rest until he gets back," she said. "The very minute he comes in, I'll send him to you."

I considered that. I couldn't do anything until he got back, and I was so tired. But lying there—closing my eyes, falling asleep, so that anyone could walk in and see me and I'd never even know it …

Fiona saw my glance go to the window, the door. "Everything's locked," she said. "All the windows, the outside doors. And, as I said, Papa is standing guard. We won't let anybody hurt you. You're safe here."

"Do you promise?" It was childish, but I wanted her to say it.

"I promise," she said. "You're safe."

Chapter 2

With a lurch I sat up and opened my eyes. I felt better—
so much better that it felt wrong to be in bed in the
middle of the day.

Cautiously I stretched, expecting aches and pains, but
there were none. I felt strong and hopeful, free from the
dread that had plagued me earlier. Maybe it was only that I'd
eaten and then slept well, or maybe it was the cheerful light
that now was filtering in around the edge of the curtains—
not the sort of light that came with heavy gray drizzle, but
clear soft autumn sunshine.

"How long have I slept?" I said aloud, testing my voice.

"How should I know?"

I jerked around, caught one bare glimpse of a male figure at my bedside, and went scrambling away from him with
a small shriek, tangling in the bedclothes, expecting any
moment to feel hands grabbing me.

"Hey—stop—I didn't do anything!"

It took a moment for the words to penetrate, but the
voice reached me instantly. I knew that voice. It was a safe
voice.

My fog of panic cleared and I saw Angus waving his
hands at me, making flapping gestures he evidently intended
to be calming.

"Shhhhhh!" he said. "You're going to get me in big trouble!"

"With who?"

"Fee, of course." He crossed the room in two long strides and eased the bedroom door closed. "She's out front messing with her dead flowers, and she wouldn't let me in the house until I promised not to disturb you." He squinted at me. "You're not disturbed, are you?"

"Not anymore." I patted my chest, as if that would help my heart rate settle back to normal.

"Good." Angus went to the window and pulled open the curtains, letting in more of the cheerful bright light. It flared in his bright hair and threw a panel of warmth across my face. "I figured you could use a little cheering up right about now, and Fee, she doesn't get that. She thinks getting well is all about lying around sipping mint tea." He grimaced. "She can just about drown a person in mint tea."

I smiled at him. "So you're here to rescue me from boredom and tea?"

"I am." He sat down on the edge of the bed, his weight tilting me toward him. He smelled like outdoors, like rain and hay, and it made me long to be outside. "You must be feeling better," he said. "When I peeked in yesterday you looked like death warmed over. You look half human today."

"Thanks," I said dubiously.

Angus grinned. "So," he said, bouncing a little on the mattress. "You want to hear my good news?"

I did.

"It's a secret, okay?"

"Okay."

"Farrell Dean and I are going to break into the Dream Recorder's house this afternoon."

I had no idea why I was supposed to think this was good news, but Angus was looking at me expectantly and I hated to disappoint him. "Oh," I said, trying to sound enthusiastic. "Why?"

"Because we need to, right?" He glanced at the door and leaned toward me, his freckled face alight. "We need to know what we're getting into over there on that other island. The experiment could be anything—a drug trial, mass hypnosis, behavior control, biological warfare. Tor even suggested electrical implants, like maybe the experimenters could zap you when you were bad." He pointed at his head and made a circular motion, and I didn't know whether he meant that zapping would make us crazy, or that Tor's idea was crazy. "The point is, that experiment could be anything, and if we don't figure it out, we're walking in blind."

This was beginning to make sense.

"You've been talking about Optica?"

Angus nodded. "The whole time you've been sick. Farrell Dean and Ezzie gave us the scoop, and since then we've been talking, arguing, discussing, planning, arguing some more." His face turned smug. "I had the idea about the Dream Recorder. She has all those books, with information going back farther than anything else. There might be hints there, right? Because that Angel guy came to this island to get twins, and if he's not super old then before him somebody else must have come, and when he or they did, somebody might have seen something or heard something, and anything interesting that happens is bound to end up getting back to the Dream Recorder eventually, right?"

"I guess so."

Angus nodded. "It's true. Everybody talks to the Dream Recorder. Except for us, of course. Alleyns don't talk to Dream Recorders. But we don't know anything, except what we already know we know, so the fact that we don't talk to her doesn't matter. Right?"

I was feeling a little disoriented, but Angus didn't wait

for a response. "And anyway she's not acting right, the Dream Recorder." He lowered his voice and leaned in again. "She's acting *suspicious*."

"She is?"

"Oh yeah. Gabriel says she won't let him in her house, and she ought to because he's a Dream Recorder himself now. He's entitled. So she's bound to be hiding something."

Or else she was just a maddening old woman.

There was a chance, though, that Angus was right. Gabriel had said something similar to me, the first time I'd met him—something about the old Ionia Dream Recorder having edited the record books, shaping what posterity saw. Maybe the surviving Dream Recorder, the Doria one, had information she didn't want to get out, and maybe that information would help us.

Angus was watching me, waiting for my reaction.

"It's a good idea," I conceded. "But she's looking for Farrell Dean—she sent those men on horseback after him. Shouldn't he stay a long way away from her?"

"Yeah, but those men, Lester and Cobb? They're stuck keeping an eye on Gabriel's house, thanks to Earl. He's pretending to guard someone there, to keep their attention. And it's not like Farrell Dean's going to come face-to-face with the Dream Recorder. That's the whole point of breaking in while she's gone."

I studied my brother. "Nobody else will go with you?"

Angus shrugged. "Haven't asked. Won't ask. Papa's all into privacy, and those books have information about everybody on the island. No way would he look at one, and he'd probably feel honor-bound to order the rest of us to leave them alone. And then we'd either have to say hey, we're grown up now, Papa can't tell us what to do, or else we'd have to give it up. And it's too good an idea to give up."

"So you haven't even told Rory?"

He glanced again at the closed door. "Rory would feel honor-bound to mention it to Papa, just because a guest's safety is involved. Although it's perfectly safe. Really, it is."

"What about Gabriel?"

Angus frowned. "It's my idea—why should I let Gabriel Drewblood take it over? And anyway why should anyone else go with us? Not one of us knows anything about Optica, so it won't do any good for us to look at those books. We might read right over the crucial parts, not even realizing what we're seeing. Nope." He shook his head. "Farrell Dean's the only one who can do it."

"Or Ezzie."

"Ezzie's not back on his feet yet."

"Or—"

Angus waved his hands, telling me no, but his eyes lit up. "You'd do it, though, wouldn't you? If you were well, I mean. Because you've got nerves of steel. Farrell Dean told us what you did, over there. All the things you did. You're something else."

I smiled at him; his enthusiasm matched my newly hopeful mood. "When are you going?" I said, lowering my eyes and straightening the blanket over my legs.

"In just a few minutes. The past couple of days I've been keeping an eye on the Dream Recorder, see, so we'd know her schedule. Farrell Dean's been doing my chores so I could watch her. Here in a bit he's going to meet me in the alley behind her house, and then he's going in while I keep an eye on her. See? Perfectly safe. If she starts back home sooner than expected, I'll delay her. Farrell Dean will scope things out, and with luck we'll learn exactly what we need to make our trip to Optica a success."

I lifted my eyes to my brother's. "I'm impressed," I said. "It's a really good plan."

He grinned. "That it is."

"And since I'm feeling much, much better—" I pulled back the covers and swung my legs toward the edge of the bed.

"Oh, no." Angus took me by the shoulders and tried to push me back down. When I resisted he let go and leapt to his feet, waving his hands at me again. "I came to cheer you up, not to get you in trouble with Fee."

"But you're right," I said, climbing out of bed. "I can't stand the thought of more mint tea." Mentally I apologized to my sister. "I think I could get completely well, if I could just get out of bed and do something useful."

Angus didn't say anything, but his brow was creased with concern.

"Truly," I said. "I've got to get out of here. In fact I'm going out, whether I'm with you or not. I can't stand being cooped up any longer."

"Fee will be furious," Angus said, but the objection was automatic.

"If it's safe for Farrell Dean, it's safe for me."

"It's safe," he assured me. Then his expression changed. "But he won't want you going in, either, I don't think."

"Farrell Dean is not my keeper."

"No, but he's crazy about you." Suddenly alarmed, Angus went on. "You do know that, right? I'm not giving anything away that you don't already know."

"I know," I said, shifting uncomfortably. "But—"

"Yeah, yeah." Angus cut me off. "Love triangle, bad-boy enchanter, Fee told us all about it."

My face turned red.

"When Farrell Dean wasn't around, of course," Angus assured me. "But the point is, Farrell Dean's been awfully worried about you. First that thing with Tristan, then you getting so sick—it doesn't seem fair to the guy, to hand him one more worry."

My face still felt scorching hot, but I ignored my own embarrassment. "He's tougher than you think," I said. "And besides, you said it was safe."

"It is—"

"And he'll see that we can cover way more ground together. If there are lots of books, I mean."

"There are *tons* of books. I saw them through the window."

"See? It would go faster with two of us."

Angus shot me a furtive look. I stood up straight, trying to convey good health and energy.

After a moment he sighed. "You really want to go?"

"I really do."

"There's no way she'll let you," he said, glancing yet again at the closed door. "She's like a dragon guarding her gold."

"I'll go out the window. We'll leave her a note so she won't worry."

"And you'll tell her you insisted?"

"Absolutely. I'll write it in the note, and afterwards I'll tell everybody that you tried to talk me out of it."

"Which I did," Angus said, giving me a severe look.

"You did," I agreed.

Angus nodded, then grinned. "All right," he said. "Get dressed and get out the window, and meet me at the stable. I'll keep Fee distracted long enough for you to get away." He stuck out his hand. "Partners in crime."

"Partners," I said, shaking my brother's hand.

Chapter 3

The alley was deserted save for a yellow cat asleep on a discarded three-legged chair in a wedge of late autumn sunshine. He was lying on his side, so utterly relaxed that he looked like a puddle of butter.

The sun did feel good; I was glad the rain of the morning had passed. But I was expecting more company than a cat. "Where's Farrell Dean?" I asked.

"He'll be here." Angus was crouched down, sorting through a pile of rubble. His sleeves were rolled up and the sun glinted in the gingery hair on his arms. There really were other redheads in the world, not just me. I was still getting used to that fact.

"Meanwhile—" Angus stood, hefted a brick in his hand, and unceremoniously heaved it through the lowest window, sending shattering glass sparkling across the ground.

"Just like that?" I said, startled.

"What did you expect?"

"Something quieter."

Angus shrugged. "I don't do quiet very well," he said.

Apparently nobody heard. At least, no one came rushing down the alley shouting at us to stop. The yellow cat glowered at us, his ears laid back against his head, but he didn't bother to get up.

Angus nudged at the largest piece of fallen glass with the toe of his boot. Then he picked up another brick and knocked loose the jagged bits of glass that clung to the window frame. I moved closer, hitching my dress up around my knees, getting ready to climb. We had seen the Dream Recorder heading off down the street, just as Angus had predicted, so the clock was ticking; if Farrell Dean didn't show, I'd do this on my own. And if he did show, then I could avoid all argument by presenting him with a done deed.

"Wait," Angus said. "There's always one more piece."

He pulled out a handkerchief and carefully swept the sill. Then he bent and cupped his hands, and when I stepped into them he boosted me up and into a small room containing only two armchairs and a small table. It was the room where the Dream Recorder interviewed people, I supposed.

"Duck out of sight," Angus said from the alley, glancing over his shoulder. Then he looked up at me, nodding in satisfaction. "Never mind. It's him."

Farrell Dean appeared beside my brother. When he saw me he looked taken aback, and then his face went carefully blank, the way it did when he was reining in his temper.

"Hi," I said brightly. "I'm better now. I came to help you."

Farrell Dean's eyebrows went up. "So I see."

"Need a boost?" Angus asked him.

"No."

Behind Farrell Dean, Angus made a face. "He's mad," he mouthed, pointing. Aloud, he said, "Any change in our plans?"

Farrell Dean shook his head.

"Then I'll leave you to it, and I'll go keep an eye on the old hag."

I felt like I ought to give him a disapproving look for his rudeness—Fiona would have—but all I could do was grin at him. He'd plucked me out of my sickbed, put me on the back of his horse, and brought me into town to do something useful for Optica.

With a final wave to me, Angus took off down the alley at a jog.

Farrell Dean crossed his arms over his chest.

"Aren't you coming?" I said, moving away from the window. "It's probably not a good idea to hang around out there."

He caught up with me in the next room. It was a dark and musty kitchen where the faucet was dripping and the sink was dark with rust. One of the cabinets had torn loose from the wall and sat loomingly on a countertop, and in the corner of the floor black flies swarmed around a pail of garbage.

"Slow down," Farrell Dean said, catching my arm and turning me to face him. In the dim room he studied my face.

"We're on a schedule," I said, pulling away. "You can scold me later."

"I don't want to scold you. I want to get a good look at you, make sure you're all right."

"I'm fine." I gave him a quelling look. "And you do too want to scold me. You just want to make sure I'm up for it first."

Farrell Dean almost smiled.

"Either that or you want to make sure you're scolding me and not Fiona."

His face changed, but before he could speak I turned away.

"Come on," I said. "The clock's ticking."

We went through the kitchen to a doorway on the other side. It was blocked by a metal grate, and through it I could see into a dim room filled floor-to-ceiling with books, hundreds of them, maybe even thousands. Shelves lined all four walls, leaving only a small threadbare rectangle of carpet in the middle of the room. This was the room we wanted.

Farrell Dean reached past me and gave the grate a shake.

"Is it locked?" I scanned the kitchen as if a key might be lying around in plain sight.

"Just jammed, I think. It's rusty." Farrell Dean pulled again and the grate came rattling open noisily, sliding sideways and folding against itself.

Other than the crowded shelves of books, the room was bare save for a few musty-smelling boxes stacked under the windows and a brass lamp sitting on the floor in a corner. There was no table, and no chairs either. This was basically a storage room. A door in the far wall was partly covered by another grate, half-open. It led to a staircase that looked very steep and even darker than the room.

I reached for the lamp, flicking it on just as Farrell Dean hit a switch on the wall and filled the room with an unpleasantly greenish artificial light that made me suddenly queasy.

"Open the curtains if you want to," Farrell Dean said, seeing my expression. "The windows look onto the alley—it should be safe enough." When I pulled the curtains open, clouds of dust motes rose into the air, lit by sunshine struggling to penetrate the dirty pane.

Farrell Dean was already pulling down a book. A cloud of dust billowed and he waved it away. When he opened the book, bits of the cracked leather cover came loose and drifted to the floor.

"Can you see well enough with just the lamp?" I said, turning off the sickly overhead light. Without looking up, he nodded.

I was fiddling with the lights because I was a little overwhelmed. It was a good thing I'd come along to help—there were so many books, far more than I'd expected. Even with two of us, we'd never get through all these in the few minutes we had. It would take days—weeks—to go through them. And what if the information wasn't even in the Dream Recorder books? Maybe it was in the musty boxes stacked under the window.

Maybe it wasn't here at all—that quelling thought flitted past and I tried to ignore it. With all these books, surely we'd find something of use.

I opened the top box, careful to not get grime on Fiona's cloak or her pretty turquoise dress. There were lots of loose papers in the box, layered in no apparent order. Some looked like dream records, their edges jagged as if they'd been torn from books, but others were grocery lists, cryptic jottings, half-finished sentences. I sorted through layer after layer, losing heart as I went deeper into the box. None of the notes here looked very promising.

"Nothing here," I said, sitting back on my heels. "Are you finding anything?"

"Actually, I think I am." Farrell Dean sounded distracted. He had a book open and was flipping pages, scanning rapidly.

I left the boxes and went to him, leaning against his shoulder so I could see what he was reading. Tilting the book toward me he began to read aloud. "The illness is passing. Most people will be functional in a day or two. The Dream Recorders are all in place."

"In place? Already?" I pressed in closer, studying the page. "But that means the Dream Recorders were there before the illness was over, and that doesn't make sense. How could anyone know that the amnesia would be permanent? How could they know they'd need Dream Recorders?"

"Exactly," Farrell Dean said, looking down at me. We were so close I could see the flecks of gold in his hazel eyes. Hurriedly I looked back down at the spiky black handwriting.

"It was all deliberate," I said. I had suspected so, but I didn't like it; I wanted this island to be different.

"What was deliberate?" Angus came into the room. "Don't worry," he said. "She's having her hair done. What hair she has left, anyway. I'll get back before they're through with her. So, what was deliberate?"

"Optica had a devastating electrical event, and Aislin had a plague," I said. "Both conveniently resulting in mass amnesia, right about the same time. And the Dream Recorders knew about the amnesia before it happened."

Angus frowned. "So they didn't just steal people from here to put in the Optica experiment," he said. "They messed with us, too."

I nodded, sorry to be the bearer of bad news.

"But they don't do anything else to us," Angus said. "I mean, we're normal otherwise, right? Or do I think we're normal but you think Optica's normal?" He went on before we could answer. "What I'm saying is, are we the control group? Aislin? We have to be the control group, because you need rescuing and we don't. Right?"

"That would be my guess," Farrell Dean said. "And Aislin's much larger than Optica, with way more people. The smaller group is bound to be the active part of the experiment."

"And we just produce twins for it." Angus nodded, turning to the rows and rows of books. "It would take some doing, to give everyone on Aislin amnesia. Who could do something like that? Who'd have that much power?"

"I don't know," I said. "Someone Sir Tom calls the watchmaker."

"He must have a lot of resources, a lot of people helping him." Angus turned to Farrell Dean. "Where do you suppose he is? Here somewhere? Or is he one of your Watchers?"

Farrell Dean shook his head. "Our guess is that he was

on the mainland, and got killed when the time of the ashes began. Sir Tom told Red that the watchmaker was gone, and that the watch was ticking itself out alone."

"Well, I for one hope Sir Tom is right," Angus said. "Good riddance to the watchmaker, I say." He looked around the room. "Okay. Good work. I'd better get back."

Just like that, he was gone again.

For awhile Farrell Dean and I flicked silently through books, through page after page of spiky handwriting recording dream after dream after dream. After that first hopeful discovery, there was nothing. Just nonsense.

"These are just plain old ordinary dreams," Farrell Dean said, putting yet another book back on the shelf. "Random things. What's the point?"

I had been thinking about that. "Tor said the Dream Recorders were trying to help people remember," I began. "He said they were trying to make sense of the memories that came back to people as dreams."

"But why would they do that, if they'd caused the amnesia to begin with? Unless that's part of the experiment— seeing what people remember after their memories are wiped."

"That could be," I said. "But the Watchers said something, that night Meritt and I spied on them. They were worrying because the past wasn't staying buried. It was bleeding through. So maybe instead of helping people remember, the Dream Recorders were doing the exact opposite. Maybe they were monitoring memories, making sure people didn't remember too much."

"That makes sense," Farrell Dean said. "If anyone remembered that he had a past, he might have tried to escape the present. But if the Dream Recorders knew what people were starting to remember, they could misdirect them. They could call memories dreams, and dreams memories. That

Grateful Day event is probably nothing but a smokescreen. Whereas—" he gestured at the books—"giant metal birds that carry people through the sky might be real."

"Yeah, right."

He grinned. "Could be. It's a fun thought, anyway."

He looked up at the row of shelves and ran a hand gently over a long row of crumbling book spines, then chose another book and opened it with steady hands. But I shivered; I didn't like this. The past should have been written in stone—it happened as it happened, and there it stayed, one sure thing set against a confusing present and an ever-uncertain future.

"What about us?" I said. "They didn't want us to remember, but they didn't do anything in particular to try to stop us, did they? In Optica they just watched us."

Farrell Dean looked at me, considering. "We were in a different situation," he said finally. "We couldn't escape, not with the wall, and the Guardians in the woods, and the sea all around. So maybe it didn't much matter whether we remembered or not."

The room had begun to feel stuffy. Fumbling with the button at the neck of Fiona's cloak, I undid it and let the cloak fall from my shoulders to the floor. Maybe I'd have better luck with a different section of books, I thought. Climbing up on the bottom shelf, I stood on tiptoe and reached for the second book on the top row. It was old, but it looked less well-worn than the other books I'd held. The edges of the pages were smooth.

Stepping back down to the floor, I gently opened it. It made a loud cracking sound as if in protest, and I flinched.

The handwriting in this one wasn't like the writing in the others I'd seen. Instead of the spiky writing, a tiny curling script ran down the page. A different Dream Recorder, then.

And something else was different. The other books had

been completely full. This one had writing on the first and second pages, and then there was nothing. Every page was blank, except for those first two.

Turning back to the beginning, I began to read.

Michael dreamed that he opened his skull, took out his memory, threw it in a barrel of burning trash, and watched as it went up in smoke.

That seemed to confirm our theory. The Dream Recorders were spot-checking to see that memories were thoroughly buried, recording evidence that they were.

When the last wisp of burned memory vanished, Michael turned to go home, but he could no longer find it because the path, mapped in his memory, now was drifting in faint ashes to the ground. Then he realized that he was forever condemned to search for home, wandering in unfamiliar places, asking strangers whether they were his wife, his mother, his brother, his son.

Michael finds his dream intensely disturbing and is not comforted by my reminder that everyone on the island has lost all but the most immediate past.

I shivered. How awful that must have been, to lose your entire past and to know you'd lost it, to lose the people you loved the most, even if they were standing right beside you.

I didn't fully understand how that could happen. Surely, no matter what, I could never forget Rafe or Meritt, or the old people who had been so kind to me. They had shaped me. They were part of who I was, so much so that if I did somehow forget them, I wouldn't be myself any longer. I'd deflate, lose my form, like clothes crumpling shapelessly to the ground when the body inside them is gone. Or would the shaping of me stay? Maybe I was more like concrete, and when the mold was removed I'd still be me …

Farrell Dean coughed, waving away a cloud of dust, and I glanced up at him. I marked clearly in my mind the strong familiar line of his jaw, the way his hair looked gold in some light and brown in others, the steady sure movement of his hands. He was solid. He was as real to me as I was. I couldn't really believe that anyone or anything could make me forget.

After a moment I went back to my book.

The next entry was dated some two years after the first, and now was written in the spiky handwriting that was more prevalent in the books.

Michael has a recurring dream representative of the typical loss-of-self anxiety that many new fathers experience. In his dream someone holds him under water until he drowns. This dream alternates with one in which he is the one holding someone under water. When the person stops thrashing Michael loosens his grip and the body rises toward him, and the dead face that breaks through the surface of the water is his own.

My hands felt unnaturally cold, as if the chilling words had affected the paper on which they were written. I didn't want to read any more, but I had to; this book was different from the others, the dreams seeming to describe how this Michael felt about his amnesia. They weren't nonsense dreams. They might hold some sort of clue.

Michael found this dream troubling enough that he actually came to me to discuss it. Putting it in the context of his life, I told him that it is normal for the father of a new infant, not to mention a colicky one like his own, to feel overwhelmed, to want to "kill" his new role of father and return to a time when he was only himself, a free agent, unburdened by the responsibilities of a family, which could easily "pull him under."

Michael rejected my interpretation, saying that the child was his best reason for living, was a light burden he was happy to bear. As we talked he became irate and called me an irresponsible quack. I do not think Michael Alleyn will be visiting me again.

Michael *Alleyn*? He must have been a member of my family. I'd ask Angus about him as soon we were back outside. Whoever he was—my grandfather, a great-uncle—I kind of liked him.

The next entry was dated a few months later.

Michael continues to struggle with depression, and he also exhibits tendencies toward paranoia. He still refuses to speak to me, so I urged his wife to get him to the hospital for cognitive therapy and pharmaceutical anti-depressant treatments. She tells me he refuses. However, his neighbor Jack Van Stavern says Michael has a knack for healing and appears quite content when tending to the ill or injured, whether human or animal. He also enjoys tinkering with scrap metal and such in Jack's tool shop. It is possible that these outlets will preserve his sanity. Otherwise, I am sorry to say, I fear there is no hope. Some have recovered well from the plague's blow and are proceeding with their lives as if nothing ever happened; others are recovering less well; but Michael Alleyn is by far the worst of all. It is possible he might even attempt to take his own life.

Was this my grandfather, Eric Alleyn's father? He might be. Papa had said Fiona got her nursing skills from his own father, hadn't he? And the Van Staverns did live right down the road.

Hastily I read on. The next entry was dated a full twenty-five years later.

Michael and Rose Alleyn have moved away from Doria. Apparently they have gone into the isolated north woods. Their exact location is not yet known, but no doubt we eventually will track them down.

It should be noted that this abrupt departure is in line with Michael's long history of paranoia and instability. It is to be hoped that he poses no threat to Rose. She has thus far seemed quite able to manage him, but if he worsens or she makes a misstep that unbalances him, there will be no one near to come to her aid.

So this was indeed my grandfather, Granny Rose's husband. My other grandfather had suggested that Eric Alleyn's father wasn't the most reliable person. From what I'd read so far, it sounded as if Grandfather had been very tactful indeed.

There was only one more entry, and it was dated the same month and year of my birth.

Michael Alleyn has drowned.

Rose did not go with Michael on his wanderings, and she did not go with him to the beach that day, for one of his quirks was that he would not permit them both to leave the house at the same time. But when Michael did not return home Rose eventually violated his rule and went looking for him, and thanks to a merciful tide she found his body washed up on the beach.

Rose, a tall woman and quite strong for her age, dragged the body into the woods near the beach and, over the course of two days, managed to dig a sufficient grave. She had no help in this, for the area was isolated and she did not want to leave the body unattended while she fetched her son. In my opinion she was not only concerned about the body, but about the effect it might have on her son, who shows evidence of inheriting Michael's unfortunate tendencies. The crabs and the water had not been kind, and the time required to fetch Eric would only have made matters worse.

While Rose appears grieved and uneasy, there is also a strong undercurrent of relief and, I am certain, guilt for experiencing that relief. I believe that Rose subconsciously is glad to be free of her difficult husband.

It should be noted that Michael Alleyn was known to be a strong swimmer and often tested his limits by going further out than was prudent. Rose believes that perhaps he went too far while trying to work off tension related to a series of dreams he had been having.

Initially Rose resisted describing these dreams, saying that she wished to protect Michael's privacy, but eventually she was persuaded to describe the outline, if not the details. In his dreams Michael saw a man who intended to betray someone he loved. In his dreams Michael was desperate to stop him. The line between fantasy and reality became so blurred that, according to Rose, Michael began traversing the island, searching for this person, hoping to prevent the projected betrayal. This irrational behavior—searching for a man he dreamed—is in keeping with Michael's history of mental instability, and his failure to locate the person he sought likely played a part in exacerbating his risk-taking behavior, as Rose speculated.

If only he had come to me, I might have been able to avert this tragedy, for I could have told him the simple truth: There is no one named Meritt on this island.

I swallowed hard. Then I read that last sentence again, but the words hadn't changed.

Meritt wouldn't betray me—he wouldn't—no matter what Farrell Dean thought, no matter what the Watchers wanted. And how could Michael Alleyn have known about Meritt, anyway? Could my disturbed grandfather see into the future?

No. I was being ridiculous. Fiona might believe in things like that, but I didn't. And anyway Meritt was only a name, and creepy, unnerving coincidences sometimes were just that—coincidences.

"Farrell Dean?" I said, my eyes still on the page. My mouth felt dry and I had a hard time getting the words out. "Have you seen any books that focus just on one person?"

"No. They're all about lots of people. Whoever happened to have a dream and mention it to a Dream Recorder. Why?"

Haltingly I told him about what I'd read.

"Interesting," Farrell Dean said, leaning against the bookshelf. His face was unreadable and his voice didn't sound quite like his own.

"It's not our Meritt," I told him. "It isn't."

Farrell Dean nodded, not quite meeting my eyes, and suddenly I wanted to be somewhere else, somewhere not with him. He knew too much. He knew me too well, and I wasn't at all certain that I knew myself.

"We're almost out of time, and we haven't even begun to do justice to all of these," Farrell Dean said abruptly, turning to survey the crowded shelves. "Let's choose fifteen or twenty and take them with us. Maybe we'll get lucky and choose one that explains the twins."

The twins here weren't controlled, measured, recorded, not like we were in Optica. Angus was right—it was the twins in Optica who were the experiment. In Optica we were watched all the time. We ate what we were told to eat; we worked where we were told to work; we bred where we were told to breed.

"Red?" Farrell Dean said, a note of concern entering his voice. "Are you feeling all right?"

"I'm fine," I said, which wasn't quite true. "Go ahead and choose some books."

"They're more or less in order," he said, scanning the shelves. "I guess the early ones might tell us more."

The light from the bare bulb glinted in his hair; his shirt sleeves were rolled up to his elbows and his shirt wasn't Optica gray. It was a normal shirt for a normal person, which is what Farrell Dean was. He wasn't a rat in an experiment; he was just collateral damage, someone who happened to be born into Optica. He wasn't a twin. He wasn't a specimen. He wasn't a freak.

Now he was looking at me, his eyes quizzical.

"You choose," I said again. "I'm going to look around upstairs."

Without waiting for an answer, I fled, still carrying Michael Alleyn's book.

Chapter 4

The stairs were narrow and unpleasant. They led to a narrow and unpleasant bedroom. Clothes were strewn across the floor, tangled with books and papers. I wasn't going to find anything useful up here. But then, I hadn't expected to. I just needed to be alone for a minute. I needed a chance to regain my equilibrium.

Standing in the middle of the room I opened Michael Alleyn's book again, running a hand over one blank page, then another. It felt as if the Dream Recorder still stood waiting for him to talk to her, as if all these empty pages were listening ears, straining to hear dreams that never came.

Here privacy wasn't stolen, like it was in Optica. Here it was voluntarily given up when people brought their most private thoughts to the Dream Recorders to be written down and analyzed. At least I hadn't done that. I hadn't conspired in my own violation.

And Michael Alleyn hadn't, either, at least not without a fight. Maybe he was crazy, my other grandfather. But I had to like him for at least trying to hold out against the Dream Recorders.

"Hey, Red," Farrell Dean called. "Time's up."

"I'm coming."

Deciding to do a perfunctory search, I nudged at the

mess on the floor with my foot; it looked like a random col-lection of debris, nothing significant, nothing the Dream Re-corder had brought up here specially, for safekeeping.

The bed wasn't made, and the pillow looked greasy. Nothing was under the bed but dustballs. Nothing was in the closet but clothes.

A wooden chest of drawers was piled high with books, jars, hairbrushes, and other odds and ends. Without touching anything I looked over it all. I reminded myself that she in-vaded people's privacy all the time, but I still felt guilty as I opened the top drawer and surveyed the Dream Recorder's underthings.

The second drawer held winter sweaters. The third held stockings and hats.

By the time I reached the bottom drawer I was thinking about Michael Alleyn again, only half paying attention to what I was doing. I slid the drawer open, knowing from the feel that it was empty, pulling it the rest of the way out only to be thorough. And as I pulled, something caught.

I jiggled the drawer. What was holding it up?

Lying down reluctantly on the less-than-clean floor, I peered underneath the chest.

Something was under there. It was taped to the bottom of the lowest drawer and had come partly loose, so now it was catching on the runner.

I pulled it free and turned it over in my hands. It was something electronic, something that looked a little like the handheld communication devices Gabriel and his men used. It wasn't a neatly labeled file explaining the experiment, but at least it was something.

Halfway down the stairs, a metallic rattling made me freeze mid-step.

"Look what I've found," someone said. "A rat in a trap."

I knew that voice, strangely soft and high for the man's

size. It was Cobb, the larger of the two horseback riders who'd been sent by the Dream Recorder to hunt down Farrell Dean.

There was another rattling noise, and a click at the bottom of the stairs. "Just in case you're inclined to run," Cobb said. "I've spent enough time chasing after you."

There was a rush of sound, a muffled bang. Something fell.

I crammed the mysterious object into my pocket and ran down the narrow dark stairs. Sure enough, the grate at the bottom was closed.

I yanked at it but it wouldn't budge. Noises were coming from the book room—sounds of struggle, grunts of pain. Pushing my face against the grate, I tried to find an angle where I could see.

There they were, against the same wall as the grate. Cobb had one hand against Farrell Dean's chest and was shoving him back against the shelf of books.

Farrell Dean grabbed Cobb's hand, trapping it against his chest, and at the same moment he dropped down, pulling the other man with him, bending Cobb's wrist in a way it was never meant to go.

Cobb grunted in pain and yanked away, but only for a second, and when he came back in he managed to pin one of Farrell Dean's arms against the bookshelf, leaning on it with his body.

Farrell Dean slammed his other fist hard against the side of Cobb's head but Cobb barely moved—he had a neck like a bull—and then both of his hands were around Farrell Dean's neck. I was so close I could see his big hands, his hairy knuckles, the way his fingertips pressed into Farrell Dean's skin.

I yanked at the grate again, shook it hard, but it wouldn't give. "Stop!" I yelled. "Let him go!"

Cobb turned his face toward me and smiled, and at the same moment Farrell Dean stopped struggling and went limp.

"Stop!" I screamed again, then, "Angus! Help!"

Cobb shifted his grip against Farrell Dean's sagging weight and when he did Farrell Dean's fist flashed up and slammed into the front of Cobb's throat. The big man made a choking sound and let go, staggering back a step or two, but then he reached into his pocket.

"Look out!" I yelled as Cobb lunged at Farrell Dean, knife glinting. They went lurching together across the room, slamming against another bookcase, knocking books to the floor, dust billowing.

Farrell Dean was fighting for his life against a man who must have had fifty pounds on him, and Farrell Dean was good at fighting people who outweighed him but the room was too small to let him play to his advantage, and I was standing and watching like an idiot, standing there behind the grate like a pawn at the mercy of the next Watcher or Guardian or random thug, standing there letting someone else decide my own life yet again, decide who lived and who died.

And so, without any clear plan but with a sudden conviction that I had to try something, anything, I dashed back up the stairs and into the dreary bedroom. Shoving the curtains aside I flung open the window and looked out. The yellow cat looked up at me, only mildly curious. Angus was nowhere in sight, the ground seemed very far away, and—whether from fright or the lingering effects of the fever—I was simultaneously sweating and shivering.

But I could do this. I had to do it, because nobody else was coming to help Farrell Dean.

I turned around and eased myself out, legs dangling, until the edge of the window was digging into my ribs. Then,

AMANDA WITT

getting a firm grip on the sill, I tried to stretch myself out full length, but my hands, slick from sweat, slipped and fell, hitting the ground hard, jarring my ankle.

It was only dirt, though, not pavement, and I rolled to my feet. Hurriedly I dashed over to the broken chair and yanked it out from under the cat. He hissed and ran off into the bushes.

The chair was unsteady but I only had to balance for a second, just long enough to get through the broken window. It took three tries and then I was up and through, a sharp sting biting my left arm as I went. A bit of glass. Some blood. I hoped it wasn't a bad cut, because I wasn't stopping to check.

I ran straight through the kitchen to the grated doorway. I hadn't heard that grate click. No click meant Cobb hadn't locked it, surely that was what it meant. Please not locked.

It wouldn't open.

Through it I could see Cobb rushing Farrell Dean, bulling him back into a stack of books, Farrell Dean falling and Cobb coming down on top of him. I couldn't get the grate open and Cobb raised one arm and the knife flashed.

"No!" I screamed, and to my amazement Cobb hesitated for just an instant and glanced over his shoulder at me.

In the same moment Farrell Dean reached for the lamp. It was too far—he couldn't quite reach it—but then he did. He gripped it around its slender neck and swung it hard against Cobb's head, the shade yanking free and skittering across the floor.

Cobb froze but didn't fall. The lamp was still plugged in, casting wild shadows around the tiny room.

I shook the grate hard, yanked again, and this time it came open and I rushed in as the knife started down and Farrell Dean swung the lamp once more, and this time the metal base made a dull ringing sound against Cobb's skull.

Cobb swayed to the right, to the left, and I slammed into him so that he tumbled onto his side instead of falling on Farrell Dean.

Cobb dropped like a sack of grain, and I stomped on his hand and kicked the knife away.

Then I stood over him, ready to kick him, sit on him, whatever it took, but he wasn't moving. Rivulets of sweat ran down the side of his face, and a trickle of blood joined them.

"Are you okay?" I said to Farrell Dean over my shoulder, still unwilling to turn my back on the violent bull of a man unconscious there on the floor.

Farrell Dean hauled himself up onto one elbow and looked at me. "Thanks," he said, breathing hard, and my eyes filled with tears.

"I'm sorry." I edged around Cobb's motionless body and knelt beside Farrell Dean, still keeping one eye on Cobb. "I shouldn't have gone up there, I shouldn't have left you, I was—it was—I'm sorry, I'm so sorry—"

"Red," Farrell Dean said, grabbing my wrist. "I said thank you. You did great. I needed a split second, and you gave it to me. You were like magic: 'Now I'm behind *this* locked grate. Now I'm behind *that* locked grate.'"

He got to his feet and helped me up too, and then I saw that his eyes were sparkling. "It was too weird—the guy just had to turn and look at you."

I swung a fist and punched him hard in the arm.

"Hey! What's that for?" he said, fending me off. He was actually smiling.

"For almost getting killed," I said.

And then I was glad Farrell Dean turned toward Cobb, because a sudden wave of exhaustion hit me and I began to tremble, or maybe it wasn't exhaustion but anger, fury at Cobb, at the Watchers, at all the people determined to control our lives.

Farrell Dean bent over the man who had tried to kill him and, yanking the cord out of the lamp, tied Cobb's hands behind him. Cobb groaned again and opened his eyes, but he didn't struggle.

"Are you really okay?" I asked Farrell Dean.

"Really." Then he saw my arm. "But you're not. You're bleeding. Let me see."

He rolled up my sleeve. It was hard to tell anything— there was more blood than I'd realized. Farrell Dean wiped at it with the tail of his shirt.

"There it is," he said, relief in his voice. "It's not as bad as it looks." He pressed hard on the cut with his shirttail, his hands streaked with my blood. He was still catching his breath and I could feel waves of heat coming off his body. What would I have done if he'd died? Unsteadily I reached out and grabbed the sleeve of his shirt.

"I'm all right, Red," he said softly, still keeping pressure on my cut. "We're both all right."

"Only because providence favors children and fools," Gabriel said, coming into the room. He did not look at all happy.

Angus was right behind him. "Hey, where'd he come from?" he said, pointing at Cobb. Before anyone could answer, he crossed the room and bent over the man. "How'd you get in?"

Cobb turned his face away. "The front door," he said in his strange high-pitched voice. "I have a key." He sounded as if he was in pain.

"Some watchman you are," Gabriel muttered, throwing Angus a dark look. "You could have gotten them killed with this stupid stunt."

Angus flushed.

"We all agreed it was a good idea," I said. "And it was. We've found out a lot."

"Not now," Farrell Dean said, with a warning look at Cobb. "We'll discuss it later. Where's the Dream Recorder?"

"She left town." Angus spoke to us, pointedly turning his back on Gabriel. "She finished at the beauty shop and got on a horse with Edgeling, and they lit out toward Ionia. I headed straight back here, and he—" he jerked his head toward our uncle—"caught me climbing in the window."

Gabriel went over to Cobb and prodded him with one foot. "What are you doing here?"

Cobb looked up at him but said nothing.

Without taking his gaze away from the man on the floor, Gabriel reached into his pocket and handed his handkerchief to Farrell Dean. "Clean her up," he said. "Then clear out. Angus, you're going to stay here with me."

"Why?" Angus didn't look happy.

Gabriel threw him one swift cold look. "Because clearly you need a lesson in what can happen to fools."

With quick movements Farrell Dean tied up my arm. Then he turned, picked up a large stack of books, and headed toward the door to the kitchen.

"Cover those with something," Gabriel said.

"Here." I took Fiona's cloak and spread it on the floor, and Farrell Dean set the stack of books on it and wrapped them up.

"Get out of town by the quickest route possible," Gabriel said. "If anyone sees you, *Fiona*, they'll wonder about all that blood. No need starting rumors."

I nodded that I understood. Farrell Dean picked up the bundle of books and left the room, but still I hesitated.

Angus was glowering silently in a corner; Gabriel was standing over Cobb.

When I hesitated he looked at me, his dark eyes unreadable. He looked like Rafe, of course, but he looked like Rafe angry in a way I'd never seen before, cold and calculating.

"What?" he said curtly.

"What are you going to do to him?"

"I'm going to get some answers."

I hesitated. "Don't ... don't kill him."

Gabriel's expression shifted. "Oh, I don't intend to do that," he said.

On the floor, Cobb closed his eyes.

Chapter 5

We walked swiftly and silently down the alley. Then I—as Fiona—casually strolled out into the exposed area, hoping no one would notice me, hoping that if anyone did, my sleeves were dark enough—and embroidered enough—to hide the blood. A couple of women were standing across the street talking, but I didn't make eye contact, and they didn't call out.

I reached the back of the leather goods store safely and waited until the two women went into a store. Then I signaled to Farrell Dean that the coast was clear. Not that he needed my help; he'd sneaked into town on his own with no problem.

From there we cut through the woods and circled the town until we reached the road that led to Eric Alleyn's, curved and hilly and lined with tall trees in various stages of losing their leaves. A few evergreens stood interspersed among the others, looking fully clothed and dignified.

As soon as we were out of sight of any buildings, Farrell Dean shifted the books under one arm and turned to me.

"Are you holding up all right?" he said. "You're bound to still be weak."

I avoided his eyes and kept walking. "I'm tired, but I'll manage." It was going to be a long walk back to Eric Alleyn's, but I wasn't going to complain. I had a feeling I was about to get the lecture Farrell Dean hadn't had time to give me earlier.

Sure enough, he just couldn't resist.

"You're not well yet," he said. "You shouldn't have gone to town."

"I didn't ask your opinion."

"So I noticed."

I walked faster, as if that would let me outrun whatever he was determined to say, but he kept pace and kept talking.

"Listen to me, Red. You were trying to help, I know, but you can't go running around like this. It's too dangerous. Your father has enemies, your uncle has enemies, and now Edgeling's thugs are after us."

"They're after you, not me. I'm Fiona." The road was muddy from the morning's rain, and I edged around a puddle.

"Yeah, well. An extra redhead's pretty hard to hide."

That brought me to a stop. "I'm not extra, I'm not a duplicate, and I'm not expendable."

Farrell Dean stopped too, irritation flashing in his eyes. "That's exactly what I'm saying. You're not expendable, certainly not to me. That's why you need to stay out of sight."

For a long moment we stood there, glaring at each other across the muddy path, but then the clear autumn sun washed over us, cutting everything clean and bright, showing more in Farrell Dean's eyes than I wanted to see.

I started walking again.

He didn't follow.

After a few yards I turned around. "I'm not going to hide and do nothing. Our friends could be dying over there."

"I know that as well as you do." His voice was steady, but I heard the edge in it.

Of course he knew. He was the one who had been

arrested and flogged. He was the one who had stood in the city circle on the very spot where Rafe had bled and died. He was the one who had come within seconds of dying himself.

"There are other ways you could help," he said. "You could hole up somewhere and go through these books while I try to round up some guns and find a boat that can fight the current. It would be safer that way. You can help without taking risks like you did today."

"But I need to." I suddenly realized I was arguing with myself as much as with Farrell Dean. Being abducted by Tristan had scared me witless; I wanted to stay safe; I wanted to hide. But if I started hiding, I'd never stop, and I'd always hate myself for putting my own safety over that of my friends.

Farrell Dean was watching me, his eyes unreadable. After a moment he looked away. Dark bruises shaped like fingerprints were rising on his neck, and I knew that when he turned back toward me, I'd see thumbprints at the base of his throat.

"I know you're worried for me," I said. "I'm worried for you, too. Cobb could have killed you."

"And Tristan could have killed you." He still wasn't looking at me. "That day, the day he took you? It was worse for you than for me, obviously. Much worse. But it wasn't exactly fun for me either. It was the single worst day of my life."

Worse than the day he stood in the city circle waiting for his mother to shoot him? I started to make a skeptical sound but stopped. If he said it, he meant it. Farrell Dean was not given to drama.

The wind shifted, bringing with it the scent of wet pine, sending a scattering of yellow leaves across the path. I followed their progress and then looked up, at the tall trees and the little insignificant clouds that could spread in a heartbeat to cover the entire sky.

I looked at the road ahead of us, leading first to my

father's house and then, sooner or later, to the beach, to the sea, to Optica. I thought about all we had to do to get there, and about what we would find when we arrived.

Including Meritt.

I saw in my mind's eye his unruly dark hair, the flash of his quick grin, the loose easy rhythm of his stride when we ran. I remembered all the nights we'd explored the blue-lit deserted streets of the city, those nights when all the world was sleeping except for us and the wardens we avoided as easily as if we were playing some harmless game.

Farrell Dean stood still, his face tilted down toward the path that scrolled away from our feet. He was strong and capable, solid and comforting and real—sometimes he felt like the only real thing in this strange new world. But once I was back in the hard cold reality that was Optica, Meritt might make the past few days look like mist, like a dream.

Taking a deep breath, I made myself speak. "Farrell Dean?"

He looked up, and at the expression in his eyes my breath caught in my throat. Hastily I looked away, and then I made myself look back again.

"I'm going to be straight with you," I said, and his face turned wary and I almost lost my resolve, but I pressed on, feeling myself beginning to blush. "You know that night? At Gabriel's house, in the dark?"

Farrell Dean nodded once. "I'm not likely to forget," he said. He took a step toward me and I could see the pulse beating at the base of his throat, could feel my own heartbeat quicken. "I don't know why I stopped it," he said. "I've been kicking myself ever since."

I swallowed. "You stopped it because you have better sense than I do," I said. "But I'm trying. I've decided that I need to think like Cline."

Farrell Dean's face lit with humor. "Interesting role

model," he said, but I could see in his troubled eyes that he knew what I meant.

"He's right, you know," I said. "You deserve better."

He shook his head.

"No, listen to me," I said. "You're wonderful. You're smart and handsome and brave and kind and funny and honest and you've been so good to me, always—"

"Stop it, Red," he said, holding up one hand and turning away, his expression pained. "I get the point. I'm great but I'm not Meritt."

It would have been easier to let it go at that—it would have accomplished what I needed to accomplish—but I couldn't do it. I'd told him I'd be straight with him, and I would.

"That's not what I was going to say."

My face was burning and I couldn't meet his eyes. "I was going to say that I might … I could … "

Farrell Dean was silent. From the corner of my eye I could see that he was standing very still.

"I could fall for you," I said, keeping my gaze on the muddy road at my feet. "I could fall hard." Now I had to keep talking, fast. "But it's true I'll be seeing Meritt again, and I don't know how that will be. I—he—for such a long time we—I only ever imagined—"

I trailed off, but Farrell Dean—ever merciful—nodded. "I understand," he said.

"No, I don't know that you do. *I* don't. Everything is so confusing." I pointed in the direction of my father's house. "I don't know how to fit into this family. I don't know what obligations I have to my father, I don't know how this sister thing works, and I have relatives I haven't even met yet. I have a *brother* I haven't even met yet.

"And Ezzie is sick and there are Dream Recorders and Watchers and wardens, and things we have to do, important things. Lives are at stake. It's all too much. I can't think about everything at once. I can't think about this, about us. I have to focus on helping our friends. I *want* to focus on that. And afterwards—if there is afterwards—then maybe I'll be able to think clearly. About us. About him and me and you."

Farrell Dean studied me for a long moment, saying nothing. Then he nodded.

"Fair enough," he said. "And thank you for being blunt. But if we're laying our cards on the table, I have something to say, too."

Something in his tone told me that whatever he had to say wouldn't make me any less bewildered.

"You don't have to say anything," I said. "I know I made you promise not to keep secrets from me, but I was hysterical at the time. I take it back."

Farrell Dean half smiled. "You can't take it back, Red," he said. "I'm the one who promised."

"Then I free you from your oath. I absolve you. I release you, unchain you, hereby give you permission to keep anything from me at any time, for any reason whatsoever."

I was trying to break the mood, trying to make him laugh, but he wouldn't play along. Instead he set the bundle of books carefully on a flat rock beside the road and moved closer to me.

"Listen to me," he said. "Just for a minute."

He waited until, reluctantly, I nodded.

"In Optica we had no choice," he said. "We bred where we were told to breed."

He was looking straight into my eyes and though I wanted to look away, I couldn't.

"You're younger than I am," he said. "You still have two years before you'd be assigned to someone. But I don't. That's one reason I jumped at the chance to help Rafe—to do more than the low-level spying I'd been doing for him for years.

Long before people started dying I wanted out of that city, out of that system. And it wasn't because I was afraid of starving, and it wasn't because I was noble and dreamed of freedom." His voice dropped until I could barely hear him. "It was because I wanted you."

Hot tears stung at the backs of my eyes.

Farrell Dean put his hands on my shoulders and studied my face. I could have moved away from him—I told myself to move away—but I didn't.

"Today's my nineteenth birthday, Red," he said. "Today's the day I didn't get assigned to someone else."

For a long moment he held my gaze. Then, slowly, he bent and kissed me. He put one hand behind my head and the other on the small of my back, pulling me close. He was warm and smelled of clean sweat and, beneath that, soap.

The road was beginning to tilt when he turned my face against his chest and held me.

"Happy birthday," I said into his shirt, blinking back tears. I felt like I was telling him goodbye.

He released me, and when he stepped back and saw my face he smiled. "Don't worry, Red," he said. "It'll be all right. Whatever happens, at least now we have a choice."

He picked up the bundle of books and tucked them under his arm, whistling something tuneless but cheerful, and then his gaze shifted over my shoulder.

Gabriel's dark blue truck was coming toward us down the road from town, and coming fast. We moved off the path and he pulled to a stop, tires crunching on the gravel.

"Get in," he said through the open passenger window. "We've got to get you away from here."

Chapter 6

A few drops of rain hit the windshield, then petered out as the sun fought through once more. Gabriel's elbow bumped mine as he shifted gears. I was in the middle of the truck cab, sandwiched between Farrell Dean and my uncle.

He drove more carefully than Tristan had—which I suppose wasn't saying much, given that Tristan drove like the madman he was. Gabriel paid close attention, skirting pot-holes in the road, avoiding rocks and tree roots, babying his truck. It surprised me, given his rather forceful personality and the urgency with which he'd ordered us to get in.

Then I remembered—Tor had mentioned that the island's trucks were getting old, that even the best mechanics couldn't always keep them going. A vehicle was a precious commodity, and the miles that could be wrung from it, limited.

Gabriel was so carefully focused on driving that I didn't want to distract him. Plus, he was still angry at us for what we'd done; his jaw was tight and his movements clipped.

Once we hit an easier stretch of road, though, I risked it.

"We can't just vanish," I said. "Papa will be worried."

"Angus knows," Gabriel said tersely. "He'll tell Eric."

"Tell him what? Where are we going?"

Gabriel eased the truck around a sharp curve. "Locria."

"Why?" Farrell Dean said.

Gabriel threw him an exasperated look, but finally stopped giving such maddeningly terse replies. "To hide you," he said. "And, if we're very fortunate, to find a boat. The Locrians have been trying to build sea-worthy vessels for years, though I've no idea whether they've ever succeeded."

A boat better than the one we'd come in would be good; but I wanted to go back to the "hide you" part.

"What did Cobb tell you?"

Gabriel looked displeased, though whether at my question or at the answer, I didn't know. "Apparently the Dream Recorder has issued a reward for Farrell Dean, and now there are a dozen or more men out looking to bring him in. They'll get paid whether he's dead or alive, though they get a bit more if he's still capable of talking."

I looked at Farrell Dean. He shrugged and opened one of the Dream Recorder books.

"She can do that?" I said. "The Isle Council doesn't stop things like that?"

"The Isle Council didn't know about it," Gabriel said. "She put word out by way of the grapevine—by its unsavory branch. Now that we've heard, yes, we can put out our own warnings. Until our response gets around, though, you need to keep out of sight."

Warnings—was that all the Council would do?

Maybe Gabriel was being elliptical. He was the Council's unacknowledged enforcer, after all.

"She's been after Farrell Dean practically since we got here," I said. "What does she want with him?" He wasn't even a twin.

Gabriel didn't answer.

Farrell Dean looked up from his book, but only briefly. "She probably wants Ezzie, too," he said, and went back to flipping pages.

I turned to get a better look at my uncle, whose face was carefully expressionless. "Ezzie's all right, isn't he?"

"He's fine."

"You don't think they can get to him, there at the hospital?"

"I left him under armed guard, and when he leaves the hospital, he'll be taken under armed guard to my house. I've already sent word."

"But why is the Dream Recorder after us?" I said, and caught the quick sideways glance Gabriel threw my way. "Yes, I said *us*. You can stop trying to spare me. Obviously she'd be after me, too, if she knew I was me and not Fiona. They're after everyone who came from Optica."

Gabriel sighed. "That's right. They are. And that includes you, Valentina. They already know about you."

Farrell Dean's head came up. "They know? How?"

Gabriel shook his head. "I don't know."

"But we've been careful," I said. "We haven't left the house together, not ever. I don't think Fiona's been away from the house at all since I arrived."

Gabriel shrugged.

"I must have done something to give myself away. But when? Rain didn't realize I wasn't Fiona, you didn't realize—who put it together?"

Gabriel shook his head again. "I don't know," he said.

"Tor wouldn't tell anyone."

"No."

"Tor's father knows," I said, "but he wouldn't tell anyone, would he?"

"No."

"So who told?"

"No doubt it was Angus," Gabriel said.

"Don't." Farrell Dean didn't quite speak sharply to Gabriel, but it was close.

I kept talking. "Did someone higher up order the Dream Recorder to track us down? Or did she decide to come after us on her own?"

"I don't know," Gabriel said yet again, sounding impatient.

"Didn't you ask Cobb?"

"Cobb claims not to know."

"But he did know about Red," Farrell Dean said.

"Yes." Gabriel apparently wasn't as irritated at Farrell Dean as he was at me, because he gave him a longer answer. "Cobb knew that the dead sister wasn't dead after all. However, he doesn't seem to know anything about another island. It's possible he thinks Valentina has been here all along, tucked somewhere out of sight."

Farrell Dean looked at me. "He could have killed you," he said. He spoke quietly, but he was angry.

"Not her," Gabriel said. "The Dream Recorder made it very clear that the girl, at least, must be taken alive."

"You still should have stayed home today," Farrell Dean said to me.

"I wouldn't have been any safer at Eric Alleyn's. If they're looking for me, someone is bound to go out there. Is Fiona in danger?"

Gabriel shook his head. "I don't think so. No one wants any trouble with Eric Alleyn." His mouth twisted wryly. "They just want the daughter Eric Alleyn already sold, as Cobb put it. The way he figures it, Eric gave up any right to you long ago, and shouldn't protest at your removal."

I started to protest that it wasn't Eric Alleyn but the endlessly creepy Tristan who had sold me and who'd persuaded the midwife to lie about it, but Gabriel and Farrell Dean already knew that.

My head began to ache; this was all too much, and I was still so weak.

We drove in silence for awhile. Farrell Dean flipped through dream records. I tried not to slump against him. He wouldn't mind—far from it—but I couldn't very well ask him to back off and, a moment later, drape myself all over him.

I sure was tired, though. It would be awful if I did manage to give myself a relapse.

"Here it is," Farrell Dean said suddenly. "I found it. This entry is about that night."

I was suddenly wide awake. I didn't have to ask which night he meant.

"Do you want to read it first?" he said, looking at me.

I shook my head. "Go ahead," I said. "Read it out loud."

Rachel Alleyn died after childbirth six nights ago, having delivered two female infants. The midwife says her death was not entirely unexpected. She was a small woman unsuited to multiple childbirth; she had suffered from extreme hyperemesis in the early months of the pregnancy; and subsequent to amniocentesis she developed a recurring fever that did not respond well to treatment.

"My poor Rachel," Gabriel said heavily. "I didn't know it was such a hard pregnancy."

He didn't know, because he'd ostracized his sister for crossing the island and marrying Eric Alleyn; he'd punished her for that for years.

The weaker baby died a few hours before Rachel did. Rachel was not told of the infant's death. The family was alone at the time except for the midwife, and when she informed Eric of the child's death and attempted to speak to him about suitable arrangements, he brushed her off. The midwife did not wish to keep the child's body in the house with other children present, nor did she wish to leave it in the barn unattended, so she herself buried the child. This was, of course, a task far beyond her duty.

Eric Alleyn, with a stunning lack of gratitude, disputes the midwife's account. I suggested that he dreamed a more amenable version of events, and wishes to believe that dream is reality, but he laughed in my face. He says the infant's body is missing, and now he is methodically digging up his pasture, ruining vast tracts of grazing areas, neglecting his children and the care of his livestock.

Opinions are mixed regarding this bizarre behavior. A few—his closest friends—almost believe him. But most say that, distraught with grief and overwhelmed by the idea of raising the six surviving children alone, Eric has simply gone out of his mind.

Others speculate that his instability is rooted in guilt for the pregnancy itself, or at the very least for not agreeing to utilize the clinical facility when Rachel's time came. Several have noted that undoubtedly Eric has always had latent tendencies toward instability—he is, of course, the son of that unfortunate Michael.

In any case, it will not be surprising when public opinion ultimately condemns him. He conspires in his own downfall by making himself more and more of a spectacle each passing day. People come to offer their condolences, and he will not leave his digging to receive them. If they cross his muddy, pockmarked pasture to speak with him, he tells them he has found no body because there is no body to be found, but can offer no alternate explanation for where the child could be. He has even admitted that he does not want to find the body, that he prefers to think his child might be alive, which has made credible the rumor that he did indeed find the corpse but, unable to face the reality of his child's death, hid it again.

(Van Stavern suggested gathering a team of men to find the body, but deferred to my opinion that, in Eric's current

state of denial, being confronted with visible evidence well might cause a mental break from which he would never recover.)

All this is troublesome but poses no real difficulties. However, Eric also has voiced threats against the midwife in front of several witnesses, and it is possible that he will tire of digging and decide to make good on those threats. We have decided to remove the midwife from his general vicinity and hope that proves sufficient. Fortunately the local doctor has agreed to replace her in providing prenatal zygosity determination via amniocentesis to expectant mothers near here. He is a man disinclined to ask awkward questions.

If being out of sight does not put the midwife out of Eric's mind, the time may come when it might be good for him to be distracted, and this could happen quite naturally. Trouble often chooses one unfortunate man with whom to make her home—and in this case, trouble is ready and willing. Eric has a long history with Tristan Oldfamily, who is remarkably easy to manipulate, as people with chips on their shoulders generally are, with Eric Alleyn being the unfortunate exception that proves the rule. Should a distraction prove necessary, one will no doubt be provided.

Also, as in the case of any tragedy, rumors will always abound. It is possible that if Eric persists in blaming the midwife, the mud he slings might stick to him instead.

Farrell Dean stopped reading. "That's the end of it," he said, putting one arm along the back of the seat behind my shoulders. "Are you all right?"

"I'm fine," I said, pulling at a strand of my hair and holding it in front of my face. Was it still just a little bit darker, or was I imagining it?

"She doesn't even pretend that this has anything to do with dreams," Farrell Dean said. "I've seen a few other entries like that, too. Ones that are descriptions of events, not records of dreams."

Gabriel nodded. "The books I inherited with my Dream Recorder shop are a mix," he said. "Dreams apparently are just a cover, a way to get people to talk to the Recorders. These books are documentation of life in Aislin. What we think, what we remember, what we do."

"Still, I'm surprised she adds so much of her own commentary in this one," I said, trying to view the entry impersonally. "It seems like she'd be afraid someone would read her books and figure out what was going on."

"She wasn't counting on people from the other island showing up—people who know what really happened to you," Farrell Dean said. "People from here probably wouldn't notice anything suspicious."

"Even the remark about Tristan doesn't say the Dream Recorder is the one doing the manipulating." Gabriel sounded grim; everyone had thought he was the one who controlled Tristan, when in fact Tristan had been carefully exacerbating the feud between Gabriel and my father.

I wasn't going to touch that topic. "It's true she doesn't come right out and admit what happened," I said. "And her books were locked up, too, so maybe she thought nobody would ever see them. But still—we got to them, and we understand them. It seems like a big risk, even saying as much as she did."

"Maybe she took the risk because Eric Alleyn threw a wrench in the works," Farrell Dean said. "They'd stolen other babies, but as far as we know your father is the only parent who kicked up a fuss. So maybe the Dream Recorder was worried that she'd be blamed."

"She had to say enough to make sure she was covered if things kept going wrong," I said.

Farrell Dean nodded. "The journals probably didn't just

sit there on the shelves. Somebody read them. She was writing for those people—the powers-that-be on the mainland, the head scientists. The watchmaker. She was making sure they all knew she was doing her best to contain the situation."

It made sense, but the timing was wrong. "The people in charge were dead by the time I was born," I said. "The watchmaker, everybody. Whatever caused the time of the ashes killed them. So why would she bother to write things down any longer?"

"Clearly the Dream Recorder didn't know what had happened," Gabriel said. The afternoon had grown dark, overcast, and as he spoke he flicked on the headlights. "Maybe she still doesn't know. Based on what you overheard, the Watchers don't know about the destruction of the mainland. Your crazy Guardian said the watch was ticking itself out. The watch is the experiment, and it lives on even though your watchmaker is dead, *because* it doesn't know that he's dead."

"He isn't my watchmaker," I said. "And watches aren't conscious entities." He was irritated with me already—through no fault of my own—and for some reason that made me want to irritate him further.

Gabriel threw me an annoyed glance and started to reply, but Farrell Dean beat him to it.

"I don't get this part," he said, and reread a portion of the entry:

Fortunately the local doctor has agreed to replace her in providing prenatal zygosity determination via amniocentesis to expectant mothers near here. He is a man disinclined to ask awkward questions.

Farrell Dean looked up from the book. "What exactly is that supposed to mean?" he said.

"A zygote is a baby," I said. "A brand new one. Before it's big enough to be a fetus." I remembered that from biology.

Gabriel nodded. "Yes. And amniocentesis is a test given to pregnant mothers."

"What sort of test is it?" I asked.

"It's so they can tell if there are any problems with the infant. Many things can be treated before the baby is even born, if you know about them. So the doctor or the midwife uses a needle to take a sample of amniotic fluid from the womb, and then they analyze the fluid sample in a laboratory. But my question is, what's this zygosity determination?"

"Determining there's a zygote?" Farrell Dean said, then shook his head. "But that doesn't make sense. You wouldn't give a pregnant woman a pregnancy test to see if she's pregnant."

"Determining whether there's one baby or two?" I offered.

"They'd know that already," Gabriel said. "Even if the mother didn't visit the clinic and have an ultrasound, the midwife would know from the heartbeats."

"You can hear the heartbeats?" I said. "Even before the baby's born?"

Gabriel nodded. "With a stethoscope," he said. "I could hear my children's heartbeats when Carol was only a few weeks along. It's a remarkable thing—hearing the mother's heartbeat, loud and strong, and the child's lighter, faster heartbeat. If there were two babies, they'd hear two little heartbeats."

"So then what's a zygosity determination test?" I said.

Gabriel kept his eyes on the road. "I can only make an educated case," he said finally. "A couple of years ago, when Martin's little boys turned out to look so much alike and everyone was upset and talking about sorcery, I set up a conference at the hospital and had the doctors explain their remarkable resemblance scientifically."

"And?"

"And apparently when it comes to twins, there are different sorts of zygotes. If twins come from two separate ova—eggs, that is—they're twins but not identical. They call that di-zygotic. If the twins come from one egg they're called mono-zygotic—that would be you and Fiona, and Rafe and me. That's why we're identical. We started out as the same person and then for some reason split very early on, with each half developing into a complete person. So presumably this zygosity determination test tells what sort of zygotes are present—mono or di."

I stared at his profile, seeing him, seeing Rafe.

"They tested the mothers to see who was going to have identical twins," I said. "So they could be prepared to steal one of them. They didn't want the other kind of twins."

Gabriel nodded, his face grim. "The midwife performed the test so they'd know when fresh subjects were about to be born."

Subjects. Lab rats.

"Then she passed the newborn subjects along to her contact person from the other island," Gabriel continued. "In your case, at least, by way of Tristan." Gabriel's voice was grim. "He wasn't one of the experimenters, but he certainly made himself useful to them."

Unsaid words hung heavy in the air.

Gabriel, too, had been all too useful to our enemies.

Chapter 7

We drove in silence for awhile, lost in our own thoughts. Clouds now completely covered the sky—and the road, too, apparently, for we were driving through a thick mist that left the windshield wet with tiny droplets. That mist moved like a living thing, swaying across the road, drifting among the trees. It fit my mental landscape. I wasn't back in the delirium of my illness, but my mind felt shrouded, my thoughts drifting at random.

After a bit Farrell Dean gestured with the book. "That's how the Dream Recorder knew about me," he said. "It must be the same doctor who treated me at the clinic. He realized I wasn't from here and told the Dream Recorder."

I covered my face with my hands.

"What is it?"

Dropping my hands, I turned to him. "Is that the same doctor who came out to see me?"

Farrell Dean's face darkened. "I didn't know a doctor came out to Eric Alleyn's."

"He did. Later than Fiona wanted him, but he came."

"What did he look like?"

"I don't know. I was out of it."

"And Fiona was there too? She didn't hide and let Eric Alleyn pretend you were her?"

I shook my head. "I don't know. I don't think so. It's all pretty fuzzy in my head, but I think I remember Fiona talking to me while the doctor was in the room. He frightened me, or maybe just startled me. I think he's why I had bad dreams."

"Why?" Farrell Dean was worried. "Did he say something, do something?"

"If he did I don't remember. I think he just looked me over and gave me some medicine and agreed with Fiona that it was a virus." But he must have said something or done something that made me uncomfortable; that had to be why I was so troubled in my sleep, and so uneasy once I awoke.

"Farrell Dean's right," Gabriel said. "At the very least Eric should have presented you as Fiona, if he really felt the need to call the doctor for a mere virus. His famous paranoia must have been sleeping for once."

There was an undertone to his comment; he was glad someone besides him had misjudged.

"Well, he's taken a lot of flack for not having a doctor involved when I was born," I said.

"How far does this range of hills run?" Farrell Dean asked, before Gabriel could answer me and before I could defend my father still further. "There's more elevation than I expected—quite a bit more than we have on our island. Other than some cliffs along the coast, we're basically flat."

It was true that the road was now cutting through hills, leaving us in a narrow channel of shadow with the cloudy sky very far away, so far that I felt as if we were driving down into the earth itself. But Farrell Dean obviously was changing the subject, and Gabriel paused long enough to announce that he was fully aware of the tactic.

"The hills span the length of the eastern coast of Aislin," he said. "And they run across the top of the island as well."

Farrell Dean turned and looked behind us. "Optica's that

way," he said. "Southeast of Aislin. If the mainland lies still further to the east, then maybe those hills explain why this island didn't suffer as much during the time of the ashes."

"You think maybe the hills blocked the poisonous ash?" I said.

"The hills, and the greater distance from the source," Farrell Dean said. "That time wasn't as bad here—Rory didn't remember any problems at all. Of course, he'd have been quite young at the time. Maybe it was worse than he realized."

"No," Gabriel said. "It wasn't bad. We had an atmospheric disturbance, but it wasn't anything more than a haze that held on too long. Nothing particularly notable, except for its duration."

Farrell Dean opened another Dream Recorder book and began flipping through it. I tried not to sag against him; I tried to think useful thoughts, thoughts that would help us save our friends, but all I came up with were questions and no answers.

And then the road was gone. First the pavement ended, and a bit later, the gravel. Finally we jostled onto a sandy track mined with rocks. There were rocks above us, too, big rocks that leaned precariously away from the hillside. If one of those rough boulders broke loose and tumbled down on us, the truck wouldn't be much protection.

Farrell Dean pulled a book from the stack he held and offered it to me, but I shook my head. The lurching of the truck, the claustrophobia of the dark hills, were making my stomach uneasy. Perhaps they'd saved my life, those hills. Mine and Fiona's. But that didn't mean I had to like driving through them. And I didn't like the trees leaning in toward us. And I didn't like the mist that spread itself suddenly in our path, only to vanish again moments later.

Gabriel glanced at me and without a word turned a

handle and lowered his window. A breeze wafted in, along with the sharp scent of pines, and the smell reminded me of the wilderland. I couldn't decide whether that made me feel better or worse.

"Gabriel," Farrell Dean said suddenly. "What are your parents' names?"

"Frederick and Mina." Gabriel shot him a look. "Why? What have you found?"

Frederick Drewblood brought Mina in today. She is troubled by a recurring dream that visits her several times a week. She has put off coming to see me because she was busy with the new baby and her little daughter.

Mina's dream is typical in many respects. She is sitting in a rocking chair holding her baby, but when she looks down at him, her arms are empty. She is cradling nothing but air. Then, in her dream, she hears a baby crying outside, so she leaves her cottage and walks out into the dark night to search for her child. She walks so far that the light from the cottage is only a distant gleam, and then she hears the thin wail of an infant. She is unsure whether the wailing comes from her cottage, or from somewhere further out in the dark, and in her dream she is paralyzed, not knowing which way to run. At this point she awakens.

I assured her that many mothers of stillborn infants dream similar dreams, but she was not comforted. Frederick says that on two occasions he has found her outside their home in the middle of the night. Once she was alone, and once she was carrying the surviving infant. He says that on neither occasion did she recognize him when he spoke to her, but that when he questioned her about the baby in her arms she explained that if she was carrying one child, she would be able to tell whether he was crying, or whether it was his brother off in the distance.

Both Frederick and Mina are afraid that she will again sleepwalk with the boy and in some way do him harm. I have told them to barricade the door and to trust that this issue will soon pass.

"Poor Nana," I said. "Do you think we should tell her about Rafe?"

Gabriel shook his head. "Tell her that her worst nightmare was true? That her dead baby didn't die, but was stolen alive, and then was executed years later?"

"Maybe we could at least tell Grandfather, someday," I said. "I'd think he'd like to know. Rafe was a good man. Grandfather would be proud of that." And anyway, I thought, he'd probably guess that his other son had been stolen, once we told him who I really was and how I'd come to be mistaken for dead. He might be growing deaf, Grandfather, but he was far from stupid.

Beside me Gabriel had grown tense again.

"Would I have been as good a man, in my brother's situation?" He lifted one finger from the steering wheel, staving off any reply. "Don't answer that," he said. "It's a rhetorical question."

But as the trees thickened around us, I could feel him brooding over it. I certainly didn't know the answer. I didn't feel like I could make even a good guess as to what Fiona would have been like if she'd been raised in my place. She was so confident, so comfortable in herself. Would she have had that same aplomb in Optica? Even if everyone else thought she was a redheaded freak?

"That entry does explain one thing," Gabriel said. "Generally babies sleep with their mothers, correct?"

"I have no idea," I said.

"You have the strangest gaps in your education."

"We didn't need to know about childrearing," I said defensively. "Rafe was a great instructor. The best."

"Of course he was," Gabriel said, then answered his own question. "Yes, babies generally do sleep with their mothers. It makes nursing easier during the night. Keeps the baby warm, bonding, mother love, et cetera. Got it?"

I nodded.

"So I should have slept with my mother until I was ready for a bed of my own. But I didn't. I slept with my sister. In light of that entry, I'd say that even with the door barricaded, my mother was afraid she'd sleepwalk with me. She was afraid she'd hurt me somehow."

Gabriel subsided again into brooding silence. Farrell Dean turned pages. Already it was beginning to grow dark—he wouldn't be able to see to read much longer. At least I thought it was getting dark; the road was so steep that I couldn't see the sky unless I leaned way forward, my chin on the dashboard.

"Sit up," Gabriel said. "If I hit a rock, you'll knock your teeth out. Or bite your tongue. You're bloody enough as it is."

I sat back and, carefully, began peeling away the handkerchief bound around my arm. The incident at the Dream Recorder's house felt like a long time ago.

"You'll make it bleed again," Gabriel said.

"No, it's stopped. It's just—" I winced—"stuck to me." I gave up. "I'll have to wait until I can soak it off." I assumed Fiona's voice. "Do you think my disreputable state will alarm the Locrians?"

That at least got a faint smile out of him. "Nothing short of amputation alarms the Locrians," he said. "And even then they aren't much bothered, as long as they can stop the bleeding."

I hoped he was only joking. "Do they lose a lot of limbs, up there?"

Gabriel half-smiled. "No more than average," he said. "Mostly the sea is what gets them. They drown."

"Like Michael Alleyn. He lived up here, didn't he?"

"Up this way. I'm not sure exactly where."

"There's a Dream Recorder book just for him."

Now that I thought about it, I didn't know where that book was. I'd dropped it somewhere on the stairs, I supposed, when Cobb was attacking Farrell Dean.

Oh well. I'd read it all already.

"It's mostly blank," I told Gabriel. "He didn't like Dream Recorders. He called them quacks."

"Eric Alleyn's father? I'm not surprised. None of the Alleyns will have anything to do with Dream Recorders or Dream Drops."

Gabriel swerved, edging the truck around a fallen tree. "I can't fathom what that might mean, though. The fact that he had his own book. He was always an odd one."

He certainly was, to leave Eric Alleyn's pleasant farm and come live up here, in these dark claustrophobic hills.

I was trying to feel grateful to the hills instead of suffocated by them, to think of them as benevolent guardians instead of as wardens rising up around us and blocking the feeble light of the muffled sun, when a flash of movement to the left caught my eye. I turned my head, but saw nothing unusual.

The trees jolted past, the undergrowth lay stagnant, clotted with brown leaves where the contours of the hills had made small valleys. Here and there a rusted barbed-wire fence sagged from rotted fence posts, and water ran in rivulets down crevices in the ground.

Patches of mist floated through the trees, gray and eerie; probably that was what I'd seen—a bit of cloud, denser than most, moving like a living thing through the dark and misty forest.

Just as I relaxed back into my seat, it happened again. From the corner of my eye I caught a sudden movement—surely not mist—but when I turned my head there was nothing. The uneven rise and fall of the hills hid too much from view.

"What's wrong?" Farrell Dean said, leaning across me to peer out Gabriel's window.

"I thought I saw something over there. I don't know. All the trees make it hard to tell."

Gabriel, I noticed, was scanning the sides of the road when he could, and glancing frequently in his rearview mirror. Farrell Dean and I stared out the windows at the gloom. The trees were dropping their last few leaves, some of them much larger than my hand, but whatever I'd seen was bigger than any leaf.

A bit later we came upon a deer standing stock-still at the edge of the road, watching us pass with wide startled eyes. Was that what it had been? A white-tailed deer fleeing from the sound of the truck? I wasn't convinced. The color and movement had been different.

We passed a large dead tree, slanted pale and precarious against a smaller birch, and then slowed to negotiate a patch of road where a small avalanche of rocks had fallen. As we eased back onto clear road, Farrell Dean's head jerked around.

"It's a horse," he said, and sure enough, there was a dark shadow just vanishing behind another rise.

"Is there another road over there?" I asked.

"Not a road," Gabriel said. "A path, of sorts, through the hills. It's pretty rough but it's a more direct way to Locria than this road."

"Lester and Cobb ride horses," I said uneasily.

"It's not Cobb," Gabriel said, and his tone was final.

We watched carefully, but didn't see the horse again.

Farrell Dean and I talked it over, and we couldn't even decide whether there had been a rider, or whether the horse was on his own. It seemed odd, for a horse to be running randomly through the trees; but even if there was a rider, he might have nothing to do with us. Lots of people rode horses on Aislin.

I was glad when we came through a break in the hills and saw lights sprinkled across the gray-blue twilight.

"Locria is bigger than I expected," I said, surveying the pretty scene.

Gabriel shook his head. "You're imaging an actual town," he said. "Those are individual homes, and the darkness between them—that's just darkness. Woods. Ravines."

"There's no town at all?"

He shrugged. "There's an uneasy collection of four or five dwellings down near the beach," he said. "And one of them is a trading post. That's the closest Locria comes to being a town proper. Now watch."

He sped up, the truck's engine revving and echoing back from the dark hills. I strained my eyes, peering past the headlights into the rapidly deepening darkness, but I didn't see anything.

"Out there," Farrell Dean said, pointing farther ahead than I was looking. "The lights."

Ahead the lights lay sparkling and cheerful against the black hills and trees. But one by one, the lights nearest us were going out, like candles being snuffed.

"They hide," Gabriel said. "The Locrians. I like to give them a little warning, so they don't have to rush. Wouldn't want my approach to cause unnecessary inconvenience."

He gave a rapid double-tap of his horn and a whole sweep of lights vanished. Within moments the entire landscape lay dark before us, swept utterly clean of the pretty spangled stars. It was only us and the darkness, and somewhere a horse that might or might not have a rider.

Chapter 8

Gabriel parked the truck at the top of a bare rise that opened out onto the sea. A handful of small houses peeked out from the woods around the clearing. All of them were dark and appeared deserted, though I could smell smoke from a fire only recently extinguished.

"If you see any Locrians," Gabriel said as we climbed out of the truck, "Don't be nosy. They're very private, and if you ask questions or seem too curious about them, they'll pull back into their shells like turtles. That's why they're useful at a time like this. If anyone shows up looking for you, they'll get no information. All you have to do is keep out of sight."

"But if we can't ask questions, how are we going to find out about their boats?" I said.

"By acting as if we know everything already. That's the only way they give out information—if they think they're not telling you anything you don't already know." He gestured. "This is the trading post."

We followed him up the wooden steps of the nearest building. Like the others, it was dark. It had a long covered porch across the front, with wooden steps leading up to the closed door.

Gabriel knocked on the door. It was wooden and it rattled on its hinges at his blows. "A man named Ernest keeps the place going," he said. "He brings things up from Doria every couple of months. He's marginally more sociable than the others."

A sudden gust of wind blew my hair across my face, and two or three cold wet raindrops hit me. I shivered and when Farrell Dean shifted I knew he was trying to block the wind for me.

Gabriel banged on the door again, more firmly this time. "Ernest!" he called. "Open up. It's Gabriel Drewblood."

"Go away," came the muffled reply.

Farrell Dean laughed shortly. "The local extrovert," he said.

"Two minutes," Gabriel said loudly. "That's all I need."

"You aren't alone," the voice said, more clearly this time.

"No, I'm not. I have my niece with me, as you can very well see—I know you're watching through your peephole. And this young man is why we're here. He'd like to see Mal's boat."

A long silence followed. Gabriel turned around and surveyed the open sand behind us, then sat down on the edge of the wooden porch. "This might take awhile," he said.

"What's he doing?" I whispered.

Gabriel shrugged. "Thinking. Eating dinner. Sneaking out the back way to confer with Mal. Falling asleep. Who knows? He'll answer when he's ready."

"And if he's never ready?"

"Then we'll try someone else." He continued under his breath. "But later. If we move too fast, we'll scare them off."

"Why can't we talk directly to this Mal person?"

Gabriel looked up at me, his eyes glinting in the wisp of moonlight. "Because I have no idea where he lives," he said. "Off in the woods somewhere, or down by the sea in a cave. Or in a treehouse, for all I know. I've met him, now and again, but only by chance."

Farrell Dean sat down beside Gabriel and they began to talk quietly about tides and boats, about the current that was preventing us from simply rowing back home. I was very tired—thinking about Fiona's soft bed almost made me regret sneaking away—but all the same I didn't feel like sitting, not after riding in the truck so long. Instead I looked around, trying to get oriented after all that wending through the mountains.

On my left a thin sliver of moon was fighting through the clouds, just in time to set; so that was west. The sea lay straight ahead of me, to the north, its tide outgoing.

Fiona's cloak billowed up in a sudden gust of wind and I fought it down. To my right were more trees and Ernest's small building. The road back to Doria was behind me, as was a faint noise that sounded like . . .

"Someone's coming!" I said, turning back toward the men. "I hear a horse."

Farrell Dean and Gabriel got to their feet and moved toward the road, listening. Sure enough, the steady clopping was louder now. Gabriel stepped forward, towards his truck, and Farrell Dean took my hand and pulled me with him into the deep shadows behind Ernest's house. Cautiously we peered around its corner, past Gabriel and his truck, down the road.

It was very dark. The tiny moon was almost gone now, dipping below the tree line, and the veil of clouds muted the stars. By their faint light I could just make out a rider as he crested the hill and entered the sandy clearing, but I couldn't begin to make out his features.

"Is it Lester?" I breathed.

"Can't tell." Farrell Dean's breath was warm against my cheek.

As best as I could tell, the horse didn't seem winded at all. If it had been the one we'd seen running beside the road, its rider must since have let it walk for awhile. As we watched, it turned its head curiously this way and that, and then reached for a tuft of grass at the base of the trees.

"Not yet," a voice said, pulling the horse's head back up.

Gabriel opened the truck door and reached inside, under the seat.

"Planning to shoot me, Drewblood?" the rider said. "I suppose you think that's a fitting means of reconciliation."

Gabriel raised his hands up in the air, showing they were empty, and turned to face the rider. "What brings you to Locria this fine evening?" he said, letting his hands fall to his sides.

"I could ask you the same thing. Though your business is rarely fit for honest ears."

"You're not going to make this easy, are you?"

"Why should I?

Gabriel laughed without humor. "Just to be gracious, I suppose. Though graciousness has never been a priority of yours."

"Not where you're concerned, no. Where is Valentina?"

"Hiding."

"Who is that?" Farrell Dean murmured.

"I don't know," I whispered back.

The rider pulled on the reins and the horse shifted, turning in a tight circle.

"Valentina!" the rider called. "Come on out."

Farrell Dean put a restraining hand on my arm, but I had no intention of moving, not until I knew who this was.

The rider called my name again, and then yet again; by the third time he was beginning to sound annoyed. I looked at Farrell Dean; he shook his head. "I don't know who it is," he said. "And I don't know what Gabriel wants us to do."

The rider wheeled the horse around to face my uncle. "Tell her to come out, Drewblood," he said.

Gabriel turned toward us. "It's all right," he said, and he sounded amused. "It's only your brother, Valentina. He's come to make sure big bad Uncle Gabriel hasn't misplaced you or endangered you."

"That's enough," the rider told him. "You've apologized, Papa tells me, but words are of limited effect when weighed against deeds."

"Which brother is it?" Farrell Dean murmured.

"I don't know. Rufus, maybe." He sounded too formal to be Mick, and I'd never met Sean, but people said he was polite to Gabriel Drewblood.

"You're mortified because you half thought your father was to blame for Valentina's disappearance," Gabriel told the rider. "Don't take that out on me. Now I'm going to get a flashlight out of my truck. Don't shoot me. I've got witnesses." He didn't sound entirely as if he were joking.

After a second a light flashed on, casting strange shadows of horse and rider against the pale sand. I peered at the rider and saw broad shoulders, dark red hair.

"Rufus?" I said, stepping out from behind the trading post, still feeling a little uncertain. He looked larger than I recalled.

"None other." He swung down from his horse on the side away from us, then came around in front of the beast, holding its reins in his hand. When he reached us, he spoke first to Farrell Dean.

"You brought my sister back to us," he said, bowing slightly. "We are very grateful. More than you can know."

Then Rufus turned to me. Taking my chin in his free hand, he studied my face.

"Fiona said you'd been sick," he said. "And it's no wonder after all you've been through. I should have dealt with Tristan Oldfamily years ago. Give me some light here, Drewblood."

The light flashed blindingly and when I raised a hand against it, the beam shone full on my arm and bloodied sleeve.

"You're hurt," Rufus said, casting a disapproving look at Gabriel.

"It's nothing," I said. "A bit of broken glass, that's all."

My brother's face softened as he looked at me.

"Never one to complain, our girls," he said. "Still, you ought to be more careful. Fiona's in a bit of a tizzy, worrying about you."

A mixture of guilt and rebelliousness washed over me. "I left a note," I said. "I didn't mean to be gone so long."

"It's just as well you were. Three men were out at the home place this afternoon, nosing around. They were looking for you, wanting to search the place. Papa put up a good fuss, for show, and then let them look."

"It was because of the doctor," I said. "That's what we think. He must have told the Dream Recorder I was back."

"Could be," Rufus said, looking thoughtful.

"Why didn't Papa let the doctor think I was Fiona?"

"Because when Papa answered the door, the first thing the doctor asked was whether Fee was having any vision disturbances." Rufus touched just beneath his eye, where Fiona had been cut by flying glass when Tristan shot the window.

"No telling how the doctor got wind of her injury," he went on. "It could have been by way of the Death Family, because they did see her when they picked up Tristan's body, or one of the boys might have said something to the wrong person. So Papa couldn't pretend you were Fee, because you obviously hadn't been cut. And he was worried enough that he wanted the doctor to check you out. You were one sick girl."

"And then the doctor must have told the Dream Recorder, and then the Dream Recorder put out a reward, and then those men came looking for me."

Gabriel broke in. "Who was it?" he said to Rufus. "Which men came looking for her?"

Rufus snorted. "Who do you think? Lennie Wright, Spike Delmaro—"

"—and Jason Jones." Gabriel finished. "Of course. They're always looking to make a quick buck."

"Usually from you."

In the glow of the flashlight I could see Gabriel's eyes narrow in annoyance. Were they going to keep sniping at each other all night?

Hastily I jumped in. "Did you really come up here to find me?"

Rufus met my eyes. "Of course I did. Do you think we'd say oh, Valentina's in trouble again, let's hope she's all right?"

Feeling chastised, I didn't know what to say to that, and it was just as well. Rufus didn't pause long enough for me to say anything.

"Locria's a good hiding place," he said, putting an arm around my shoulders as if to take the sting out of his earlier words. "And if anyone has a seaworthy boat, it'll be someone here. Fortunately no one else knows you're looking for a boat, so with luck none of the bounty hunters will bother to come this far."

He jostled me slightly, in what I supposed was a fond-but-gruff brotherly way, and let me go. "I brought supplies," he said, nodding toward the locked trading post. "You did leave unexpectedly, after all. Otherwise Fiona would have loaded you down."

Going to the other side of his horse, he opened a leather saddlebag. After a moment he came out with two parcels, which he handed to me. One was a large loaf of bread, and the other was half a round cheese.

No sooner had he handed them to me than a large raindrop smacked onto my hand. Dozens more followed, pattering loudly in the tree tops and on the roof of Gabriel's truck.

We hurried for the cover of the trading post porch, reaching it just as the sky opened and let out a flood of water. This wasn't a gentle rain—it was possibly the wildest I'd ever seen, blowing in at us from the sides of the porch, dripping through flaws in the roof. I wondered if being right beside the sea had something to do with it—maybe the wind was snatching up seawater and flinging it at us, in addition to the rain falling from the clouds. I would have asked, but was afraid of sounding foolish.

In any case, while being on the porch was better than being in the open, it was clear that if we stayed there very long we'd soon be wet through.

The men didn't seem concerned. Gabriel set his light down on the porch, and I knelt in its circle of light and spread open the packages, shielding them with my body from the rain. Rufus handed me a knife and I began to hack at the food. I knew Fiona would have made a better job of it, but I didn't much care at the moment. I was tired and cold and hungry, and getting increasingly wet, and somewhere out there in the dark people who meant harm were searching for me.

"There's a well just over there," Gabriel said, pointing out into the driving rain. "And come daylight we can do some fishing."

That was the first it had occurred to me that we'd be spending the night. I looked around, but between the darkness and the rain I couldn't make anything out. "Where will we sleep?" I said, passing around the cheese and then backing against the trading post wall, trying to find a spot where I wouldn't get drenched.

"You'll sleep locked up safely in the truck," Gabriel said. "I'll back it into the underbrush so it won't be exposed to casual view. And unless the rain slows, I suppose the three of us will take shelter in the bad house."

Rufus gave a grim nod.

"The what?" I said.

Gabriel chewed and swallowed before answering. "The bad house. That's what they call it. It's an empty house, and in poor repair, as most abandoned houses are. But it has a roof and walls, and a fire pit with a stone chimney. It'll be better than catching our death of cold on this porch."

The rain was pounding on the tin roof, and I raised my voice to be heard. "Why can't I stay there too?"

Gabriel merely smiled, so I turned to my brother. He glanced at Farrell Dean, managing to look both uncomfortable and forbidding.

"We'd all be together," I protested. "There would be chaperones."

"I'll sleep in the truck," Farrell Dean said.

"No, the truck will be safest for her," Rufus said. "And more comfortable. If you need anything, Valentina, honk the horn and we'll all come running."

But I didn't want to sleep alone. It was dark, and I'd been kidnapped, and men were out looking for us, and who knew how many Locrians were peering at us from the trees as we sat in our circle of light.

"I don't want to stay by myself, and I don't see why I should have to," I said.

"Don't be stubborn," Rufus said. "That house isn't a pleasant place to stay. The truck will be much better. Take my word for it."

"I don't want to take anyone's word for it. I want to stay with all of you."

"Tough," Rufus said.

I looked at Gabriel.

"Don't look at me," he said, raising his hands as if in surrender. "I'm only the estranged uncle." The glance he gave Rufus had a malicious glint.

Rufus stared at him for a long moment, then sighed and ran a hand over his face. "Valentina, you wouldn't like sleeping in the bad house. A woman died there."

"Is that all? People die in all sorts of places. I don't mind sleeping where someone died."

"She was murdered." Now Rufus's eyes were on mine. "She was killed by her husband. He tortured her first, held her hands into the fire, her face, punishing her for some imagined trespass. He was drunk, and even when he wasn't drunk he was a brute. He moved up here because he'd been run out of every civilized area."

Rufus paused just fractionally, and then went on. "After he killed his wife he went on living in that house, and then a few months later the house killed him. I suppose that was poetic justice, but it was ugly. The whole thing was ugly."

"The house killed him."

He nodded. "A cross timber came down, one of the roof supports. It knocked him flat and pinned him, and in the wreckage something caught fire. He burned to death."

"And you think the house did it. On purpose."

I meant to sound skeptical, but the dark clearing, the curtain of rain streaming off the edge of the porch roof, the all-around desolation of the place brought uncertainty to my tone.

"Don't be ridiculous." Rufus gestured off into the distance, presumably toward the so-called bad house. "He didn't take care of the place. It was bound to come down on him sooner or later. But it's still not a pleasant place to sleep. It's safe enough—they've braced the roof back up and patched the walls a bit, which is as far as Locrians go to extend hospitality toward guests—but it's damp and untidy, a burnt shell. It reeks of misery."

He glanced at Gabriel, who nodded and cleared his throat. I waited for him to say something, but he didn't.

After a long silence, Farrell Dean turned to me. "I'll arm wrestle you for the truck," he said.

Rufus laughed shortly and held out a hand into the pouring rain. "If it stops raining, I'll sleep in the truck bed," he said, and glanced at Farrell Dean. "I'm her brother. It's only fitting."

"But I have seniority," Gabriel said. "That, and ownership of the truck."

As the men tried to lighten the mood I looked at the rain, which had settled into a quiet, steady rhythm. It wasn't going to stop, not anytime soon.

I'd be sleeping by myself that night.

Chapter 9

Though I was damp from the rain, Fiona's cloak was warm. The bench seat was as soft as my bed in Optica, if not as soft as the beds in Aislin. The truck doors were locked and windows were cracked just a tiny bit—only enough to let in some air and not enough to let in the rain, much less a human hand and arm, should anyone try to reach in while I slept.

But someone could still come creeping out from the undergrowth and peer in the windows at me, and I would never know—unless I woke with a sudden start, thanks to that sixth sense that tells you when someone's eyes are fixed on you. Then I would open my eyes and see someone looking through the rain-streaked glass just a few inches from my face.

I was never going to get to sleep.

Gabriel had let me keep the flashlight, and I flicked it on. Now I was sitting in a brightly lit fishbowl.

Hurriedly I pulled Fiona's cloak over my head, making a tent over me and the light. Her cloak was thick—with luck it completely blocked the light from view. I was going to assume that it did; I certainly wasn't going to stick my head out to check.

Now I was in a stuffy tent in a truck in the rain. I held

my hand over the light and watched my skin turn red. I examined the cut on my arm—it had gotten soaked by the rain, earlier, and I'd peeled off Gabriel's ruined handkerchief. Now it was nothing but a thin red line, pretty unimpressive considering how much it had bled.

Having exhaustively examined my injury, I still didn't feel sleepy. I felt nervous and anyway, it wasn't very late. I couldn't be expected to sleep just because it was raining and I had been sent "to bed" to stay dry.

The stack of Dream Recorder books was on the passenger floorboard; that would give me something to do.

Snaking out one hand, I snagged one. It wasn't the one with my birth in it, which was fine with me. The less personal my bedtime reading, the better.

Lucinda Marcos dreamed that she turned into a metal bird. She ate hundreds of people, and with them in her belly she flew away. On the other side of the ocean she opened her beak and the people walked out.

Yes, nonsensical dreams like that—plain old random dreams—those were what I needed tonight.

Bill Trink dreams frequently about singing. In his dreams many people gather together, facing beautiful panels of stained glass, and sing in four-part harmony. He is able to repeat bits of the lyrics to some of the songs, but finds them baffling. Why, he asks, do the people in his dreams persist in singing about crosses? Why not triangles or squares?

I told him that he is not dreaming about geometry, but about exclusions. When one wishes to exclude an item on a list, one crosses it out. No one likes to deprive oneself of choices, and Bill admits that he is more indecisive than most.

He then took it upon himself to ask around, and when he

discovered several others who dream of crosses as well, he told them that they too had decisiveness issues. He also learned that Joseph Gold and Marian White dream about stars pinned to coats, and wanted me to interpret that for him as well. I told him they would have to come themselves, that I could not work with secondhand dreams.

I yawned. Surely I wouldn't suffocate myself under Fiona's cloak. Just to be sure, I folded the edge back a tiny bit, letting in air down by my knee.

Margo Trail frequently dreams that all the color has been drained out of her life. She wanders around looking for something to do, some way to be useful, but no one will let her help. They tell her she is too old. Then a tiny redheaded girl runs up, holds out her hand, and asks Margo to take her for a walk. Margo is delighted.

Margo is getting older and so it is not atypical for her to be concerned about her changing role in life. However, her dream is unusual in that it ends happily. She cannot explain the redheaded child. She is aware that the Alleyns have a daughter with red hair, but as they live in Doria and do not often come to Ionia, Margo believes she has never seen the girl. I assured her that she must have seen her without being aware of it.

Hmmm. I wanted to meet Margo.

Esme Whitehouse dreams she is trying to cook dinner, but when she opens the cupboards, they're empty. She tries one and then another, opening dozens of cupboard doors, but finds only bare shelves. Then she turns and sees that her kitchen table is crowded with people, thin and hungry, waiting to be fed, and she is horrified and mortified that she has nothing to give

them. At least Alice's boy has a bag of apples, she tells herself;
at least he won't starve. Note: There is no one on Aislin named
Alice.

Now that was very strange. How could Esme
Whitehouse possibly be dreaming about Farrell Dean and his
mother?

I read the next dream—a silly one about people having
surgeries to change the shapes of their noses—and then I began skimming, flipping pages, searching for I didn't know
what. When I finished that book I picked up another—a
much later one, according to the dates, and with different
handwriting—and began skimming rapidly through it, scanning dream after dream after dream.

All these people pouring out their secrets, exposing
their hearts. It made me sick.

The next few dreams were nonsensical ones, and I was
starting to get sleepy. I began to read less carefully, flipping
pages before my brain really understood what my eyes had
seen.

Midway through the book I froze. Surely that hadn't said
what I thought it said.

I backed up and read more slowly.

Keith Foster has had recurring dreams about Fiona Al-
leyn. He believes the dreams are more likely to come after he
has taken Dream Drops, and expressed his intent of abstaining
from them for a time. I was able to persuade him, however,
that it is better to get his subconscious urgings out into the
open; repressing them would surely be more disastrous, in the
long run, than facing them.

Keith dreams that he is following Fiona Alleyn, spying on
her, making notes in a book about her every move. He watches
her in the most private situations, which embarrasses him, but

she is unlike anyone he has ever seen, and he can't take his eyes off her. He is simultaneously repelled and attracted.

Keith finds this dream terribly upsetting. "Why should I be interested in a mutant freak?" he says, and when I press him—in what way is Fiona Alleyn a mutant freak?—he cradles his head in his hands. "I don't know," he says. "I shouldn't have said that. She's a perfectly normal young woman. A nice young woman, well respected. I shouldn't be thinking about her this way at all. I think I must be losing my mind."

I yanked the cloak off of my head and reached for the horn, but as I moved I caught a glimpse of the next dream, and I let my hand fall without summoning the men.

Will Bright dreamed that he was standing in the middle of a circle of a large crowd of people. A man wearing black clothes walked up to him and without warning set his clothes alight. Will felt the heat, smelled smoke and singeing flesh, and then someone threw water over him. It was very cold and coming so suddenly after the terrible heat, it knocked the breath out of him. The dream concluded with steam rising from Will's body and obscuring his sight as he desperately tried to see what was happening around him.

Of course.

I should have realized sooner. I should have seen it the very first time I spoke with Gabriel, that day I fainted at the sight of him. He had told me his dreams about his lost brother, dreams I knew were true. That wasn't some random cosmic coincidence, and it wasn't because twins had once been one person—though surely that helped, of course it helped, that had to be why the experimenters wanted only identical twins.

Gabriel had dreamed about Rafe because the Dream

Drops made him dream about Rafe. That was the experiment. The *dreams* were the experiment.

And so the dream records weren't just to keep track of surfacing memories that might cause problems. The dream records were lab books.

The Dream Recorders on this island wrote down dreams, and the Watchers on the other island could tell whether they were real or not, because the Watchers watched us—me especially, twins especially—so they'd know what we were doing, and if our twins over here saw us doing something we really did do, then the scientists knew that the experiment was working.

The rain was drumming noisily on the truck roof and I pressed my hands over my ears, trying to think.

To think. Thinking my own thoughts, here in the privacy of the rain, in the locked truck.

My mouth went dry. I'd always known I was watched—at meals, in bed, in the shower—but I'd believed that at least my thoughts were my own.

The stinging of my eyes told me I was crying and I swiped away hot tears. I wasn't going to call the men. I didn't want anyone to know this, not yet. It was too upsetting, too humiliating. I'd had nothing that was mine alone. I'd *been* nothing that was me alone. The Watchers and wardens had kept track of me. The scarred warden—he was surely Keith Foster's twin brother—had obsessed about me. Angel had spied on me when I'd thought I was alone with Meritt. And even my thoughts had been exposed, laid bare to the dreamers on this island.

They'd known how I'd felt about Meritt, the dreamers. They'd known how I'd hated being different, being the freak. They'd known all my secret pettiness, my playing up to Farrell Dean so he'd give me his food—because Cline was right about that, even though I hadn't admitted it even to myself, and the dreamers would have seen it. They'd know the worst about me.

No, that wasn't exactly so. *Fiona* would know the worst of me. Only Fiona, and whoever had heard her describe her dreams. What must she think of me?

But—

Hope rose suddenly. Michael Alleyn had thought the Dream Recorders were nosy quacks. Eric Alleyn also didn't approve of Dream Drops—Tor had said he didn't, and Angus had said none of the Alleyns ever had anything to do with Dream Recorders. So that meant Fiona had never taken any drops. And she'd certainly never mentioned dreaming odd dreams, not even when I'd told her about Optica, not even when I'd told her about Meritt. She'd only had vague dreams about hunger, just as I'd had vague dreams about the sea.

I'd have thrown my arms around Eric Alleyn's neck, if he'd been with me. As it was, I blew a kiss in his general direction, south toward Doria, and in my relief I laughed out loud, in the blessed privacy of Gabriel's truck. Then I laughed again, at myself, for being so upset and so elated in the space of a couple of minutes.

Of course this meant Sir Tom was right—the watching had nothing to do with my hair. I was watched so the experimenters could compare my life to whatever my sister saw in her dreams. Or would have seen, if she had taken Dream Drops. That's why I was watched, not because I was a mutant freak. At least, no more a mutant freak than any other identical twin. No more a mutant freak than the scarred warden, whose own brother was watching him watching me.

That was weird. Why would they do that? Why would they let a twin be a warden? Wasn't that like being inside the experiment and outside it, all at once?

But the wardens didn't know everything; maybe they didn't even know they were in an experiment. Or—my heart leaped again—maybe Optica wasn't the primary subject of the experiment. Aislin was. *Fiona* was. And I was in the control group, or something approaching a control group. Yes, I'd grown up without a family, without freedom, without any number of riches that Fiona enjoyed; but at least I wasn't the one being actively experimented on. I was only watched.

Fleetingly I felt ashamed for being glad my sister might be the lab rat they were experimenting on, rather than me, but actually, thanks to Eric Alleyn, she wasn't. Thanks to him, she wasn't given Dream Drops, wasn't tricked into spying, into reading my mind. Good old obstinate, opinionated, prickly, contrary Eric Alleyn. I was beginning to really love that man. He essentially had opted Fiona and me out of the experiment.

And this was the answer we'd been looking for—this was the information Gabriel and Papa wanted. So we could go now, as soon as we had weapons and supplies and more people. We could go back to Optica without fear that the Watchers would spring something dangerous on us. We knew the experiment was about mind reading.

Mind reading …

It made the violation of the cameras seem almost quaint by comparison. No wonder Sir Tom felt guilty about his part in it. No wonder he hadn't wanted to tell me. And besides, what had he said? *Some doors, once opened, can never be shut again.* Knowing someone might be out there listening to my thoughts certainly would have been an unsettling open door. I could have ended up being paranoid my entire life, trying to hide, even inside my own head.

Sir Tom had been right to keep me in the dark, I had to admit. I should have trusted the old Guardian more.

The rain eased, just a bit, and the change in the sound of the drops hitting the windshield brought me back to the little truck in Locria. Suddenly aware that I was sitting there fully exposed again, I pulled Fiona's cloak back over my head. My legs felt cramped from sitting cross-legged so long, and I stretched out on the seat. Then I clicked the light off.

I wasn't sleepy, but there was no need to run down Gabriel's flashlight battery when I didn't need the light. I was going to lie there and think—think secretly, privately—about what I had learned.

Chapter 10

A bee was buzzing around my head. It must be a very large bee, because it was very loud, but I couldn't spot it. I wasn't afraid of bees but I was cautious around them; I didn't swat at them like some of the field workers did.

With a start, I sat up and pulled Fiona's cloak off my head. I was in Gabriel's truck, in Locria. The rain had stopped and dawn was just thinking about coming—the sky above the trees was still dark, but not determinedly so, and birds were singing.

And I hadn't been dreaming, not exactly. Something was buzzing—not a bee—but something hard in my pocket. What was that?

I struggled with the skirt of my dress and finally came out with the source of the noise. It was the little communicator-like object I'd found upstairs at the Dream Recorder's shop. I'd completely forgotten about it.

A yellow light was blinking on a raised button on the side. There were other small buttons as well, but I couldn't tell what they were in the dark, and I didn't want to turn on Gabriel's light. I was about to do something I almost certainly shouldn't do, and I didn't want anyone—not the Locrians, not Farrell Dean and the others—to see.

I pushed the button with the yellow light.

The buzzing stopped and the light turned green and, at the same time, something sprang out from the top of the object. It was a wire. An antennae, probably. I was lucky it hadn't poked me in the eye.

Nothing else happened. I held the object in both hands and waited. I wasn't going to press any other button to speak; I wasn't that stupid. But the Dream Recorder was something akin to a Watcher, and I wanted to know who communicated with her. It might be the midwife, or Edgeling, or the doctor. It might be someone else, someone we didn't yet know was involved.

"Come in, Jean."

The voice seemed familiar. Who was that? It must not be Edgeling or the doctor—their voices I wouldn't know.

"Answer me, Jean. Are you there? You ought to keep your transmitter with you—sloppiness is not acceptable, not even now."

My heart began to thud. I knew this voice. It was Angel.

And I shouldn't have been surprised. Of course Angel could communicate with this island; otherwise how would he know when to come steal a baby?

Angel paused, and I heard a thumping sound, as if he might be drumming his fingers on the transmitter. "Jean, are you dead? Are you conferring with Rowena? I'm a bit perplexed, because it seems your transmitter is receiving, and yet you do not answer. Perhaps you're experiencing a malfunction. If you can hear me, listen closely: I'm looking for a red-headed girl who goes, believe it or not, by the name Red."

Suddenly I felt uncomfortably warm.

"Yes, it's an asinine name. A primitive descriptor, signifying only the most superficial trait. Valentina is too sentimental but at least it has some imagination. I would have done better. I should have kept her, named her something meaningful, something that marked her as mine."

"But I'm not yours," I said.

"Ah. Good morning."

I shut my eyes. How stupid could I possibly be?

I hadn't expected him to hear me; I'd thought there would be a button I had to push to be heard, like on Gabriel's transceivers.

"I know you're there," Angel said. "You might as well speak to me."

True enough. And maybe if I talked to him I could get more information, though the thought of speaking with the person who had stolen me from my home made me feel queasy with distaste and something oddly like humiliation.

"So you don't belong to me, you say?" Angel sounded strangely interested in my remark.

"That's right."

"To whom, then, do you belong? Your mother is dead."

"Thanks to you," I said hotly.

"No. You're speaking from emotion, not reason. Your mother died in childbirth. It happens, especially in rural areas without modern medical care."

He was blaming my father, like everyone else did.

"You don't belong to Eric Alleyn," Angel said, making it not quite a question, and a little shock ran through me.

"You know his name?"

"Of course I do. Why wouldn't I?"

"And you know what he named me. You called me Valentina."

"Haven't you realized? I know everything."

His tone was mocking, but I couldn't tell whether the mockery was directed at me or at himself. And anyway, I didn't care.

"You knew our names," I said. "You knew us as people, as a family, but you stole me anyway. You didn't care what you did to us."

"You're making inferences that the facts do not warrant."

"I know for a fact that you stole me."

"I don't deny it," Angel said, sounding both exasperated and amused. "Technically I purchased you, but I was aware that I was buying stolen goods, and if I hadn't bought you I would have stolen you. But don't worry—you don't have to thank me for it."

Thank him?

"What did I do with you, after I took you?" he went on, and when I didn't reply, he pressed the point. "Where did I take you?"

"To a place where my family wasn't. To a place where I was a freak, alone and lonely, where I didn't have anybody."

There was a long silence. First I hoped I'd shamed him; then I thought no, he was too far gone to be shamed.

"Meritt would be hurt to hear you say that," Angel said finally, quietly.

"Meritt isn't my family. It's different."

"I know the difference. So does he, for whom did he have?"

"You."

There was a brief pause.

"He always said you were clever," Angel murmured. "But you aren't as clever as you think you are. Whom did Meritt have? A dead mother, like you. And, like you, a father who was separated from him. No siblings, no cousins, no flesh and blood of his own in that blighted city. He was all alone."

"So Meritt doesn't have family in Optica," I said. "That's a shame, but it doesn't have anything at all to do with you stealing me."

"It has everything to do with it. I thought you would be company for him."

"You stole me because of the experiment," I said defensively. "You stole me because I'm a twin. You weren't stealing a friend for Meritt—why would you? There are lots of people in Optica, lots of people his own age. You didn't have to steal someone from across the sea for him."

Angel didn't answer, and in the silence I began, uncomfortably, to think over the ramifications of what I'd said. Was I actually saying I would rather I'd never met Meritt? Of course not—how could I say that? But the price had been growing up without a family, without Fiona and Rory and my father—

"Meritt cares for you," Angel said, and now his voice was cold. "I'm sorry to hear how little you care for him."

"I do care for him," I managed, though my throat was suddenly tight with unshed tears. "I care for him very much."

"You have a strange way of showing it."

"Where is he? Is he okay?"

"You have no right to ask. You say you're sorry you ever met him, and your actions prove as much."

"What do you mean? I've never done anything to hurt Meritt." I'd tried to protect him, in fact; I'd been arrested protecting him.

"You left him," Angel said.

"But I—"

"You abandoned him at the very moment when he needed you the most. You got in that boat and you left him to face everything on this island alone."

"But I didn't mean to leave—I tried to row back, surely you saw that—"

"You should never have set foot in that boat. I offered to take you to my son; in good faith I promised to take you to him. Instead you chose to run away."

Outside the window, the world was gray and still. "Is he hurt? Please tell me. Is he in trouble?"

"I will ask the questions. How did you get hold of that transmitter?"

"I … it was … " I didn't know what to tell him. I didn't know whether he was on our side or not. He was Meritt's father, and Ezzie thought he was on our side, but he had stolen me from my family and was working with the Dream Recorders and the Watchers and the experimenters.

"It's a simple enough question," he said. "Jean would never have given it to you."

"No. She …" Hurriedly I changed the subject. "Angel, I want to come back. But I don't know how to get there. The boat—the currents—can you tell me how to do it?" He must know how—he'd come to steal babies, and surely not only when the currents were right.

"You endangered my son by leaving, and you will endanger him still more by returning," Angel said. "If you come back, he'll be forced once again to choose between your life and his."

The Watchers would demand me as proof of Meritt's loyalty, that was what Angel meant. He didn't know that I already knew about that problem; he couldn't know what Farrell Dean had overheard, the night before he almost died in the city meeting.

"What if no one knows I've come back?" I said. "Then I wouldn't endanger him. I could stay in the woods, I could hide—"

Angel interrupted me. His voice was so quiet I had to strain to hear. "If you come back and my son dies to save you, I will kill you for it. That is a promise."

"If Meritt died to save me, I wouldn't want to live."

"Then we understand each other."

Suddenly there was a noise in the background. Angel said something I couldn't catch and I thought he was going to cut the transmission, but he didn't. The line stayed open, crackling and whistling, and I wondered what he was doing. I hoped he'd come back; I had to try to get more information.

As I waited I watched the grayness going lighter at the tops of the trees and tried not to think, tried not to weigh my years with Meritt against my lost years with my family. Thinking about it made my heart hurt.

The transmitter crackled again, loudly, and a voice spoke right into it, making me jump. "Red?"

"Meritt!" I almost dropped the transmitter, slamming my elbow against the truck door in the process.

"Are you all right? Are you safe? Where are you—what's happening? I was so afraid—I thought you'd been killed—Angel wouldn't tell me—"

He broke in, laughing. "I'm fine, Red. It's okay. Take a deep breath."

My arm was tingling painfully from the blow to my elbow, but I was afraid to set down the transmitter so I could rub it.

"You're with—he's your—did you know that he's—"

"My father." He laughed again, this time with disbelief. "My father, a Guardian. Wild, isn't?"

"Did you know? How long have you known?" And what exactly did Meritt know—did he know about the twins, the kidnappings? I didn't know whether Angel had told him anything at all.

In the background Angel said something.

"That's too dangerous," Meritt said, apparently talking to Angel. I wanted Angel to go away. I wanted to be alone with Meritt, even if we were alone with an ocean between us. I wished that I could see him—the last time I'd seen him he'd been standing on the cliff, watching us leave, and I hadn't heard his voice since the night he left me in Farrell Dean's prison cell, since the night he kissed me and then walked out the door to put himself in danger in order to protect us.

"Meritt? Are you there?"

"I'm here." I couldn't see him but I could imagine him as clearly as if he were there with me, sitting in the little truck in the underbrush, all alone with me in the gray silent dawn with the birds singing around us, the rain from the night before turning to mist as the sun hit it. I could see his face, the striking cheekbones, the lightning quick grin, the way his gray eyes lit up when something caught his interest. His dark hair would be too long—it always seemed to be too long—and he'd be running a hand through it, fidgeting, thinking, laughing, talking.

Then from across the sea he did start talking, fast, the way he sometimes did, so fast I could hardly catch it all. "So you made it to another island? And Farrell Dean—is he okay? That was good, Red, that you got him into that boat and away. That was the best possible thing to do. Is he with you?"

"Not right now," I said. "Right now I'm alone. Meritt, after the city meeting, when you didn't come to the orchard, we thought—" I couldn't bring myself to say we'd thought he'd been killed.

"Nah," Meritt said, reading my mind. "The Watchers talked big, but they didn't do anything. I told them they'd almost made a terrible mistake, that if they'd shot one of my closest friends, nobody would ever believe I'd support them. I said people would think I was faking my support, that I was spying on them instead of joining them. I said the whole thing would have blown up in their faces."

"And they believed that?"

"No, of course not. But they believed that I believed it, so it worked."

But the Watchers wouldn't let him keep everyone safe, all his friends, not if they wanted a sign of loyalty. For all I knew, maybe Meritt had come after me on the cliff because he had to make up for protecting Farrell Dean.

I wanted to ask. I wanted to ask and then tell him I understood, but I wasn't completely sure I did, and anyway, now that I was talking with him it seemed like such an insult to even bring it up. Maybe he would turn me in, and maybe he should, to save all the others. But I couldn't ruin the moment by talking about it.

"The Watchers want me to join the Watcher Council," Meritt was saying. "We're negotiating, I guess you'd say. Coming to terms."

I already knew that—and he knew I knew, because we'd spied on the Watchers together. Maybe he'd forgotten that I knew.

Or maybe Meritt couldn't talk freely in front of Angel, either.

"I hope it works out," I said, picking my words with care. "You'll be able to do some good that way. You might be able to protect my old people—are they still all right?"

Angel was talking again, saying something to Meritt that I couldn't quite make out. I so wanted Angel to go away.

"So far they're okay," Meritt said, as if there had been no interruption. "And there haven't been any more city meetings either. They've locked down the city, though. Extra wardens on duty, early curfews, no talking at meals. They're furious about the people who got out. So now I have to get them to trust me, get them to believe I'm on their side, and then we're good to go."

"How are you going to get them to trust you?" I said. *Without me there to hand over,* I added mentally.

"Oh, you know. Flatter them, tell them how smart they are, let them think I agree with everything, that I'm hanging on their every word." Suddenly he was talking fast again. "It's sickening, but it's only for a little while, just until I'm all the way in, just until they trust me. I mean, they're suspicious of me, but they want me on their side because they know my father's a Guardian, and even a sort of defunct Guardian is way better than no Guardian at all, and that's going to win out in the end."

It didn't seem very tactful, calling Angel a defunct Guardian, and I suddenly had a terrible image of Angel killing Meritt while I listened, helpless, from across the sea.

But he wouldn't hurt his son, would he? He was mad at me for endangering Meritt, so surely he wouldn't hurt him himself. Still it might be best to find something else to say, something to distract Angel, just in case.

"Meritt," I said, "Who's your mother? Do you know?"

No—that was stupid—I'd probably just made matters worse. I should hurry and distract Angel from my distraction, but for the life of me I couldn't think what else to say. I couldn't tell Meritt about the experiment, or that Angel had kidnapped me, or about my twin sister, or about Rafe's twin brother. There was nothing I could safely say in front of Angel.

Because what if Angel wasn't really helping Meritt? Or what if he was helping him now, but would stop if I exposed him for what he was? Or what if Meritt turned his back on his father, disgusted and repulsed, and Angel decided to punish us all for making his son hate him? Angel was simply too much of an unknown quantity.

I couldn't hear Angel, but in the long pause I had the feeling Meritt was listening to him. When Meritt finally spoke again, his voice was neutral. "Rosella," he said.

Crazy Rosella.

I didn't know what to say. Luckily Meritt didn't notice my silence; in the background, Angel was talking again.

"Not until it's absolutely safe," Meritt said.

"What are you talking about?" I said.

"The sea current. Angel says you want to come back, but the sea isn't safe right now."

It was pitiful but I couldn't help myself; I had to say it. "I didn't mean to leave you, Meritt. It was an accident. I wish I could come back. I'm trying to. I'm trying as hard as I can."

"Hey, don't cry, Red—you're not crying, are you? Listen, I wish you could come back too. I miss you and besides, there's a problem you could help me with. You know that other Guardian—the old one, Tommy?"

Sir Tom—but Meritt called him Tommy, the same as Angel did.

"Is he hurt?"

"No, nothing like that," Meritt said. "He's fine. But he won't work with us. I tried to talk to Judd—there's something I need him to ask his father about—but the old man won't let me near him. He's got some crazy notion that Angel's his enemy, and since I'm Angel's son he thinks I am, too. I've tried and tried to tell him otherwise—and Cline and the others have told him too—but he won't let me in the stockade, and won't let Judd come out to talk to me. If you were here you might be able to talk some sense into him."

"Can't you ask Warden Rhoda instead of Judd's father?"

I didn't even like saying that woman's name.

"No, I can't ask her this," Meritt said. "It's complicated. See, we always thought of the wardens as a single unit, right? All for one and one for all. But it isn't like that. They have factions, and I'm trying to play one faction against the other. Divide and conquer. Rhoda's on one side, and Warden Karl and his buddies are the other. So I need an in with them, and Judd's it. But I can't get to him. If you could just talk to Tommy—"

Angel said something else in the background.

"Meritt," I said. "Ask Angel—"

I hesitated, wondering yet again how much Meritt knew, trying to find words that wouldn't expose Angel as a kidnapper and make him angry at us.

"Angel might know a safe way to come back before the current shifts, and then I—"

"No," Meritt said. "It's too dangerous. You could drown, or get washed who knows where. But it's a shame because it really is a problem, not being able to talk to Judd."

I had another idea. "Does Sir Tom have a transmitter that connects with this one? Or can you get one to him?"

"To—oh, to Tommy?" His voice turned thoughtful. "Maybe I could. It's a little tricky—he has all these crazy boo-by traps set up. It's like an obstacle course getting anywhere near him—but maybe I could do it." He paused. "Yeah. I think I could. That's a good idea. Then you could convince him to cooperate."

"Don't try if it's too dangerous," I said. "And watch out for those wild men, Meritt. They're really vicious."

He laughed. "Don't worry. I'm learning from the best. You wouldn't believe the tricks Angel knows."

Wouldn't I.

"My light's blinking," Meritt said. "I think the battery's dying."

"Meritt—listen—I could be really careful, and find a sturdy boat, but I don't have an engine and we can't row against the current—let me talk to Angel, please, just for a minute—"

Meritt spoke over me, his voice less clear than before. "Red? Are you there? I can't hear you. If you can hear me, be careful, okay? I'll call you again as soon as I can. Bye, Red. I miss you. Stay safe."

The transmitter turned to static. The little light on top, which had been green while we were talking, turned back to yellow. Then it went dark.

"Bye, Meritt," I said. Trying hard to blink back the tears that blinded me, I pushed the button and watched the anten-nae pull itself back inside.

Lifting the edge of Fiona's cloak, I mopped my tear-streaked face.

And now I should go tell the men what had happened. But I needed a minute, first, to recover. I hoped they wouldn't suddenly appear while I was still unnerved.

The bad house was out the back window, toward the sea. Turning to make sure the others weren't coming, I could see it in the thin morning light, just its dark outline. It looked sinister, black against the lightening world, but probably that was only because of what they'd said about it.

Out the driver's side window, through the scraggly brush, I could now see bits of Ernest's trading post, while in front of me lay the empty clearing, the pale sand dull and flat in the gray early light.

I turned my head to look out the passenger window and shrieked.

Someone was looking back at me.

Chapter 11

It wasn't a long shriek, and maybe it wasn't loud, except inside the truck. The man staring at me heard it, obviously—his eyebrows came together—but he didn't otherwise react. And I didn't yell again, or honk the horn to call the men. I couldn't. I was stunned by the man outside the truck. I had never seen anyone even remotely like him.

His honey-colored hair was long and pulled back from his face, twisted into dozens of snake-like braids that hung past his shoulders. His skin was a pale warm gold, his eyes were such a pale brown they looked gold, and as the sun cleared the top of the trees its yellow light glinted on three gold rings that were stuck straight through one of his ears.

The most dramatic thing, though, was the drawings. They were black, winding, complicated spirals and vines, and they scrolled from the fingertips of his left hand up his arm, around his shoulder, and down his left side, where they disappeared into his pants and then emerged with his left ankle, scrolling all the way down to his toes.

I could see all this because all he had on was a pair of raggedy trousers, but he didn't look cold though I was cold, even fully clothed, in the truck, and with a cloak.

He wasn't a particularly big man, but every square inch of him seemed honed sharp. Distinct rows of muscles played down his abdomen. It was hard for me to judge how old he was—maybe twenty, maybe older. He seemed sort of timeless, and for a heartbeat I thought maybe I was delirious again. But I could smell the oil from the truck's engine, and I could see the man's footprints in the wet sandy soil, and he looked solid enough, though he did have that I-could-vanish-without-a-word look about him, like a wild creature.

If he did vanish without a word we'd have lost another chance to find out about the boats, and who knew when another Locrian would deign to show himself? This was the very first one we'd seen.

Hurriedly I reached over and rolled down the window, just enough to make myself heard, but not enough that the man could grab me, if he were so inclined, which he didn't seem to be. He was simply standing there quietly, perfectly still, examining me as I was examining him.

"Hello," I said tentatively.

He nodded once.

I wanted to ask who he was, but Gabriel had said the Locrians didn't like to be asked questions, so instead I said, "My name is Red."

He nodded again—once—but he didn't reciprocate with his own name, and he didn't say anything else, either. He only stood there, his gaze drifting thoughtfully across my face. Why didn't he speak?

Maybe he *couldn't* speak.

Maybe that was what the strange designs meant, that he wasn't like other people, that he couldn't talk. How was I going to communicate with him if he couldn't talk?

While I tried to figure out what to do—should I try to see if he could write? Should I encourage him to use hand gestures? Should I come right out and ask if he could talk, or would that be terribly rude?—his gaze drifted away from me, toward the trees. He was going to get bored and wander away, and it would be my fault for dithering around like this.

But even if he couldn't talk, he could hear—he'd nodded, so he could hear—so maybe if I kept talking, if I said something interesting, he'd stay put.

"I'm not dead," I blurted. "And I'm not a mutant either."

Again his eyebrows came together, and no wonder. I sounded like a lunatic.

I tried again. "Please don't go," I said. "You startled me. I'm not making much sense. I meant to say, I came here from another island."

"Not in a truck."

He'd spoken! And he was smiling, just barely. He could talk *and* he was making a joke.

I smiled too, and it was a real smile, a relieved one, though my face felt stiff with the salt from my tears. "No, I didn't come in a truck. I came in a boat. I landed down near Doria, on the beach there."

He took a step closer, and I saw with relief that I definitely had caught his interest.

"Not a boat with an engine," he said. His voice was very quiet, so quiet that the sound of the sea would have overshadowed it, had not each word been spoken with crystal clarity.

"No. It was a rowboat. We had oars."

"You cannot row against the current," he said, hooking his thumbs into the waistband of his pants. "It is very strong."

"Yes, but that was good for us. It took us where we wanted to go. And for awhile, before we hit the current, we could row."

"You knew directions to this land."

"Yes, we had directions. But we can't go back to our island until the current changes, and that's weeks and weeks from now."

"Rowboats are limited in what they can do."

"Yes."

I saw how this worked, this Locrian thing. If you wanted to know something, you made it sound like a statement, not a question. The other person either let your statement stand, or corrected you, and that was how you learned what you wanted to know.

For a long moment we studied each other. Then the man shifted, putting his hands on his hips, the black drawings writhing as he moved.

"That is Gabriel Drewblood's truck," he said, and I nodded. "Gabriel Drewblood has a niece with red hair. She lives in Doria."

"She's my sister. I'm Gabriel's niece too, but the niece you're thinking of, that's not me, even though she looks like me." I sure hoped he was patient, or else I'd drive him away with this tangle. "Her name is Fiona," I said. "We're identical twins. We were born together and we look alike but we're not each other. I was stolen when we were babies, and taken away to that other island."

"I have heard about the baby sister who died," he said, and something glinted in his pale gold eyes and I knew he was being tactful. He'd heard about crazy Eric Alleyn digging up his pasture, that was what he'd heard.

"That was me," I said. "I was the baby who died. Only of course I didn't die—they only thought I did, except when they were thinking I'd been stolen. Or sold. The midwife lied, and of course the lights for souls confused things." I took a deep breath. This wasn't at all like me, but I was rattled—I'd been yanked out of sleep by Angel, had spoken with Meritt, and then fast on the heels of all that had been presented with this apparition.

Fortunately the apparition nodded as if I were making perfect sense.

"You came to Locria to find a better boat," he said.

"That's right!" Either he was Ernest, or he had talked to Ernest.

"A boat that can fight the currents."

"Yes. A boat that can take me home. I have friends over there who are in trouble—in danger—and I have to get back, or else they'll die. I have to take guns to them, and people."

"It is a bad island."

I thought about that. "Some people there are bad, but some are good. Just like here."

He weighed that comment.

It was time. I didn't want to scare him away, but I was going to try to get some answers, if I could, using the Locrian method. I rolled the window the rest of the way down and, leaning out, said, "You have a boat."

"Yes."

Okay, good. I had been pretty sure he had one, given his interest in the one I'd come in.

"You have a boat that can fight the currents," I said.

He nodded.

I wasn't sure what to ask next. Maybe I could ask to see the boat—or did that count as asking questions? I certainly couldn't say, "You'll let me see the boat." That might be the Locrian method, but it sounded way too presumptuous.

I decided to take a chance.

"You're Mal," I said.

He smiled in a way that lit up his whole face.

Then, like the sun going out, the smile vanished. Mal looked away and I craned around, leaning farther out the window, to see what it was he saw.

Gabriel was striding towards us through the under-brush, Rufus and Farrell Dean not far behind. They all looked bleak and unrested, their faces drawn. And while they probably didn't mean to seem aggressive, with all three of them hurrying like that—and with Rufus looking as cantankerous as our father—it was no wonder Mal was edging toward the thicker woods.

Hurriedly I extricated myself from the window, fumbled with the lock, and swung open the truck door.

"Good morning," I called to the rapidly approaching men, putting myself between them and Mal. I could feel him right behind me—he hadn't vanished yet—but he'd be gone in a heartbeat if they kept barreling toward us. I held up one hand and frowned at them, trying to signal for them to stay back.

"I think you've met Gabriel before," I said over my shoulder. "The one with the red hair is Rufus, my oldest brother. He's a little grumpy but he means well. And the other one is Farrell Dean. He came with me from the other island."

Mal was a little further back now, a little closer to vanishing. Desperate, I tried to think of something to say that would keep him. "He's the one who'd like to see your boat," I said. "He's good with mechanical things, and he won't hurt the boat. I promise."

The men had paused—reluctantly—a short distance away. Farrell Dean looked tense, but he nodded a greeting politely enough. "I won't hurt your boat," he repeated.

I glanced over my shoulder at Mal; he was studying the group with his strange gold eyes.

Gabriel said something to Rufus out of the side of his mouth, and Rufus answered equally quietly. He looked more uneasy than the other two; he kept glancing at Mal's designs and then away again, as if trying not to stare. Clearly he'd never seen the man before.

Mal nodded, as if to himself, and took a few steps away from the woods, toward me. When he did Farrell Dean came forward too, looking protective.

"It's all right," I told him. "Stay where you are."

Mal edged right up beside me. "The other island has many troubles," he said, in that quiet voice that made me feel as if I might only be thinking the words. "You were in an experiment. That is why you had to escape."

Startled, I nodded. "How did you—" I began, but stopped myself before I completed the question. Could I ask, or would he vanish at a direct question? I'd better not risk it. Besides, it was pretty easy to guess how he knew; the men had no doubt been talking last night in the bad house; it wouldn't have been hard to eavesdrop on them.

"I'm only just figuring out about the experiment," I said, just to say something while I figured out how to direct this conversation where it needed to go.

"That is why you want a boat," Mal helpfully clarified. "To stop the experiment."

"Yes. Well, technically the experiment is probably over." I felt some perverse need to be completely honest with this strange man. "But the people in charge over there don't know that. So they're still experimenting on us. And besides that we don't have enough food, so they're going to kill some of us to make sure there's enough for everyone else."

Mal nodded. "That is bad," he said.

"It is. And we don't have time to build a boat with an engine that can fight the current. If we have to start from scratch, everyone we love will be dead by the time we get back to Optica."

Mal considered this, his eyes scanning my face, his brow wrinkling with concern. To my surprise I realized my cheeks were once again wet with tears.

The men shifted restlessly, trying to keep an eye on the Locrian without staring at him, shooting quick glances at him and then at each other, at the sand, at the choppy sea.

"Optica is a long way away," Mal said eventually, hooking his thumbs into the waistband of his pants again. That seemed like a good sign—that was his comfortable stance, I thought. Maybe he wouldn't vanish, at least not if the other men stayed put. Rufus was looking awfully impatient.

"I don't know how far away Optica is in miles," I said. "It took us a couple of days when we were drifting and rowing." I hesitated, risked another question-statement. "Your boat can go that far."

"My boat can. The engine cannot. The engine can go twice around this island. Sometimes. It is not enough."

That was bad news. I glanced at Gabriel. He gave a miniscule nod, but I didn't know how to read that.

"You don't have another engine?" I tried. "I mean—you have another engine. A better one."

Mal shook his head. "No. I have one engine, and it will not go far."

Farrell Dean cleared his throat. "Rufus has a lot of engineering experience," he said. "And I have some myself. Not with boat engines, but with other sorts. Tractors and cars and trucks."

He paused, but when Mal kept watching him attentively, went on. "Maybe between the three of us we can adjust your engine so it can go further."

"To Optica."

"To Optica," Farrell Dean agreed.

Mal didn't immediately answer, but he didn't walk away, either. He stood there, perfectly still, with his gaze resting on Farrell Dean and his mind clearly elsewhere. The wind kicked up and sprinkled us with raindrops from the trees above, and the sea was choppy with gray harsh waves.

The silence stretched on, longer than I knew how to interpret. I hoped Mal was considering our request. Maybe he was just waiting for us to go away.

Finally I couldn't stand it any longer.

"I don't know why you should help us," I said.

Gabriel sighed heavily and gave me a warning look, but I ignored him.

"We're strangers," I continued. "And we want something you made, something you worked hard for. We'll take good care of your boat and we'll try to bring it back to you, but we can't promise, because we could all get killed over there and then you wouldn't get your boat back. So you really don't have any reason to help us." I swallowed. "But I still hope you will."

Mal studied me, his pale gold eyes unreadable. Then he turned slightly and pointed at his shoulder, the one with the scrolling black design. "You see this," he said.

I glanced at the men, but they looked as baffled as I felt. Of course I saw the design. You'd have to be blind not to see that design.

Mal's eyes met mine and he nodded encouragingly. I moved a little closer to him, trying to see anything other than those dramatic black marks. The treetops were swaying in the wind, dappling shadow and light over us all; anything subtle, I wouldn't be able to see.

Something on his shoulder. A mole? A scar? The man was so peculiar, it could be anything at all.

"You have a birthmark," I said finally, trying to sound sure of myself. I thought there was a birthmark, a strawberry mark, but the designs pretty thoroughly obscured it.

Mal nodded. "Yes," he said. "Some people call it an evil sign."

"It's just a harmless birthmark," I said. "Sometimes people have them. They don't mean anything."

"That is what my mother said. But he said no, the boy is bad, throw him out."

I winced, and Mal watched me expectantly.

He was giving me something—he'd told me something that he knew for a fact I didn't know. This must be very important. It was a test, perhaps. But I didn't know where he was going with his revelation, or where he wanted me to go.

The thin watery sunlight faded, and as it did the temperature seemed to plunge. My skin prickled with goose bumps but it didn't matter; I'd have stood there in the clearing until I froze to death, trying to figure out how to persuade this man to help us get home.

"I never knew my mother," I said finally. "But she wouldn't have thrown me out. Especially not for something I couldn't help, like a birthmark."

"No," Mal agreed, crossing his arms over his chest. "She wouldn't"—something shifted in his eyes, and I knew we were talking about his mother now—"but then she died and he threw me out."

"Who threw you out?" Rufus's voice was too loud in the quiet clearing. "Was it your father? How old were you?" I tried to catch Rufus's eye, to warn him not to scare Mal off with questions, but he was focused on Mal.

Of course. I kept forgetting that Rufus was a father.

Mal was hesitating, watching Rufus a bit warily. He didn't walk away, but I could see he was struggling. It wasn't just some perverse Locrian convention, then; he was truly uncomfortable with questions. And the Locrians were all like this? How did they ever get anything said?

I tried to think of a statement to help him through.

"You were very young," I said, guessing.

It was feeble, but good enough. Mal held up one hand, fingers spread. "Five," he said. "I was five. He said the devil was in me and must be burned with fire. She tried to stop him and it was very bad, and in the night I woke up outside in the sand and the rain, and she was there beside me, dead."

He told this appalling story matter-of-factly, and somehow I felt that was the best way to respond.

"That's the worst thing I've ever heard," I said.

He nodded. "It was a bad time." He looked past me, past all of us. "A bad house."

All three men flinched.

Gabriel and Rufus hadn't mentioned a child. They glanced at each other, and Rufus shook his head. Neither had known. They hadn't known there was a child, and they hadn't known it had been Mal's family who had lived there.

Now I understood why the skin on his left side, half-hidden beneath the drawings, had a puckered, shiny quality. I'd thought it had something to do with the drawings; now I wondered whether the drawings were meant to hide the scars from the burns.

Mal was watching me. He seemed to be waiting patiently. But for what? I had nothing wise or comforting to say.

"What your father did was wrong," I said, feeling helpless. "He was a very bad man."

"Yes," Mal said, rocking a little on the sand. "But when he was bad, someone else was good."

"Someone took you in," I said, guessing. "Someone tended to your wounds, and fed you, and kept you warm."

Mal nodded. "I was strange, and a stranger, but he took me in," he said. "That is why I am alive."

Then I understood. I looked at the other men, but they were staring at us blankly, each of them thinking about what Mal had endured, none of them hearing what Mal in his odd way was saying.

I looked away from them, straight into the pale gold eyes.

"You're going to help us," I said, and it was not a question but a fact.

He nodded at the four strangers before him. "I am."

Chapter 12

Farrell Dean stood knee-deep in the cold sea, doing some-thing to the part of the engine that went under water. He was caked with sand and salt, and streaked with engine grease. His shirt was off and sometimes when he turned I could see the scars on his back. They had turned a pale pearly pink, standing out sharply against his skin.

"What if they can't do it?" I said.

"If they can't, no one can."

That wasn't exactly reassuring.

"And it's pointless for us to stand here watching them," Gabriel said, as if I'd argued otherwise. "We're wasting time. No telling how long it will take us to persuade someone to let me administer their Dream Drops."

We were going to track down people whose dreams seemed like Optica dreams, see if they knew anything that wasn't in the Dream Recorder books, and then attempt to persuade them to take the drops that night and—with luck—discover helpful information about the current situation in the city.

I didn't like this plan—it seemed too much like becom-ing an experimenter myself—but Gabriel said it could make all the difference in the world to our assault on Optica.

At the moment, though, we were still standing on the

beach, watching the work going on at the edge of the sea. Rufus was making notes on a clipboard, and Mal was in the boat, which was half on the sand, half in the water.

Gabriel had been in a foul mood all morning, ever since I'd told the men about the mind-reading aspect of the experiment. And all morning I'd been sorting through dream records, which managed to be both unsettling and tedious. Despite having spoken with Meritt, despite having found Mal and his boat-building skills, I wasn't in a much better mood than Gabriel.

Farrell Dean wasn't acting quite right either. All day he'd been unnaturally quiet, and not meeting my eyes. The last time he'd acted like this, he'd diverted our boat away from Meritt and carted me off to Aislin. What was wrong now? I didn't know. Maybe it was nothing more than a bad night. Sometimes it took awhile to shake off nightmares, even in broad daylight.

The wind kicked up, blowing my hair across my face. I shoved it back, tasting salt on my lips.

"So I guess nothing bad happened in the bad house last night?" I asked Gabriel.

"Nothing ever *happens*," Gabriel said. "It simply isn't pleasant there, that's all. Try not to be scornful of matters you don't understand."

"I'm not! I'm worried about Farrell Dean, that's all. He's not acting like himself."

Gabriel sighed.

Crossing my arms over my chest, I turned away from him, belatedly realizing that the noise I'd been hearing wasn't only the sound of the waves. Someone was standing near us—Pearl, a hugely pregnant woman, the only other Locrian who had ventured into our horrifying presence. I didn't know who Pearl was or why she'd come back when everyone else was still hiding. Was she Mal's wife, or whatever they had up here? She looked older than he was, but that didn't necessarily mean anything.

She was standing only a few yards behind us, making a sound somewhere between humming and singing, and I'd have said she was looking out to sea, except for the fact that her eyes were shut. Then she began to sway, still making the chanting noise, rubbing her enormous pregnant belly. Her long skirt tangled around her legs as the sea wind rose and fell and shifted. Her feet were bare and her toenails were stained a rich purple, as were her fingernails.

"What's she doing?"

Gabriel shrugged, clearly considering such things beneath his notice.

Another gust of salty wind blew my hair across my face yet again, and chill bumps rose on my arms. Farrell Dean waded out of the water and reached for his light blue shirt, which was hanging over the edge of the boat. He pulled it on and stood looking out across the water—toward something unknown, because we were on the north of the island. Not toward home.

Home.

I touched the transmitter in my pocket.

Mal said something I couldn't hear, the sound carried away on the wind. Rufus flipped back a few pages and nodded. Farrell Dean reached down and sorted through a box of tools, coming up with a wrench that he handed to Mal in the boat. The boat that might—or might not—get us home.

Who knew what was happening there?

I hadn't heard back from Meritt and it had been hours now, and there were traps in the woods, and wild men. Meritt could be as sick as Ezzie—worse maybe—and it would be my fault for suggesting he try to get the transmitter to the old man.

"I hope Meritt's not in trouble," I said, half to myself.

Beside me Gabriel made an impatient sound. "Meritt this, Meritt that. I'm sick of the sound of his name."

Startled, stung, I turned to face him.

"Don't give me that look," he said. "Of course Farrell Dean is out of sorts. And as there's no one else here to say it, I will. You're behaving like a little fool. Rafe should have talked some sense into you."

Rafe.

This man, this stranger who wore Rafe's face, thought he could invoke Rafe against me.

"Rafe liked Meritt," I said, struggling to speak calmly. "Farrell Dean does too. He's our friend."

"He's Farrell Dean's rival. And he's the son of the man who stole you from us."

"That isn't Meritt's fault! He's helping us. He—"

"Blood is thicker than water. His father is our enemy, and that boy will side with his father. And while we're on the topic, you never should have answered that transmitter. Attracting Angel's notice is dangerous, an unnecessary risk."

"I told you, I didn't mean to answer it! And they're on the other island—it's not like Angel can get to us."

"You don't know what he can and can't do. For all you know, he has a tracking device in that transmitter. His people could be on their way to Locria right now."

I tried not to glance back toward the road, but I couldn't stop myself.

"You don't know why he was contacting the Doria Dream Recorder," Gabriel went on. "If you'd listened instead of talking, you might have learned something. But no—you had to speak. You'll get yourself killed one day, acting rashly. Or Farrell Dean, more likely. If that matters to you at all."

"Of course it matters!"

"You don't act as if it does. This isn't the first time you've put him in danger. You could have gotten him killed sneaking into my house in the night, making me think he was an agent of my enemy, or—"

"It's not my fault you thought Eric Alleyn was your enemy."

He raised his voice. "Or, at the very least, that Farrell Dean was wrongly interfering with my niece, and under my own roof."

"You're the one who jumped to conclusions about my father. You can't blame me for—"

"Strangers can't be trusted, not until they've proven themselves. Farrell Dean could have been a spy, and then—"

"A spy! For all we know you're the one who—"

Even though the red haze of anger I knew some things were best left unsaid, but Gabriel's darkening expression told me I hadn't stopped soon enough.

"Don't think the thought hasn't occurred to me," he said bitterly. "Someone betrayed my brother. I am well aware that it might have been me. All those years, Rafe was plotting, spying on the Watchers, collecting allies, patiently training up children to place in strategic positions, and I played right into the enemies' hands, blabbing my crazy dreams to the Ionia Dream Recorder so he could pass them on to the authorities on your island."

"You don't know that happened," I said. "And even if it did, you couldn't possibly have known. It was an accident."

Gabriel laughed harshly. "An accident Eric Alleyn would have avoided. Eric Alleyn, who never took Dream Drops."

"They didn't press him to," I said. "He isn't a twin. They didn't care if he took them or not. He wasn't haunted by dreams of a lost brother."

My uncle didn't acknowledge the point, except to make a dismissive gesture with one hand.

His gaze shifted behind me and I turned.

Mal and Rufus were coming toward us, walking unevenly across the soft sand. Rufus looked very large beside Mal, and rough, as if his frame had been cut with a less precise tool. And even now, after spending half a day with Mal, he kept glancing at the black designs and looking perplexed.

Farrell Dean was still down by the water, sorting through the box of tools. His shirt was unbuttoned and flapping in the wind. His gold-brown hair was longer than I'd ever seen it, and as I watched he gave an impatient jerk of his head, shaking it out of his eyes.

"Good news and bad news," Rufus said. He was talking to Gabriel, and speaking civilly enough, but couldn't quite bring himself to look at our uncle. Instead he was looking at the space between us. "It's not hopeless, but it's going to be difficult. If we can do it, it will take awhile."

"Of course it will take awhile," Gabriel said. "If it were easy, Mal would have done it long ago. Red and I will head back to Ionia—we've other matters to attend to."

"Will you have to sleep in the bad house again?" I asked my brother.

Rufus shook his head. "Mal says we can stay with him."

Behind us Pearl was still humming.

"With Mal and Pearl," I said.

I was fishing for information, and Mal knew it. He smiled faintly. "No," he said. "Pearl lives with her family. Her family is not mine."

Because he had answered my unasked question, because I was out of sorts, because the Locrian method was so unwieldy and irritating, I blundered on.

"I guess your family is the man who raised you. Will he mind having visitors?"

Rufus frowned at me; Gabriel stifled a sigh.

Mal didn't answer, and no one else spoke. Even Pearl stopped her humming. Everyone stood there carefully not looking at me, except for Mal, an expression in his eyes I took for reproof.

The wind shifted, bringing with it a distantly sour smell, seaweed or kelp or some other slimy thing. Down at the water Farrell Dean found whatever he was looking for, tossed it into the boat, and started toward us. I could see him taking in our odd tableau, my flushed face, the men's averted eyes. All I'd done was ask a simple question—why did they have to act like I'd spit on my mother's grave?

Hoping Gabriel wouldn't notice, I felt again in my pocket, touching the hard cold transmitter.

Unexpectedly, it was Mal who took pity on me. "The man who raised me is gone," he said, just as Farrell Dean reached us. "He has been gone a long time. Now I live alone."

His kindness—in contrast to Gabriel's grumpiness—pulled me up short. "I'm sorry," I said. I meant I was sorry for being nosy, but Mal took my apology a different way.

"Gone is not the worst thing," he said, his gaze shifting to the hill behind me, to the half-ruined shell of the bad house.

Gabriel gave me a quelling look, as if he thought I might otherwise keep blundering on, sticking my foot in my mouth and generally threatening good relations with the Locrians.

"We're heading out now," he told Farrell Dean. "I'll send a man up to check your progress in a day or two. I'd leave you a transceiver, but they don't work across the mountains." He reached out to shake hands. "Good luck."

Then Gabriel held out his hand to Rufus. After a moment's hesitation, Rufus shook, though a little gingerly, as if he thought it might be some sort of trick.

"And good luck with the old people," he said. Dropping Gabriel's hand, he turned to me and ruffled my hair. "Be careful," he said.

"I will."

Farrell Dean finally looked at me, and I expected him to tell me to be careful, too, but he simply raised one hand in casual farewell and turned to join Mal at the crate full of parts.

So much for wanting to protect me always.

Rufus lifted his clipboard and began flipping pages, but Gabriel stood watching me, his expression inscrutable.

To hide the tears prickling in my eyes I turned and walked away.

Chapter 13

"We're here."

I sat up, blinking. My neck felt stiff because I'd been sleeping propped against the truck window, but other than that I felt better than before. A nap had seemed like a good way to avoid conversation with my cranky uncle on the long drive down from Locria, but I'd also really needed it.

We were parked in front of a neatly kept house on the outskirts of Doria, a house handily on the way to Ionia, where the other possible twins I'd found in the dream records lived. A path edged with stones led to a porch freshly painted a clean bright white, and lights in the windows shone in cheerful contrast to the overcast day.

We climbed the wooden steps and Gabriel knocked on the door.

When it opened, revealing a pretty woman with long blonde hair, I took a step forward before I could stop myself.

"Cynda!" I said.

The woman before me blinked, her hand still on the door as if she might close it in our faces.

"Sharla," Gabriel corrected me, and then spoke to the woman. "We'd like to speak with you, if you can spare a few minutes of your time."

The woman shrugged and opened the door wider. "It

wouldn't be prudent to turn Gabriel Drewblood away," she said, but her smile took the sting out of the words.

She led us into a small but comfortable room decorated all in red and white. It was a very pretty room, with frills and patterned fabrics, a very feminine room. Somehow, though it was late autumn, the room smelled like roses. I wasn't exactly an expert on home design, but from what I'd seen in other houses, it didn't seem like a place where a man lived.

Sharla invited us to sit down on a couch, and she took a rocking chair. As soon as we were all seated, Gabriel began.

"This is not Fiona Alleyn," he said. "This is her sister. She has been living on another island."

The explanation took awhile. Sharla listened carefully, without interrupting or asking questions, her face growing a little pale. She was shapely and plump, just like Cynda, and she had the same neat deliberate movements. It was amazing—and it was especially amazing to think that Cynda, of all people, had a sister on another island. Cynda, who had said talking ducks were more likely than other inhabited islands.

"We found your dreams this morning," Gabriel concluded. "The ones about the walls and the men. You can see why we felt it necessary to speak to you. We're going over there, and we need all the information we can glean."

Sharla leaned forward, the rocking chair creaking gently against the wood floor. She had grown a little pale as Gabriel talked, but when she spoke her voice was as easy as if she were discussing flower arrangements.

"Do you know what the Dream Recorder told me?" Sharla said. "I went to her with these terrible dreams, and she said I was mentally disturbed. She said how could I marry Lars, when I was dreaming every night about other men? And about walls, about being dreary and trapped? So I broke it off."

Her pale face suddenly flushed with excitement, and her

blue eyes began to sparkle. "But now we can get married. I can't wait to tell him!"

Gabriel smiled at her, but I shifted uncomfortably; I knew something he didn't.

"Are we finished?" Sharla said. "I want to go find Lars."

"Not quite yet," Gabriel began. We'd given her information, but she'd told us nothing.

"That's all right," Sharla broke in. "I have to come up with a good story first. I never told Lars about the dreams, and it might not be wise to tell him even now—he might not understand the distinction between dreaming my own dreams about other men, and dreaming someone else's."

There was a second of silence—just a second, while we thought about the implications of secondhand unfaithfulness—and then I spoke up.

"Before we go, we need to know if you've had any other dreams."

Sharla frowned.

I pressed the point. "Your sister is in trouble, and so are my other friends. Have you had any other dreams about Optica recently? Anything that might help us?"

"I really don't like to think about those dreams," Sharla said. "And, really, I don't especially like that you even know about them."

"I'm sorry—but please, if there's anything you can tell us about what's going on over there, it could save lives. It could save your sister's life."

Sharla pursed her lips. "To be honest with you, I don't think my sister sounds like a very nice sort of person."

I couldn't believe my ears. "But she is nice," I said. "She's my friend, my good friend—and she isn't a relief worker by choice. It's her job. She was assigned."

Sharla gave a pointed little shudder.

If she was going to be so selfish, then I'd go right ahead

and tell her the bad news. "Cynda's a relief worker because she was removed from the breeding pool," I said.

Gabriel didn't know what was coming, but he held up a warning hand just the same.

I didn't stop. "They didn't want her to have children because there's something wrong with her," I said. "Something genetic."

Something very bad, apparently, for them to have ruled a twin out of the breeding program. Twins were more likely to give birth to other twins—we were their best bet for future subjects, as the Watchers had said.

Sharla stared at me. I waited for understanding to dawn in those pretty blue eyes: Something was wrong with Cynda, and therefore something was wrong with Sharla.

Sure enough, after a moment her eyes grew round and her hand went to her stomach. "Oh," she said. "I can't believe it. I totally forgot."

"You forgot you have a genetic problem and shouldn't have children?"

Gabriel gave me a look that told me my diplomacy skills were sadly lacking.

But Sharla shook her head. "No, it's not that," she said, gently patting her stomach. "I forgot that she was part of me. I was thinking of her as a ghost who got into my head. A dream. But she was me."

My eyes met Gabriel's.

"It's true that all identical twins start out as one zygote," he said. "And then they split into two. It happened to Red and her sister. It happened to my brother and me."

Sharla shook her head. "I was special," she said. "There's never been anyone else like me. My mother said so."

Hadn't she been listening? I was a twin, Gabriel was a twin, identical twins were everywhere.

"I almost became two babies," Sharla went on. "But one

of them didn't develop properly. She was like a growth on my stomach."

Gabriel leaned forward, interest flickering in his eyes. "You're the Downing baby?"

Sharla nodded and patted her stomach again, contemplatively.

"I didn't realize," Gabriel said. "That was, what? Twenty years ago? I only heard that the Downing baby required surgery for a rare genetic abnormality. I never knew there was a twin."

"Yes," Sharla said. "We didn't like to talk about it. But she was there. They surgically removed her from me, and then I was fine. I got all the organs."

Again, it was as if we hadn't just told her about Cynda.

Sharla turned toward me. "Are you sure that's my sister over there?" she said. "Because she died, you know. She didn't have enough organs to live. She died during the surgery because there wasn't enough of her to be a person."

"Yes, she's your sister. She looks exactly like you." I hoped my face didn't show how disgusted with her I felt. "That's how the experimenters work. They steal one of the twins, and then lie and say she died at birth."

"And she can't have children?"

"Right."

"I can," Sharla said complacently. "I got more organs. If she's alive, what's she doing for organs?"

I looked at Gabriel; he could very well handle that one.

"The organ problem apparently was a complete fabrication," he said. "Your sister was fine after the surgery, just like you."

Sharla shook her head. "I can show you the scar," she said, running a hand down her abdomen. "But I won't. We shared organs, and when they separated us, I got them. She was like a growth on me. She had no organs and she died."

126

"She has organs!" I said.

"She doesn't have a womb. You said so yourself."

Gabriel gave me a helpless look. No one had said anything about a missing womb. I was on the verge of concluding that Sharla's genetic problem was that she was maddeningly slow, but I had seen something in the shallow blue pools of Sharla's eyes.

"Your sister is good at that too," I said. "Better than you are, in fact."

Sharla blinked at me, miming puzzlement.

"She can seem helpless and not too bright. She can evade questions and lie and look totally innocent the whole time. She had to learn all that to cope with the wardens. So you aren't fooling me. Now tell us what you've dreamed, and then we'll go."

Sharla looked at me blankly for a long moment. Then she smiled—not altogether nicely—and intelligence sharpened in her eyes.

"I'll say it one time, and one time only," she said. "Then I never want to think about that horrid place again, and I don't want you knocking on my door asking about it. I don't want you talking about it, either, not to anyone. I thought the Dream Recorder might be able to give me some advice, or I'd never have gone to her. I certainly wouldn't have gone to her if I'd known other people would be reading her books." She gave Gabriel a reproving look.

"I apologize," he said. "But I am a Dream Recorder myself now, you know. For Ionia."

She didn't look impressed. "I did have another dream about men who were dressed in black clothes," she said. "Other than the usual dreams, I mean. This time there were several men at once and I was talking to them. I was telling them that someone had been tampering with their precious cameras."

I made a sort of strangled noise and Sharla gave me a brief assessing look, as if making sure I wasn't going to be sick on her new furniture.

"Who was tampering with the cameras?" Gabriel said.

Sharla shrugged. "A weird name. Honor. Nobility. Something like that."

I was shaking my head. This couldn't be true.

"Meritt," Gabriel said.

"That's it. Meritt. He's broken a lot of rules. Out after hours, tampering with surveillance." Sharla looked at her fingernails. "He's a friend of mine, but really, he of all people should know that sometimes it's not about friendship. Sometimes you have to take care of yourself."

My mind was blank with shock. She had turned him in; Cynda had turned Meritt in to the wardens.

"She wouldn't do that," I protested.

Sharla shrugged. "Why not? He deserves it. He's done the exact same thing."

Understanding hit; the walls of the pretty room seemed to close in around me. She'd done it because of me—Meritt was in danger because of me. Cynda must have heard from the wardens that Meritt was being pressed to turn me in, and she had turned him in first. Maybe she was trying to protect me. Or—unfortunately, it was possible—maybe Cynda was trying to build up favor with the wardens against the coming hungry winter. She was very good at shoring up her standing, and she didn't like being hungry. No one did.

"What do you mean?" Gabriel was saying. "What has he done?"

Again Sharla shrugged. "I don't know. I just know, that's all. He looks out for Number One."

I was shaking my head. Gabriel glanced at me, a mixture of pity and contempt in his eyes, then turned back to Sharla.

"When did you have this dream?" he said. "Is it recent?"

"Very recent. I dreamed it just last night." Sharla stood up. "Yesterday evening, if you want to be exact. I took a late nap. Now, if that's all you need?"

Meritt didn't even know the danger he was in. I'd talked to him that morning and he'd been so hopeful, so sure everything would work out fine. He didn't know what Cynda had done. What would happen to him? Would the Watchers kill him, or would they be afraid to, because of his father?

"I'm sure you have other places to go, people to see," Sharla said, smiling with sudden artificial brightness. She steered us through the red-and-white room and to the door.

On the porch Gabriel turned back to face her. "We were hoping you might take Dream Drops tonight," he said. "If you saw something helpful, it could make all the difference in the world to your sister and the others over there."

I didn't know why he bothered; Sharla wasn't going to help us.

Sharla tilted her head prettily. "No, I don't believe I will," she said. "The drops don't actually help me dream, do they? Because dreams aren't true. What the drops do is make me see reality. More of it than I ever want to see again." And once again, a look of distaste for her sister crossed her face. It irritated me, but at the same time—

For whatever reason, Cynda had betrayed Meritt. And if he had returned to Optica since I had spoken with him, it was even possible she'd gotten him killed.

Chapter 14

"Stop treating me like a baby." Rain was dressed all in close-fitting black. She looked mad, and she looked dangerous. "*She's* going. You can't let her go and make me stay behind."

"*She* is safer with me than not." Gabriel, looking every bit as angry and dangerous as his daughter, turned and eyed me narrowly. "She has a bad habit of disappearing, and that's not going to happen on my watch."

Rain put her fists on her hips and glowered at me. I was sitting on the couch beside Aunt Carol, who was the only cheerful person in the room. Gabriel had been in a foul mood all day, and Rain had grown progressively more grim as she heard about recent events—events I'd experienced and she'd missed out on. She even seemed to think that getting cornered by Cobb was a thrill of which she'd been deliberately deprived.

Beside me, Aunt Carol tried to make peace. "Rain, darling, your father is only trying to keep you safe. You know Mr. Edgeling isn't going to be at all pleased, if he discovers people stealing his guns."

Rain opened her mouth and pointed at me; before she could speak, Carol went on. She wasn't drunk, but she was a little fuzzy around the edges. "I know, dear," she said. "But this is her project. And everyone who knows Fiona has a soft spot for her, so if Mr. Edgeling catches Red, maybe she can just toss her beautiful red hair, and —"

"Mother!" Rain cut in. "That's ridiculous."

"Don't speak to your mother that way," Gabriel said sharply.

Rain took a deep breath. "Sorry," she said. "But really, Mom—yes, everybody knows that everybody in the world is fond of sweet little Fiona and her beautiful red hair, but that won't magically protect her—or Red—if she's caught breaking and entering and burgling. She'll be in every bit as much danger as I'd be in. More, because the Dream Recorder wants to get her hands on her. There are actually people out looking for her, and nobody's looking for me."

"That's true," Carol said, nodding.

"So why can't I go? I want to help."

"You can help by staying out of the way." That was Gabriel.

"Red can't even fight!"

"Fighting's not on the agenda."

"You hope."

"Oh, for heaven's sake," Carol said, looking up at both of them. "Gabriel, dear, let her go with you. If the nurse needs help with poor Ezzie, I'll be here. And the old people won't be any trouble. They've had their Dream Drops, and they're sound asleep. They won't need any attention until morning."

Three people had agreed to try to help us—Esme, sister of my friend Estelle, the former cook; Margo, sister to old Mariella; and Will Bright, who was Louie's brother. I was pinning my best hopes on him—because of all the people in Optica, Louie was one of my very favorites, and he was also a smart old man.

The three old people were settled down the hall, as was Ezzie, with a suspiciously muscular male nurse looking after everyone. I thought he was probably a security man who'd had—I hoped—some medical training.

"I'm not worried about what's going on here," Gabriel said, looking at his wife. "That's the point."

"I know." Carol tucked a few strands of graying blonde hair back into her chignon. "But bear in mind she'll be with you, and that's the safest place for anyone to be."

Unexpectedly, Gabriel's face softened.

Carol smiled at him and turned to Rain. "Do exactly what your father tells you," she said.

Rain still looked angry, but she had the good sense to keep her mouth shut. As for me, I felt as if I'd missed something. When had Carol won the argument?

Carol patted me on the knee. "And you be careful," she said. "Mr. Edgeling is not a very nice man."

Gabriel was frowning at me. "You can't go dressed like that," he said, and Rain grabbed my hand and yanked me up off the couch, and in a flash we were running up the stairs to her room. Behind me I heard Gabriel say something to Carol in a low voice.

"You know how she is," Carol replied. "If you left her behind she'd find some way to follow you. This way is safer, don't you think?"

In the bedroom I pulled the door shut while Rain hurried to her closet and began digging through it, flinging rejected clothes here and there until she found what she was looking for: another pair of black pants and a black shirt.

"They'll be too big," she said, tossing them to me. "But they'll have to do."

I was already pulling off my dress.

"Find me a safety pin," I said, and Rain yanked open a dresser drawer so hard it rattled against its anchors. She left it hanging open and brought a handful of pins to me, and together we tightened the pants and fastened the neckline of the shirt so it didn't gape to my naval. Then I pulled the transmitter out of the dress pocket and tucked it in my pants pocket.

"Good," she said, looking me over. "You aren't scared, are you?"

I shook my head, but Rain had turned away and was digging through another drawer, flinging scarves that fell with soft swishing sounds to the floor.

"Here," she said, handing me a long black lace shawl. "Can you cover your hair with that?"

I looked at the shawl dubiously; it was ten or twelve feet long. But I still hadn't found the black cap that had gone missing when Tristan Oldfamily abducted me, and I certainly did need to hide my flaming hair.

"Or—I know," Rain said, yanking a box out from under her bed and upending it onto the floor. Her room, which had been perfectly neat when we entered, now looked as if it had been ransacked.

"Here. Try this." She was holding a finely knitted black stocking. Before I could take it she pulled the open end over my head and crammed my braid up under it.

"Now hold still." Twisting the stocking, she knotted it on top of my head. Then she grabbed a pair of scissors from her dressing table and snipped off the extra.

"There," she said, eyeing me with satisfaction. "Now you're ready for the dark."

We ran back down the stairs. Gabriel was standing by the front door with Earl and my brother Mick. They were all dressed in black, and they all had handguns in black holsters under their left arms.

Earl nodded at us, and Mick caught my eye and winked. Dark stubble covered his jaw, and his green eyes were mischievous. He was my most handsome brother. I'd thought brooding Rufus was the most dangerous, but seeing Mick tonight made me wonder. He looked like the sort of person who'd start a fight just to see what happened.

"There won't be any talking once we leave the main road," Gabriel said. "So listen up. Mick?"

"They have dogs, but they bring them into the house at night," Mick said. "The barn is set a good ways away. It has two doors—the big front one, which will be barred from the inside, and the small side door that will be locked with a key. That's where we'll enter. Earl, Red, and me."

"I'll stay outside and keep watch," Gabriel said. "Rain, you will too."

I thought she might protest, but she merely nodded.

"I want you watching the front of the house," Gabriel said. "Not close enough to alert the dogs—but near enough that you'll see if anyone comes outside. If someone does, click the transceiver."

He handed her a small transmitter—not like the one I carried, but the ones Gabriel had for his men. They worked for a range of a couple of miles, no further.

"Once means you're telling Mick's group to stay put," Gabriel said. "Twice means get out of sight but don't run. Three times means run. Five means all clear."

Rain nodded.

"Repeat the signals," Gabriel said. "One—stay. Two—hide. Three—run. Five—safe."

We repeated them three times before he was satisfied. Then he nodded at Mick, who resumed his explanations.

"The weapons should be under a trapdoor beneath the third stall," he said. "We'll work fast, and we won't take the weapons all the way back to the truck—I have a temporary shelter set up about halfway there. It's camouflaged and if we have to leave anything there it's not likely anyone will find it before we can get back."

Gabriel looked at me. "When I'm not with you, Mick

and Earl are in charge," he said. "Do exactly as they say. Do not under any circumstances take it into your head to improvise."

"Got that?" Mick said, and the look he gave me was dead serious.

I nodded. "Got it."

"If something goes wrong," Gabriel said, "you girls are to clear out. Head straight for the truck and drive away. Don't wait for any of us. We can make our own way back."

Rain's face was impassive. Earl made a clicking sound with his tongue and she looked over at him. He shook his head once. Rain's expression darkened, but she nodded.

Then Earl's gaze flicked over my face, passing on before I could look suitably obedient or focused or whatever I ought to be looking. I couldn't read anything in his glance, and I hoped there was nothing there to read.

I had thought I'd sneaked past Earl when I'd broken into Gabriel's house to visit Farrell Dean, but as it turned out, Earl had heard me. Had seen me, in fact, through the door that connected the bathroom and bedroom. He'd let me go right on in to Farrell Dean, and only after listening at the hall door—and hearing nothing but silence and some virtually inaudible whispering—did he go upstairs to tell my uncle about "Fiona's" little visit.

Since it had all turned out okay, I was glad Earl had gotten the better of me. I'd been more than a little worried about my uncle's flimsy security here at his house. Woof the dog was close to useless, no doubt about it, and I'd successfully slipped past the outside guard who, I'd learned, was no longer in my uncle's employ. But Earl was on top of things.

"Valentina," Gabriel said, jerking me out of my thoughts. "Leave the transmitter here. We can't risk the noise."

Leave it?

I started to object, but Gabriel was right. The transmitter buzzed when someone called, and it wasn't a very quiet buzz.

I pulled the transmitter from my pocket, thinking quickly. There was a small table near the door. If I left the transmitter there, I could palm it on the way out. I wouldn't take it all the way to the Edgeling barn with me—I'd leave it in the truck, and that way I'd be out of Meritt's reach for a much shorter length of time.

"I'll leave it here," I said, setting it on the table.

"I'll give it to Carol," Gabriel replied, and held out his hand.

Mick sat beside me in the back of the truck. Rain and Earl sat up front, with Gabriel.

"Come here, baby girl," Mick said, putting an arm around my shoulders. He smelled like pine trees. "Gabriel didn't want to say so in front of Aunt Carol, but you're a crucial piece of the plan tonight."

My heart gave a sudden thud. "All right," I said, and was glad my voice sounded strong and unconcerned. "What do you want me to do?"

It was too dark to really see his face. "I don't have a key to the barn," he said. "My contact person got crossways with Edgeling and he fired her before she could make an impression of it. But there's a tiny wee door—used to be for hens, now it's for the rat terrier."

"What's a rat terrier?"

"A dog, a little one that chases rats out of the hay. He can come and go at will during the day, and at night they shut and latch the little door, to keep coons and possums out. So all you have to do is get through that door—I'm pretty sure you're small enough, if you squeeze a bit. Then you can unlock the regular door for Earl and me. That door's a deadbolt and all you have to do is turn the catch. Think you can manage all that?"

"Sure."

"Good girl. Now, just wait 'til you see what I've got for you in that barn. According to rumor, and rumor never lies, Edgeling has been collecting guns for thirty years. Buying them, stealing them, borrowing them and never returning them. Just as if he knew we'd need a nice fat armory to rob one day."

"Does Edgeling ever do anything with all his guns?" I asked.

Mick laughed softly. "Just having those guns is enough to persuade most people to take his point of view," he said. "Edgeling fancies himself a player, separate and apart from whatever agreement he had with the Dream Recorders. He has fingers in a hundred pies, but always on the hush hush. Rumor has it that he'd like to find some hold over the Council, some way to control the island through them, but our Council members are bulletproof. They're all either squeaky clean, like Tor's father, or they don't care who sees their dirty laundry. And they don't bully easily, either."

We didn't talk any more after that. We sat companionably side-by-side in the dark, bumping gently down the main road. Mick, the night, the excitement—it all reminded me of sneaking out with Meritt, back in Optica. And tonight I was helping Optica, though no one there knew it.

I wished Meritt knew.

Eventually Gabriel pulled over. He didn't pull onto the side of the road; he pulled completely off it, into a small clearing hidden from the road by brush and trees. The Edgeling place was somewhere between Ionia and Doria, off the main road a bit. We'd have to walk in for about half a mile.

Mick swung out of the truck bed and I followed. He reached up to help me, but I was already on the ground, and I heard him give an uneven breath that had to be a silent chuckle, and in the darkness I smiled, too.

Gabriel shut the truck door with hardly a sound and we were off, moving silently through the trees. The moon was waxing—I'd seen it as we left the house—but it was late now, past midnight, and the moon had set, leaving the night dark except for the few stars whose light made it through the heavy trees.

Half a mile is a long way in the dark. I focused on the dark shadow that was Rain ahead of me, and tried not to tramp noisily on dry leaves or get swatted in the face by a swinging branch or turn my ankle on a rock or dip in the ground. I was so intent on those things—on seeming like I knew what I was doing, more or less—that I was surprised when we arrived at our destination.

As soon as I realized we were there, I realized something was wrong. First I smelled smoke. Then I saw light flickering through the trees. Then I heard voices.

This wasn't a sleeping farm. It was wide awake.

Six or eight dark figures circled around a big fire in the clearing, midway between the house and barn. The figures went in one direction, then in the other. They were holding hands. They were chanting something. The sound made the hairs on the back of my neck stand up.

A hand touched my arm. It was Gabriel. He pointed to the ground, telling me to stay put. I nodded. Gabriel and Rain stayed, too, hidden with me deep in the shadows, but Earl slipped off in one direction and Mick in another.

The figures around the fire stopped circling and broke into cries that would have sounded like cheers, except they weren't happy, but angry and excited. Then the figures gathered around something on the ground, and then they separated again, their dark shapes mingling and crossing in the firelight.

I shivered, and not from cold. What was this?

We watched the figures for what felt like a long time. Sometimes they held hands and ran around the fire, sometimes they flung their arms up to the sky and screamed long, blood-curdling cries. Sometimes they laughed hysterically and sat down on the ground. Once two of them stumbled away together, into the woods, and came back a few minutes later. They tossed more wood on the fire and red sparks shot high, as if trying to attack the cool white stars.

Finally Mick and Earl came back.

"Drunk," Mick breathed. "And as a bonus there are plenty of people for Edgeling to blame. Let's do it."

Gabriel hesitated, looking at me.

"It'll be fine," Mick said. "I'll take care of her."

"All right. Be fast."

Gabriel started giving Rain instructions as the three of us started off. When we neared the barn we stopped, studying it from the protection of the trees.

The circle of light didn't reach the barn; against the brightness of the fire it was cloaked in deep shadows. I could see the big double doors for horses, on the side of the barn facing the fire, and I could see that the side toward us— toward the trees—had a regular-sized door. But I couldn't spot the dog door.

"Over there," Mick murmured. I followed the direction he indicated and saw, on the wall nearest the fire, the dim outline of a small rectangle, right down by the ground. "I'm going with you," he said in my ear. "You ready?"

I nodded. For a moment Mick watched the people by the fire; they seemed to be winding up a particularly complicated dance.

"Now," he said.

He and I ran for the barn while Earl stayed behind, in the shadows of the woods. We crouched down by the little door and Mick swung open the latch. I froze for a second, trying to decide whether to go feet-first or face-first, then sat down and stuck my legs through the hole. My hips were a tight squeeze, and then I didn't know if I'd get my shoulders through at all. But by raising my arms above my head and angling my shoulders, I just managed to wriggle inside.

The door swung shut behind me and I heard Mick latch it. I couldn't see anything in the pitch-black barn, but I could smell hay and manure and hear something moving around—horses, I hoped. When my eyes began to adjust I saw a row of stalls in front of me—five of them, all with horses inside. Above the stalls was a hay loft. A ladder near me led up to it.

Most of the wall to my right was taken up by large double doors. Around their edges I could see flickering light from the fire. The other walls were lined with a plow and other farm equipment, but the whole middle of the floor was clear. I wouldn't have to worry about tripping.

I got up and moved left, looking for the dim outline of the outside door. When I found it I turned the bolt and opened it just a crack—not too far, for fear someone besides Mick and Earl would see. Then I moved back and stood against the wall.

Seconds later the door swung open and two dark forms entered; then the door shut.

"Valentina?"

"Here."

"Good job," Mick said softly. "Now for the guns. Don't get kicked by the horse. Every time you approach, pat his rump so he'll know you're behind him." He was pointing at the third stall, where a large pale horse stood.

Earl went first, shoving away the straw and opening a trapdoor in the floor. He swung himself down inside and Mick and I followed him into the stall, where I stayed as far from the horse's rump as I could manage.

Then Earl began passing guns up to us. When I had an armload of guns, Mick made a pile on the ground for Earl and another for himself, and then Earl climbed out of the hole in the ground carrying a bucket full of ammunition. He lowered the trapdoor, covered it with straw, and we hurried to the door.

Earl reached for his transceiver and clicked five times. In response we heard five clicks.

"All clear," Earl said, and in seconds we were in the dark woods once more.

It was impossible to run holding armloads of long guns. We walked, slowly and carefully, following Mick. Behind us we could still hear the whoops and chanting of the people around that blazing, smoking fire. The woods, by contrast, seemed clean and cold, and I was glad when we were far enough from the barn that the sounds faded. The longer I stayed on this island, the bigger and stranger it seemed.

Mick's hiding place was a hollowed out boulder, almost a cave, hidden by a clump of dense bushes. I don't know how he knew about the place—there were a lot of things about Mick that I suspected I'd rather not know. He pulled back the branches and brush, and we carefully piled our loads inside.

Then we went back and did it all again.

We made the trip six times. By the last trip my arms were aching and the people cavorting around the fire were beginning to seem silly instead of sinister. The horse had started moving out of the way when he heard us coming, his breath coming in exasperated little puffs. Every time, Earl went in first and checked the barn before Mick and I went in. Every time as we finished, he lowered the trapdoor and carefully covered it with straw, leaving it just as he'd found it.

"Hey," Mick said softly as we waited by the door, our arms full of our last loads. "Do you know what that is?" He nodded in the direction of the fire.

"What?"

"Dark Night."

"I don't know what that is."

"Last night of October. Devil's night, some call it. They're calling down all the forces of evil and darkness in the world. Trying to, anyway."

I wished he hadn't told me.

Earl started toward us across the barn, his arms full of weapons. As he reached us the transceivers clicked. This time they clicked twice.

Hide.

"Here," Mick said, laying his guns on the ground against the wall. While we set ours down he left and came back almost immediately with a stack of horse blankets, which he dropped in a haphazard pile over the guns.

"The hayloft," he said. "Quick."

Earl was already climbing the ladder. I followed, but Mick didn't. Instead, he went to the end stall and slipped in behind the horse.

We'd barely made it up the ladder when the barn door banged open. Earl and I stayed low, dropping flat on our stomachs behind the nearest bales of hay.

"But we agreed," a man's voice said. He was angry and his speech was slurred.

"You agreed," another man said, and my heart began to pound. He didn't sound the least bit drunk.

There was a scraping sound and then a dim flickering light filled the barn. A candle or lantern, probably. Was that Edgeling? Now that he had light, what if he saw the blankets, knew they were out of place?

I turned toward Earl; in the ambient light his eyes were calm.

"I said you could use my property for a bonfire," the second man went on. "A fire. That's all. I did not say you could call down curses, or whatever you're doing, on all and sundry."

"You said you don't believe in curses," the first voice said, sounding sullen.

"So what? That doesn't mean my animals don't."

"We didn't curse your animals," the first man said.

"No, but casting a powerful curse is like throwing a stone into the water, wouldn't you say? It ripples out. Did you protect my animals? Did you surround them with—what is it, parsley? Turnips?"

"Sage," the first voice said. "But that's for people. And don't make fun." He sounded as if his head hurt.

"All I'm saying is you didn't take steps to protect my property," Edgeling said. "So if anything happens to any of my animals in the next twelve months, it's down to you. Do you agree?"

"You set me up," the drunk man said. He was whining. "You could do anything—weed out your weakest calves, blame it on me, make me replace them. Not fair."

Edgeling laughed. "You just gutted a black cat on my lawn and read the future in its intestines. Do you call that fair to the cat?"

"Entrails," the drunk said.

"Excuse me?"

"You call them entrails during a magical rite. Intestines—that's clinical. Doctors say intestines."

Beside me, Earl smiled faintly.

"My mistake," Edgeling said. "But the point is the same."

"I don't get your point," the drunk said testily. "But all right. Whatever. I'll be responsible for your animals. But only for one month, not twelve."

"Your curses aren't powerful enough to last a year?"

"Stop making fun. I'll agree to one month, and no more."

"You'll agree to six months."

"Three."

"Three it is. Now shake on it."

I supposed they shook hands.

"And sign on it as well. Look, I have it all written out, and I'm altering it to three months."

Paper rustled.

"What do you mean, sign? Why should I sign your paper?"

"Because you're drunk. You might not remember this conversation, come morning."

The other man gave a low skeptical laugh. "You're a believer, aren't you?"

"I don't know what you mean." Edgeling's voice was cold.

"This paper—it's bound to the spirit world, isn't it? And if I sign it, they'll know me."

There was a short silence. Then Edgeling sighed. "You've found me out," he said. "This paper binds you to keep your word. If you don't, the spirits will make your hair fall out and your bowels loose."

"For how long?" Now the drunk sounded crafty.

"For the rest of your life, you idiot. Now sign!"

Paper rustled again.

"Now you had better get back to your party," Edgeling said. "We wouldn't want your guests to miss their host."

"It's not a party. It's a rite."

"Right, wrong, whatever. Go make sure your friends don't set my woods afire."

The door opened and then there was silence, but the pale light from the candle or lantern remained. Earl's eyes met mine and he shook his head.

Edgeling was still inside.

For a long time we listened. I could hear cries now and

then from the fire outside, but nothing else. What was Edgeling doing down there?

Finally he spoke.

"I know you're in here," he said.

No one answered. If only Mick could get behind him—but he couldn't, not if Edgeling was standing by the door we'd come in. Gabriel could come in behind him, though. Surely Gabriel would do something.

"Who are you?" Edgeling said. "Jenkins? That would be my first guess. But I can have as many as I like, given that you're treed."

A horse whinnied softly.

"It was a good plan, Jenkins, I give you that," Edgeling said. "Steal my horses while I'm drunk and dancing by the Dark Night fire. But I don't dance, you see. Or drink when other people are setting fires on my property."

Sudden movement from below interrupted him. An unearthly shrieking split the air. The horses all gave startled neighs and then hooves pounded.

"Stop!" Edgeling shouted, and past the edge of the bale of hay I saw a black horse flash past, Mick low on his back—I knew it was Mick, but his black clothes and hair blended with the horse and his face was turned into its neck, making him nearly invisible.

A thud rang out and the big double doors swung open. Shrieks rose from outside. I could see the fire, dark figures raising their arms high.

Beneath us Edgeling was cursing. Then more hooves thudded and he flew past my field of vision on a second horse, a dappled one, and like Mick vanished from sight.

Earl's transceiver clicked three times, paused, clicked three times again.

"Go," Earl said, leaping from the loft without touching the ladder. The barn doors were wide open—we were fully exposed—but one glance told me the people outside were all facing the distant woods, watching Mick and Edgeling as they tore away.

By the time I climbed down the ladder and made it to the small door Earl had snuffed the lantern and moved the blankets. He piled a heavy armload of guns on me—we had to manage Mick's share as well as our own—and took the rest himself.

"Let's go," he said, and we hurried out into the night. I wanted to look over my shoulder at the bonfire, at the dark figures, but if I looked I might trip so I kept my eyes fixed ahead of me, toward the darkness, toward the faint sounds Earl made hurrying through the undergrowth.

Then Rain was right beside me and, after a few seconds, someone else. I risked a quick glance. Gabriel. Without stopping, without slowing down, he took some of the guns from Earl, and Rain did the same for me, and then it was easier to hurry.

We reached the boulders where the stash was hidden and shoved our guns inside, then ran again, hard, toward the truck. Earl was in front and by the time we made it to the clearing the truck was on, humming softly in the darkness. All three of us jumped into the back and then we were moving, pulling out onto the road, turning towards Ionia.

"Mick," Rain said, panting.

"Stay down," Gabriel said, reaching out and yanking her flat. He was crouched low, the top of his head beneath the sides of the truck bed. I was low, too, but only because I'd fallen when I climbed in.

"Mick's fine," Gabriel said. "I've seen him ride, and he's on the better horse."

The truck bed was cold metal, and I shifted position, trying to protect myself from the worst of the bumps. "Will Edgeling know it's Mick?" Rain asked.

"I hope not," Gabriel said. "But even if he does, we've got his stash."

"He thought it was someone named Jenkins," I said, and I felt a little sorry for the mysterious Jenkins.

When we reached the causeway out to the Drewblood house Gabriel let us sit up. It was low tide, and the causeway leading out to his house was wider than I'd ever seen it, the center gravel path flanked by wide stretches of wet dark sand.

We passed Nana and Grandfather's dark house and continued up the narrow road to Gabriel's. Earl pulled to a stop in the open yard area outside the fence, and we piled out of the back.

A guard was waiting at the gate, Woof at his heels. Three others guards, I knew, were stationed around the perimeter. As Rain and I approached, the guard at the gate swung it open for us, and then shut it behind us. Gabriel was still outside the gate. Earl was still in the truck.

"Aren't you coming in?" Rain said, and her father shook his head.

"We'll scout around a bit," he said. "Watch for Mick. If we get the chance, we'll collect the guns. If not we'll do it later."

She didn't say anything, which probably was wise, given the look on her face.

"You two were a big help tonight," Gabriel said. "But I want you out of this now."

Rain said nothing. She wound her fingers through the cast iron fence and watched as the little gray truck rounded the bend and faded from sight.

Chapter 15

In the dark living room Carol was asleep on the couch, the transmitter on the cushion near her hand. Gently I picked it up and turned to follow Rain upstairs.

"Hey," a voice called softly. Looking toward the hallway, I saw a dark figure topped by a white bandage. Ezzie.

I hurried over to him and flung my arms around his neck, but he stiffened and I released him, afraid I was hurting him. Lamplight filtered to us from the open door of his room down the hall, but his face was in shadows.

"Are you all right?" I kept my voice low so as not to wake Carol. "How do you feel?" It was the first time I'd seen him since Rory and Angus had brought him to the hospital.

"I'm not too bad, considering," Ezzie said. "But you'd best not come too close."

"You aren't contagious." I sounded more sure than I was.

"Not unless I suddenly take an urge to bite you or scratch you or something."

It was too dim to see his expression, but I was pretty sure he wasn't joking.

"You aren't going to do that."

"Says who?"

"Says me, and anyway you might not be contagious at all. Maybe only the wild men can pass it on."

His silence made me suddenly awkward.

"I'm sorry," I said. "I shouldn't call them that."

"It's what they are." His voice was flat. "But I didn't call you over here to lay my problems on you, Red. I wanted to give you something."

He felt around in the pocket of his bathrobe, and pulled out something that glinted in the dim light. "I snagged it when Meritt got us free of the wardens."

He handed the object to me. It was a key.

"It unlocks handcuffs," he said. "It might be useful, when you go back."

"When *we* go back."

Ezzie snorted.

"But you're doing better—"

Ezzie held up his hands. "I don't want to have this conversation," he said. "Not now. Look here—I got you something else, too." This time it was a tiny bottle.

"Dream Drops." He gestured down the hall. "I sorta looked in on the old people when the nurse had his back turned. They're all sound asleep, dreaming about Optica if we're lucky. And there are plenty of these bottles."

Turning the small bottle over in my hand, I watched the golden liquid inside shift thickly, like oil. Cautiously I opened it, and a strong scent of peppermint filled the air. Hurriedly I recapped the bottle, as if the very scent of it might take me over. These drops had caused so much trouble, so much grief. They had, perhaps, tricked Gabriel into causing his own brother's death.

"I thought they might be useful," Ezzie said.

I didn't want to disappoint him, but I didn't see how they could help.

"I can't see Optica with these," I said apologetically. "I can only see what Fiona's doing."

Ezzie nodded. "I know. I get that. But maybe you can

use them to bargain with. Bribe a warden or something, or threaten the Watchers. I don't know."

"Okay." I dropped both items into my pocket, where they clinked gently against each other. "Thanks, Ezzie."

He shifted uneasily. "Sure wish I could be more use," he said. "But I can't think how. Unless you set me loose on the Watchers."

He wasn't trying to be funny, but the image made me laugh. "Our secret weapon," I said. "A tame lunatic."

After a second, Ezzie chuckled softly. "Consider it a standing offer," he said, and then his voice went dead serious. "Use me however you can." Before I could answer he was turning away.

"Ezzie—"

But he didn't stop. He waved one hand at me and vanished into his room. Then the door closed, shutting away the light.

Upstairs Rain was sitting cross-legged on her bed.

"Take that thing off," she said crossly as I came into her room. "You look ridiculous."

I hadn't realized I was still wearing the makeshift cap. Obediently I pulled it off and sat down beside Rain, dropping the transmitter between us on the coverlets.

Rain's face was very white. "I still can't believe he left us," she said. "If anything, I'm a better fighter than he is. Even Earl says so."

I didn't answer. I certainly didn't have any advice about her issues with her father. Kicking off my shoes, I tucked my feet up beneath me.

"Get up," Rain said, flinging herself off the bed.

Assuming that she'd decided we should get ready to go to sleep, I stood up. The pale blue rug felt dense and soft beneath my feet. Behind Rain the pale thin curtains moved like ghosts, stirring in the wake of her passing.

"You've never been trained, right?"

It took a moment before I realized what she meant.

"You mean trained in fighting?" I said. "No, but I'm really good at running." I was trying for humor—I'd had enough intensity for the evening—but Rain's eyes narrowed.

"You can't always run away," she said. "Listen. This is what Earl says. Girls are too polite. They let people get too close because they don't want to seem distrustful. Then when they get grabbed they're surprised, because that isn't supposed to happen. It paralyzes them. So the key is to remember: It can happen to you. You can get grabbed, and you can get hurt."

"No, really?"

Rain glowered at me. I smiled sweetly and sat back down on the bed.

"Get up," Rain said. "I'm going to show you some basic moves."

I stayed put.

"Get up!"

"It's late and I'm tired," I said. Before the words were out of my mouth Rain had jumped on the bed behind me and wrapped one arm around my neck.

I leaned forward, pulling myself off the bed and her with me. We landed with a loud thud on the floor and rolled, and because she was heavier gravity helped me end up on top. I didn't want to hurt my cousin, but I didn't want her hurting me, either, or playing stupid games, so I elbowed her hard in the stomach and wrenched myself out of her grasp, yanking out a few hairs in the process.

Getting to my feet I backed against the bedroom wall, eyeing her warily, rubbing my stinging scalp. Rain stood up, her eyes glittering, and ran at me. I stepped aside at the last possible moment and she hit the wall with the side of her foot—she would have kicked me hard if I hadn't moved—and then spun toward me again, but I was already gone, over by the balcony windows, ready to climb out.

"Good instincts," she said, putting her hands on her hips. "You used my weight against me, and you have the patience to wait to make your evasive move most effective. But there at the start? It would have been better if you hadn't let me get a grip on you to begin with. Rear choke holds are brutal. The only thing that saved you was the fact that you were on a bed."

She was moving around me in a half circle.

"Stop it," I said, sliding up the pane of glass. "I'm tired."

"That's when they like to come after you."

"Rain, let's do this tomorrow."

Rain dropped to a half-crouch. Wearily I watched her. "I'll sleep at Nana's," I said, swinging one leg outside. "She might be senile, but at least she doesn't attack me at two in the morning."

"It's later than that," Rain said. "And you aren't going anywhere. The guards won't let you."

And I didn't really want to be wandering around in the dark alone, not with the Dream Recorder's thugs out looking for me.

"So I'll hang out with the guards instead. See you in the morning," I said, and waved.

Then I saw the transmitter on the bed. "The light's on!"

"Nice try." Rain lunged at me.

"Stop it!" I dodged and tried to get to the bed. "Really, Rain. Look at the transmitter!"

A flicker of doubt crossed her face and she glanced over her shoulder. I didn't wait for her reaction. I sprang toward the bed and grabbed up the transmitter. As I did, it began buzzing. I hit the button and the antenna scrolled out.

"Hello?" I said. "Meritt, are you there? Hello, hello, hello? Meritt?"

"Red Girl?"

"Sir Tom!"

"So you made it to the island," he said. "Young Meritt wasn't lying."

"Is he okay?"

"Last I saw. So what did you find over there, on that other island?"

Rain sank down on the pale blue bedspread, her eyes fixed on the transmitter.

"I found my twin sister," I said. "And Rafe's twin, too. And others—there were lots of us who were stolen."

I sounded accusatory; maybe that wasn't strategic, but I couldn't help it.

"So it's true," Sir Tom said quietly. "I was afraid it was."

That brought me up short. "Didn't you know? You were Head Guardian. You had to have known."

"Any big operation, the right hand doesn't know what the left is doing. That's to be expected. A safety precaution, because power corrupts and knowledge is power."

"But Angel said you knew—he said you felt guilty for your part in the experiment."

"Oh, he did, did he? Well, I'm not ashamed to say he's right about that. It's right to feel guilty if you are guilty."

"So you did know?" I was thoroughly confused.

A wry chuckle cackled out of the transmitter, so loud it made me jump.

"I knew about the experiment," Sir Tom said. "Of course I knew that. But I didn't know about the kidnappings. Now, I knew all along that I didn't know some things. But knowing I didn't know wasn't the same thing as knowing *what* I didn't know."

Rain blinked.

"I thought the entire project was built on volunteers," Sir Tom continued, "brave patriots in Optica and their more ordinary counterparts back home who were making the chicken's contribution to breakfast instead of the pig's."

Okay. Volunteers. It sounded crazy, that anyone would volunteer for this sort of thing, but maybe they didn't quite know what they were getting into.

But I wanted clarification about the "back home" part. "So you didn't know about this island? You thought our siblings were on the mainland?"

Sir Tom didn't answer me. Instead, his voice dropped to a mutter. "The problem is, when he finally knew what he hadn't known, then he knew he could have known if he'd wanted to know. Give up your life for your country? Certainly. It's done all the time, in every generation. Give up your memory? No one's that noble. He should have known better than that."

Rain's eyes met mine.

"Sir Tom," I said, deciding to change the subject. "Is everyone all right?"

There was a long pause.

"Sir Tom?" I said again.

"Well, I won't lie to you, Red Girl. Your black friend has gone missing."

"My—do you mean Ezzie? He's here. He came here the same night we did. But he's sick, Sir Tom. He's really sick. It's some sort of animal parasite."

"I'm sorry to say that's to be expected. He'll find himself vulnerable, now, to things of that sort."

My heart fell. "So Ezzie's truly different now, because the wild man clawed him."

"Because poor Nolan clawed him, yes."

"And Nolan is sick. He's like an animal."

"He can't help that," Sir Tom said. "That was my fault."

"Because you sent him to investigate what had happened on the mainland? You couldn't have known that would happen. You were the—they had a duty to investigate."

"There were laboratories," Sir Tom said sadly. "Laboratories developing biological weapons. In the destruction, they were breached."

Rain breathed in sharply, looking both horrified and fascinated.

"You mean this thing was intentional?" I said. "Somebody *wanted* to make people act like animals? Why?"

Sir Tom gave a humorless chuckle. "You won't have heard the old stories," he said. "They make it sound like becoming part wolf makes a man superhuman, but that's nonsense. Humans are at the top, developmentally speaking."

"But why would anybody want to do that to someone else?"

"To make our enemies degenerate, turn on each other. Then we could pick off the survivors easily enough, like hunting wild game."

I swallowed. "Ezzie had surgery," I said. "They did brain surgery on him to remove cysts."

"Ah. Well, child, maybe that'll do the trick."

He didn't sound like he thought so. I didn't think so either—I was just telling him, that was all. "The cysts came because he caught one type of wild animal disease," I said. I couldn't at the moment think what Rory had called it. "You're saying he could catch others, too. But maybe he could stay in the city, away from that sort of thing. Maybe that way he'd be okay."

"I don't know, Red Girl. All I know is what happened to my men. No doubt they caught other things, secondary infections or what have you, like Ezzie caught. But I'm fairly certain it's the primary infection that—well, there's no need to talk about this. Not now."

"I heard you tell Alice that the illness nurtured the seeds. I was hoping that maybe, if Ezzie had good seeds, he wouldn't become like those others."

Sir Tom was silent for a long moment. "The line between good and evil runs right up the middle of the human heart," he said finally.

"So why does the bad have to win?"

"Maybe it doesn't. Maybe you're right, Red Girl. I'm no expert."

"Is there nothing else we can do? No medicine, nothing like that?"

Sir Tom sighed. "There are no magic pills, no. At least not in my pockets. This is the hand he's been dealt. But the game's not over, and it just may be that he holds the cards to win. Stranger things have happened. Now you tell me this—how'd Ezzie get to be on that other island?"

"He found some old boat in the stockade."

Sir Tom cackled. "Did he, now? A bathtub would float better than that so-called boat. Angel made it, and Angel's good at many things, but boat-building's not one of them. He's too impatient, for one thing."

"He didn't use that boat to steal me." Good grief, now I was using the interrogation strategy I'd developed in Locria.

"No, because I sank his nice boat after he stole you."

Hmm. I tried again. "So you knew he had stolen me."

"Well, he certainly didn't give birth to you. I heard you crying, see, in the woods, and so Angel had to explain. Well, he enjoyed explaining, truth be told. He enjoyed rubbing my face in my ignorance, telling me about all the stolen ones while I held you in my arms." Sir Tom's voice turned dreamy. "Ah, you were just a tiny mite. A pretty little thing. A fairy child, from the water and the wild."

Goosebumps rose on my skin.

The old man went on, changing Louie's lines. "Come

with a demon, hand in hand, to a world more full of weeping that you could understand."

Rain widened her eyes and I hurried to pull Sir Tom back to normal conversation.

"So you took me into the city and gave me to the nanny mothers?"

"I did no such thing," Sir Tom said indignantly. "I told Angel to take you back to your folks."

"But he didn't."

"No," Sir Tom said. "He didn't. But I thought he did. I thought so until you showed up on my doorstep the other day and proved me an old fool yet again. So you see, Red Girl, your life in Optica was my fault. My failure, as a general and a man. Angel taunted me, told me about the big settlement on the far side of that other island and the few forlorn misfits on the near side, told me that island was a feeder league for this one, told me all kinds of things until I told him to stop talking and take you back, and afterwards I sank his boat. I didn't want him tormenting people on that other island; and I didn't want any to-and-froing with the mainland, either, not with that contamination at large. But I sank Angel's boat too late. Or too soon, it seems. For now, of course, we could do with having it."

My head was starting to ache, and I still hadn't done what Meritt needed me to do.

"Is everyone all right over there?" I said, looking for a natural segue. "Judd and everyone else?"

Sir Tom sighed. "More or less. For the time being."

"Why? What's wrong?"

Sir Tom's voice rose. "What's wrong is young Meritt! He's taken up with his good-for-nothing father, and if they have their way this rebellion will never get off the ground!"

"No, it isn't like that. Meritt's helping. And Angel is, too. Ezzie told me so. When the wardens arrested him and the others, Angel and Meritt helped. They attacked the wardens and helped them escape."

Sir Tom snorted. "That they did. They set the rabbit loose so the dogs would chase it."

I stared at Rain, baffled.

"A decoy," Rain said. "A diversion. Get the Watchers to look outside the city, so they'll forget to pay attention to the danger inside."

"Who's that?"

"It's my cousin. Rafe's niece. Her name is Rain."

"Well, Rain, you've hit the nail right smack on the head," Sir Tom said.

"I don't know what you're talking about," I said. "All I know is that Meritt is on our side. And he's in trouble—Cynda told the Watchers about him. They know he's been sabotaging their cameras. You'll tell him, won't you? Please?"

"I doubt I'll be seeing the boy."

"But he needs to see you—at least he needs to see Judd. He's trying to turn the wardens against each other—divide and conquer—and he wants you to let him talk to Judd, so Judd can help him do that. So Meritt can help free Optica."

"He is not trying to free Optica," Sir Tom said. "He's trying to take it over." For once he didn't sound theatrical. He also sounded old and tired.

"No," I said. "You don't understand. He's trying infiltrate the Watchers, but that's so he can help us."

"Same way he helped your Rafe?" Sir Tom said.

Rain's eyes narrowed.

"What do you mean?" I said, turning away from her.

"I mean just this: Young Meritt wasn't supposed to be out there that night, the night Rafe got arrested. Cline was."

"Cline told you this?"

"He did. It was Cline's job, to pick up those sedatives. And at the last minute young Meritt said no, he'd go, even though the switch didn't make any sense. Because Cline, he's a cattleman, and with no arrests, just a few minor incidents like any young man might have on his record. So Cline, if he gets caught, it's not going to be any big deal.

"But young Meritt? He already had quite a record, and he's your electronics specialist. He's crucial, if you're going to spy on someone in that city or keep someone from spying on you. The wardens pick him up again, especially out there with Rafe and his illegal sedatives, and the whole rebellion could go up in smoke. So why's young Meritt out there? He's a smart lad. Why'd he go and take a risk that could ruin everything? Just because he wanted a little fresh air, a night out with a pretty girl?"

I was shaking my head; Sir Tom went relentlessly on.

"Maybe he went because he knew there was no risk, Red Girl. Maybe young Meritt didn't have anything to fear, out there that night. Maybe he was ready for the uprising to be quashed. And maybe he wanted to see it with his own eyes, make sure it happened like it needed to happen."

"That's not true!" I said, though in my mind's eye I was seeing Meritt standing on the sidewalk at the opening to the wall, catching his breath, talking to Warden Rhoda.

"He wasn't expecting you to throw a wrench in his plans," Sir Tom said. "Think of it, child. Rafe dead, the city meetings terrorizing everyone else. The rebellion would have been over before it seriously began, if you hadn't lit out for the wilderland."

I shut my eyes. "No—you don't know him. Meritt loved Rafe. He would never hurt him."

Sir Tom sighed. "Think it through," he said.

"If he knew what was going to happen that night, why would he take me with him? It doesn't make sense."

"I wasn't there, child. You tell me. Why did he need a witness?"

I didn't know, and I didn't want to think about it. I wanted to defend Meritt. "He saved Farrell Dean," I said.

"Red Girl, you're the one who did that. All young Meritt did was cut the lights, and he could talk himself out of that corner easily enough. Cline tells me Optica's gear malfunctions all the time."

Yes, but at just the right instant? Sir Tom was so dead set against Meritt that I didn't know where to start; and before I could say anything else, Sir Tom spoke again.

"My light's flickering," he said. "You're cutting in and out. Here's the bottom line. The stockade has been depleted. Angel cleared it out, and I haven't had time to locate his new stash because we're under constant attack. One wave of wardens after another. They just keep on coming—and somehow, Red Girl, they conveniently knew exactly where to find us. And the climbing boy, he's been shot."

"Joe?" I said. "How bad is it?"

"He's not dead, but two inches over and he would be. Shawna's a good girl, she's seeing him through, doing her best, but she's not a doctor. So with those two out of commission, I've got five able-bodied soldiers. And one of them's a boy I'm trying to keep steady, and one of them's a tender-hearted woman who can't bring herself to shoot at real live people, at least not ones she's spent the last twenty years cooking dinner for. So that leaves me three. Cline, Harding, and Liza."

He sounded suddenly tired. "They're good soldiers, Red Girl. They don't complain. But they're wearing out. Now tell me you've got good news."

I swallowed. I wasn't finished defending Meritt, not by a long shot, but that would have to wait.

"I do have good news," I said. "We're bringing help. I don't know when, exactly, but soon. Farrell Dean's building an engine for a boat—rebuilding an engine—so we won't have to wait for the current. And we have a lot of guns—a whole lot of them—and ammunition. We'll bring supplies and fighters, Sir Tom. Plenty of things. Just hold on. Please, Sir Tom. Hold on."

"Oh, I'm holding on," he said. "What else can an old soldier do?"

Chapter 16

My head was splitting. I pressed my hands against my temples and wished Rain would stop talking. But no—she had questions.

"Who's this Meritt?" she said.

"My friend."

She gave me a wry look. "Obviously. Give me more than that."

"He's my very best friend," I said.

"Better than Farrell Dean?"

Everyone kept taking Farrell Dean's side against Meritt, but they didn't even know Meritt. For that matter, they didn't really know Farrell Dean. For all I knew, he'd been acting odd in Locria because he didn't want to succeed with the engine; for all I knew he wanted to keep me away from Optica and Meritt, just like he'd taken me away from Optica and Meritt before. Maybe he was going to sabotage Mal's work.

All right—that wasn't very likely. But still.

"Meritt has been my very best friend forever," I said, and if Rain caught the evasion, she didn't call me on it. "And no matter what Sir Tom thinks, Meritt wants to help. Sir Tom doesn't like him because he's Angel's son, and he won't give him a chance, just because of that."

I started to say that Gabriel wouldn't, either, but

remembered just in time that he was Rain's father. "It isn't fair," I said instead. "He can't help who his father is."

Rain nodded. "All right. Let's work this out. Why do you suppose Meritt was out there when Uncle Rafe got taken?"

"I don't know. But it's not like Sir Tom makes it sound. I'm sure about that. Meritt wouldn't turn Rafe in. Rafe was—we—he was like my—"

"Okay, okay." Rain was holding up her hands to stop me. "Could this Cline person be lying?"

I wished. I couldn't see it, though. Cline would hit someone in the face, not stab him in the back. Cline was just mistaken. There was no way Meritt could be responsible for Rafe's arrest.

"Red?" Rain's voice was like a sledgehammer on my brain. "Sorry if it's painful, but we need to figure this out. Tell me exactly what happened the night Uncle Rafe got taken."

Haltingly, I told her. The blue electric lights, the wet pavement, the intermittent glare of the spotlight. Warden Rhoda. Rafe. Running away. Turning myself in so Meritt wouldn't get caught.

Rain listened without comment until I was finished.

"Just for a minute, play the devil's advocate," she said. "Why would Meritt have taken you with him, if he knew what was going to happen?"

By then I had the answer, but I couldn't say it.

"So you'd see it," Rain said gently. "So you'd know he couldn't stop it. So you wouldn't suspect he was involved, and you'd make sure no one else thought so either."

I was shaking my head. "He took me with him because he didn't know there was a problem," I said. "I know he didn't know, because Rafe got killed. Meritt would never be involved in that. I don't know why he traded places with Cline, but I know he would never have done anything to hurt Rafe."

"All right," Rain said, her voice noncommittal. "Let's

move on. You didn't know why you were meeting Rafe?"

"No. I didn't know anything about the rebellion, not then. I didn't even know there was a rebellion at all."

"If Meritt's your best friend, why didn't he tell you?"

That was a sensitive point with me, but I shrugged as if it weren't. "Farrell Dean didn't tell me either."

Rain tilted her head. "But Farrell Dean didn't take you along on his missions, did he?"

Reluctantly I shook my head.

"And Farrell Dean isn't your *very best friend.*"

"It was safer that way, all right? Meritt was protecting me. If I got picked up by wardens—like I did—then I couldn't tell what I didn't know."

Rain said nothing.

"Don't try to turn that into something sinister," I said, keeping my voice even with effort. "That's just Meritt."

"Go on."

"He's always been careful that way. More careful than most of us. When you're watched all the time it's safer not to say anything at all. Not if it's important."

"So you're not saying he lies, just that he keeps quiet."

"Right. He doesn't lie, not to me." I was forgetting the argument now, almost forgetting Rain's presence, thinking only about Meritt. "Sometimes when he doesn't want me to know something, he'll straight-out say he isn't going to tell me. And other times he'll change the subject. And sometimes I'll think he's answered me, but then I'll realize later he hasn't, at least not all the way."

Rain raised her eyebrows. "He's more dangerous than a straight-out liar," she said.

"Why?" But I already knew the answer. "Because a barefaced liar can be caught out. But Meritt can't."

"He's slick," Rain said, nodding. "He's charming, am I right?"

Oh, yes. Meritt could charm the leaves right off the trees, without even really exerting himself.

"You want to trust him, so you do half the work for him. But he's definitely slippery."

"And you know what? Maybe that's actually a good thing," I said, flinging the pillow away from me. "Sir Tom can't do anything, not with what he's got—a few guns, a handful of untrained soldiers. You heard him. He's in trouble, and we might not get there in time—they could all be dead before we show up. So maybe infiltrating the Watchers, making a difference from inside, being slick and charming—maybe that's our only hope. Maybe Meritt is our only hope."

Rain wasn't arguing with me—she was merely listening intently—but all the same I was beginning to get angry.

"And wouldn't it be better that way?" I said. "Maybe nobody will have to die, if we do things Meritt's way. Shouldn't Sir Tom be happy if Meritt can protect hundreds of people without having to kill hundreds of others? He should have agreed to work with Meritt. He should have let Meritt talk to Judd. He should go find Meritt right now and warn him that he's in danger, that a so-called friend has put him in danger, when all he's doing is trying to save her life and everyone else's."

Rain's expression was unreadable.

"What?" I said, spoiling for a fight.

"Not a thing," Rain said, picking up the transmitter and turning it over in her hand. "If Tristan were still around, I'd get him to look at this," she said.

Catching my expression, she shrugged. "He wasn't crazy all the time," she said. "Just when it came to your folks. I'll have to ask Dad who his new tech guy is going to be."

"Why?" I said. "Tell me what you're thinking."

Rain looked up at me from beneath her lashes, then lifted her head and looked me straight in the eye.

"You know what I'd do, if I were Meritt? I'd take my transmitter to Sir Tom, if that seemed like the strategic thing to do—if it would help build your trust, or if I really did need access to this Judd person. But I'd make sure the power was low. Letting Sir Tom have a single conversation with you is one thing. Letting him have constant access to you is something else entirely. So I want to show this to a tech person and find out if there's a way to limit the length of a transmission, by either draining the battery or some other way."

I stared at her.

"But that transmitter ran low before," I said. "When I was talking to Meritt."

"So he said."

"You think he let me talk to Sir Tom just to manipulate me? Just to pretend he was being open and up-front?"

"I didn't say that. But I'm sure he'd rather us support him and Angel, if we manage to get over there. Instead of Sir Tom."

"We weren't talking about Angel," I said. "We were talking about Meritt."

"Well, I want to talk about Angel now. What does he want? Does he want to control Optica, destroy it, liberate it?"

"I don't know."

"You'd better do some thinking, then." Rain leaned forward, so close that I could smell the woods and the smoke from Edgeling's bonfire on her clothes. "If you ask me, that's the million dollar question. What does Angel want?"

Chapter 17

It was almost dawn when the men returned. Rain and I both had fallen asleep, but we must have been sleeping lightly because we woke when Woof gave a happy bark outside.

I felt stiff, and frozen from sleeping on top of the covers, and I guess Rain did too, because she shoved a blanket at me and wrapped one around herself. Then we started downstairs.

Over the stair railing I saw Gabriel bending over Aunt Carol on the couch, rousing her.

"We're back," he told her as she sat up groggily. "Go on to bed now."

She passed us going up as we came down, her graying blonde hair disheveled, her eyes barely open enough to see where she was going.

"Where's Mick?" I said.

Gabriel waited until Carol was out of sight before he answered. He looked tired—there were dark circles under his eyes—and something was wrong. I could see it in the way he stood, half turned away from us.

"Where is he?" I said again, my heart constricting.

Gabriel tried to smile, but only managed to look pained. "Mick's right here," he said. "He's fine."

From the shadows near the door two figures appeared, moving slowly. Mick's dark curls were standing on end and he was leaning heavily on Earl. I would have thought his black clothes were wet, but the smudges of red on his hands told the real story.

"He doesn't look fine," Rain said as I ran to him, tripping over the edge of my blanket in my haste.

Mick's face was pale, but he looked at Rain and his green eyes lit up with mischief. "Looks can be deceiving," he said, putting his free arm around my shoulders.

Rain was circling us, looking him over. "I don't see any injuries," she said. "Whose blood is that?"

Mick looked down at his clothes. "Midnight's," he said. "The horse. Bullet just grazed him."

"Edgeling shot his own horse?" I couldn't believe it.

Mick shrugged. "He didn't mean to," he said.

"You mean he was aiming at—"

"Probably we zigged when he thought we would zag," Mick said.

"But if—"

"Never any point in thinking about the ifs," Mick said, and winked at me. "Gunfire's a good way to spook a horse, get me thrown."

"But if that's what he wanted to do, then why didn't he shoot straight up in the air?"

"And that's when Dad got there?" Rain said at the same time. "When the horse got shot?"

My brother shook his head and chose to answer Rain, not me. "No," he said. "That's when I got thrown. Edgeling followed the horse, not me. I trekked three miles through the woods, more or less, two of them after I wrenched my ankle stepping in a woodchuck hole. Not a very thrilling injury, I'm afraid. Just clumsy Mick not watching where he was going."

I got the point. Of course we wouldn't go around telling

people he'd been injured while stealing a horse—or while stealing guns, for that matter.

Rain was crouched at Mick's feet, checking his ankle.

"It's awfully swollen," she said, looking up.

"Hurts, too," Mick said. "Never thought I'd say this, but I was mighty glad to see Uncle Gabe once I finally made it back to the road."

"He called on the transceiver," Gabriel said. "We couldn't go in looking for him, because he didn't know exactly where he was. So we cruised up and down waiting for him to show."

"Does he need a doctor?" Rain asked.

Gabriel shook his head. "He needs to ice it and stay off it for a couple of days, and then it should be fine."

He turned to Mick. "Go get cleaned up and get off that foot. Earl will show you where."

Earl made as if to help Mick out of the room, but Mick hesitated, looking at Gabriel. I couldn't make sense of the expression on his face—questioning, concerned.

Rain looked at me, clearly thinking the same thing I was. Something was badly wrong. Something worse than Mick's ankle.

"I'll tell the girls," Gabriel said to Mick. "If that's all right with you."

Mick nodded. Then he and Earl made their slow way out of the room.

"What is it?" Rain said. "What happened?"

Gabriel looked at her, and then at me. "Earl and I got the guns," he said, nodding toward the door. "They're in the truck under a tarp."

Rain caught something in his look that I didn't, or else she'd already suspected. "You went back," she said, her tone accusing. "You went all the way back to the barn."

Gabriel nodded. "It was too good a chance to miss," he

said. "All that chaos, nobody watching the farm. Edgeling was just asking for a visit from someone with sticky fingers. We got the last of his guns and found some explosives that might come in useful."

"But what's wrong?" I said. "Something happened. What is it?"

Gabriel didn't delay any longer. "We found this," he said, putting one hand in his pocket. "Edgeling had it in his hidey hole. I don't know what it means. We'll have to ask your father."

He pulled out a small black object with a glass front and held it out to me.

"That's one of the wireless cameras," I said, taking it from Gabriel and turning it over in my hands. "Meritt and I found one just like it, set in the wall in the wasteland outside of Optica."

"What else can you tell me?" Gabriel asked, and I thought back to that night at Rafe's little house, Meritt bent over the camera, excitedly explaining all about it.

"It's more advanced than the normal cameras," I said. "Smaller, wireless, very high tech. The regular cameras are just out there in the open, where we can see them, but this kind is hidden. The one we found was corroded inside. Meritt said it hadn't been used for a long time."

"Back up a minute, Daddy," Rain said. "Did you say you'd have to ask Eric Alleyn about it?"

Gabriel was studying the camera device again, but he nodded absently.

"What would he know?" Rain said. "He's not exactly the most technologically savvy person on the island."

Gabriel sighed. "I hope he knows something," he said. "The camera was wrapped in this." He put his hand in his pocket again and pulled out a handkerchief. When he smoothed it out on the arm of the couch I could see that it was very finely woven. A distinctive blue and gold scrolling design was embroidered around the edge in the tiniest imaginable stitches. At the corner were initials: MA.

"Whose is it?" I said, just as Rain said, "Alleyn, but what's the M? Mick?"

"Close," Gabriel said. "Mick was named for him."

"Michael Alleyn," I said.

Gabriel nodded. "Eric Alleyn's father," he said. "Your other grandfather. The one with a habit of running away."

Chapter 18

"Can't we get moving? It's nearly morning. We can wake the old people up and find out if they saw anything, and then we can go."

"Wake them, and risk cutting short a dream of Optica?"

Gabriel was right, but I didn't like it.

"Sit down, Valentina."

"Red," I said irritably, flicking back the velvety curtain and looking out at the darkness beyond. "They were watching my grandpa. There was a camera hidden in his house."

In the darkness Gabriel settled a cushion beneath his head. He was stretched out on the couch, and everyone else had gone to bed, but I couldn't stop pacing.

"*Possibly* that camera was in Michael Alleyn's house," he said. "And possibly not. We don't know where it was placed, or where he came upon it, or if he even did."

"It was wrapped in his handkerchief."

"There are dozens of possible explanations for that. Perhaps his handkerchief was lost or stolen, and Edgeling picked it up and wrapped the camera in it."

"I don't think so."

"No," Gabriel said. "We should bear other possibilities in mind, but I don't think it's a coincidence either. There are too many peculiarities having to do with Michael Alleyn. The fact that he had his own Dream Record book, his reputation for being paranoid—and his suspicion of the Dream Recorder in particular."

Mollified by his concession, I turned back to the window. Once again I pulled back the curtains, searching for a dawn that was still some hours away. The window faced east, but there was no hint of morning.

Just to be sure, for comparison I crossed the room and looked out the west-facing window beside the front door. Was it any darker at all in this direction? I tried to fix the shade of darkness firmly in my mind, and went back to the eastern window. But the darkness in the room, the darkness between the darknesses outside the windows, confused me.

So I went back to the western window and did it all over again, trying to shake off the sense of urgency that had been growing ever since I'd learned that Cynda had betrayed Meritt. He was all on his own over there, without support, and everyone was against him, and now there were cameras here too—for all we knew, someone in Optica was watching us, listening to us plan, seeing our every move.

"I'd thought I might catch a few winks, but clearly that isn't going to happen," Gabriel said, sitting up. "Not with you flitting back and forth like some demented ghost."

I stopped my pacing and faced him. Still dressed in the black clothes he'd worn to steal Edgeling's guns, he was only a dim silhouette there in the darkness, a shadow that could have been anyone. A shadow that could have been Rafe.

"It's not supposed to be like that here," I said, and then I had to stop and fight down the lump in my throat. "They aren't supposed to watch you the way they watch us."

A few drops of rain pattered against the window, carried by a sudden rising wind, and the lonely sound made tears come to my eyes.

"They aren't watching any longer," Gabriel said after a

moment, and for once his tone was not ungentle. "That camera is here, wrapped up. It isn't in your father's house."

"There are bound to be others."

"Could be, but if Michael Alleyn found one, he'd have taken the place apart checking for more." Gabriel lifted a hand to his face in a gesture that had become familiar to me. He was running a hand over his short beard, smoothing it, and I was glad he had that beard. Otherwise he'd look exactly like his dead brother and I'd fling myself at him and start bawling like a baby. I was so tired, and so unsettled. I wanted Rafe. I wanted things back the way they were.

"I want to go home," I said aloud, without meaning to.

Gabriel didn't snap at me. "I know," he said. "We're working on it. We have guns now, and tomorrow I'll send someone to check on the engine. And we'll talk to your father, see what he knows or can guess about that camera."

A figure moved into the room from the hallway, startling me. Gabriel flipped on the lamp as Esme came into the room, still pulling her bathrobe on over her long nightgown.

"I'm sorry," she said unevenly. "I'm so sorry. I don't even know if it's real, but it's terrible."

Gabriel went to Esme and put an arm around her shoulders. "Tell us about it," he said, steering her to the couch. "All you have to do is tell us what you saw, and we'll take it from there."

I couldn't seem to move. The cold pane of glass beneath my fingers anchored me in place. It would have been less frightening if it had been anyone but Esme—her sister was such a calm, matter-of-fact sort of person. I remembered the day of the first city meeting, when everyone else was so tense, and Estelle's only concern was that I got breakfast. If Esme was naturally calm like her sister, something awful was happening in Optica.

Esme took a long breath and pulled the edges of her

blue bathrobe tightly together at her throat; she was chilly, like Estelle always was, even though she was plumper than Estelle ever had a chance to be.

"I'm sorry," she said again, her eyes going to the window behind me, where drops of rain streamed gray and gleaming down the glass. "I'm not usually such a ninny."

Then she sat up very straight and looked me in the eye. "This is what happened," she said. "I was confined in a room with a lot of other old people. We were frightened and tired and wanted to go home to our own beds, and the room was so crowded we couldn't even all sit down at once. Margo—I mean, Mariella—was with me. She isn't as strong as I am, and of course she's a few years older. She was so exhausted she was literally asleep on her feet, propped against the wall. I was worried about her."

Crossing the room, I sat down beside her and she reached over and took my hand. Her fingers were cold.

"You did it," I said, astonished. "You actually dreamed about Optica."

Esme squeezed my hand. "Yes," she said. "And now I know it's a real place, not some odd figment of my imagination. It's my own sister's life that I'm seeing. Her troubles."

"What else happened?" Gabriel asked, and Esme flinched.

"Will stood up on a chair and got everyone's attention," she said. "Not Will, but his brother. Louie. And he said the very thing I'd been thinking: If we didn't do something, we all would die. 'You know we're not well prepared for the winter,' he said. 'You know we've all been wondering what the Watchers have planned to save us. Well, we're it. We're the plan. With us gone, the young ones can live. Now, if the city doesn't want to be burdened by us, fine. I for one don't want to take food out of the mouths of babes. But why not let us fend for ourselves?'"

Esme's hands began to tremble. "So we decided that the next time a warden came, Louie would create a distraction and the others would rush the door. We didn't know if we'd succeed. We didn't know if we could make it to the woods, or if we could survive out there. But we didn't want to be put down like animals."

She stopped talking, but she didn't let go of my hand. The rain drummed loudly against the window, then quieted. I waited for Gabriel to comment, but he said nothing.

"They aren't dead," I said. "They're still alive, and Louie has a plan."

Esme didn't look at me. "That's not the end of the dream," she said. "A warden came in, and Will fought with him. Louie, I mean. He struggled with the warden, and the rest of us tried to get out the door. Some of us made it. About a dozen, I think. But Mariella didn't."

"You mean she's still trapped?"

Esme shook her head. She did look at me, then, and her eyes were compassionate and wet with tears.

Letting go of her hand, I got up and went back to the window. I ran my fingers over the window, wanting to wipe away the drops of rain that beaded the pane like tears, but the glass wouldn't let me. They were dying, over there in Optica. Mariella had died.

I remembered the day after Rafe's city meeting, when people were shunning me, when Mariella had stopped in the street and waved at me, right there in front of everybody. She had seemed so unsteady on her feet, and I'd worried that she might fall and break a hip.

And now she was dead.

Behind me, Esme spoke to Gabriel. "I have a confession," she said. "After the nurse left last night, I took extra drops. I know Will thought increasing the dosage might compromise the integrity of our dreams, but I've never been a big dreamer, and I didn't want to waste an entire night. Is it possible I mis-dreamed? I don't want to lead you astray, of course, but I can't help hoping I've imagined this whole thing."

Gabriel shook his head, and in the window reflection I saw him glance my way. "I'm afraid your dream is accurate enough," he told Esme.

We'd told her nothing specific; we'd only told her that she had a twin sister who was in danger. We hadn't mentioned the upcoming killings, or that Optica was starving, or that the people in Optica were afraid of the woods. We hadn't even told her the names of the other old people, the ones over there in Optica. We had been as scientific as possible.

When Gabriel spoke again, I thought at first that he was speaking to Esme. "Are you all right?" he said.

But it was Margo who answered. I turned to see her moving slowly into the room, one hand against the wall as if to keep herself upright. Her lavender shawl, half on and half off, trailed behind her.

"I've had a terrible dream," she said.

Esme rose from the couch and hurried to her side. "I saw it too," she said, putting an arm around Margo's shoulders. "Oh, my dear. I am so sorry."

Margo nodded; her eyes were vague. "She was very brave, wasn't she?"

"Yes. She was." Esme's eyes went to me. "The warden raised his gun at Louie, and Mariella stepped in front of it. She—"

She broke off, steadying Margo as the older woman lowered herself onto the couch. Margo looked terribly frail, gray-faced and shocked.

"She accomplished what she intended," Margo said, speaking carefully, as if every word required effort. "I wanted him to make it out with the others. He's such a capable man, and I've grown so old and weak. Most likely I wouldn't even be able to make it to the woods, much less be helpful when it came to surviving out there. So I did what I could."

"Your sister was very brave," Esme said, patting her hand. "*Mariella* was brave."

Margo's gaze focused a bit. "Yes. My sister. It felt like me, though not as if I were making decisions. I was there, but I was only along for the ride."

Then she looked at me and, faintly, smiled. "Before it happened she was sleeping," she said. "I dreamed my sister's dream, and she was dreaming about you. You were lost, and she was worried. In her dream she went to look for Rafe, because she knew he would find you."

My cheeks were wet with tears.

"It was a dream within a dream. And then she woke up." Margo's voice faltered. "And then she fell asleep once more."

Gabriel fumbled in his pocket—his awkward motions the only indication he wasn't perfectly calm and collected—and offered her a handkerchief. She nodded her thanks and began to wipe her eyes, while I stood there at the window, frozen.

What did it do to you, to feel your twin dying?

And we had done this to her; we had asked Margo to take Dream Drops, to see if she could spy for us on Optica. She could have died herself, from the shock of it.

"I'm glad I was with her," Margo said. "At least she didn't die alone. Do you suppose she knew I was there?"

"Surely she did," Esme murmured comfortingly, though how could she say? I had no idea whether the twins in Optica sensed an eavesdropper in their minds. None of my old people in Optica had ever mentioned feeling like someone was with her, but of course, they wouldn't. If anyone had, we'd have thought she was unhinged, driven a little crazy by the constant surveillance.

"Come on in," Gabriel said.

Will Bright was standing in the doorway, watching us all. Unlike the women he was fully clothed, right down to his shoes.

"Did you make it all the way to the woods?" Margo asked anxiously.

Will looked down at the floor. "All I saw was rubbish," he said "As I expected. Waste of time."

"But—"

Esme put a restraining hand on Margo's arm, murmured something in her ear. She was probably reminding the other woman to be scientific, I thought, reminding her not to tell Will details he didn't already know. But something in Will's demeanor made me think such caution was unnecessary.

Gabriel apparently had the same instinct. "Are you sure about that?" he said, standing up and crossing over to Will. "Apparently it's been an eventful night in Optica."

Will Bright glared at him. "This is poor strategy all around," he said. "We could dream something about Optica that's only a dream, and then we'd be leading you into terrible danger. Giving you misinformation."

"This is untried territory, certainly. We'll be careful. And if your dreams correspond, that would be a clear indication of their veracity."

Will shook his head.

"I could steer you wrong," he said. "Just because I dreamed one dream that was accurate—" he flinched, and I knew he was thinking about Louie in the fire—"that doesn't mean every dream I have is reliable. It's crazy, what you're asking. It's too risky."

I left the window and crossed the room to him, so angry I could hardly get the words out.

"It's worth the risk," I said. "We're trying to save lives. We're trying to save your *brother's* life, like Mariella just did.

Did you hear what they dreamed? Were you listening? Did you have the same dream?"

"You can't be making life-or-death decisions based on anything I dream," Will said, taking a step away from me. "Anything I see is only a possibility, not a certainty. And as I said right from the get-go, I reserve the right to not tell you what I dream, if I think it's of questionable veracity."

He looked like Louie, right down to the hands twisted with arthritis—he even sounded like Louie, with a twangy sort of drawl—but he acted nothing like his brother.

"Your brother used to play games with me," I said, determined to get through to him. "He taught me to make three-dimensional shapes out of string. It was just a child's game, but he liked playing it with me. He said he remembered it from when he was little."

Will Bright's eyes flickered across my face.

"When Farrell Dean and I came to this island we didn't know what we'd find," I said. Farrell Dean's name felt odd in my mouth, but I ignored it and went on. "We didn't know if anyone lived here. But Louie had told Farrell Dean how to dig on a beach for clean water, so we knew we'd survive."

Still there was no reply.

"When Louie almost burned up in the city meeting, and the man who saved him got killed instead, Louie did something strange just before the lights went out. I don't know why, but maybe you know."

Gabriel was watching me intently, but Will didn't look interested at all.

"He folded his hands together, like this," I said. "And then he bowed his head and started talking—"

"Time to get moving," Will said curtly. "I have business to tend to today. I'll try again tonight, but I make you no promises." And with that he turned and left the room.

"What's wrong with him?" I said, turning back toward

the women on the couch and struggling to keep my voice down. "Does he even care what happens over there?"

The two old women looked up at me. They had their arms around each other, and Esme was rocking gently, as if she were holding a small child instead of an elderly woman.

"I suspect he cares all too much," she said.

Chapter 19

Frankly, I was getting a little tired of being bossed around by my Uncle Gabriel.

"It's on the way," he said. "And I can't waste time doubling back later. I've a lot to get done today."

Well, I had a lot to get done today too.

I needed to warn my father and sister that somebody might be watching, that there might be cameras in their home. I needed to find someone who could figure out how to make the transmitter call out, so I could ask Sir Tom to find my old people out in the woods before the wild men did.

Most of all, I needed to hurry up and get back to Optica before everyone I loved there was killed. Already I was too late; Mariella was dead. Even if we could somehow instantly be back in Optica with weapons and people, we would still be too late for her.

Before I could make my point, Gabriel stopped the truck by the side of the road and got out. It surprised me—we'd only been driving for a few minutes.

"Come on," he said impatiently.

Giving him an annoyed look—which he ignored—I climbed out of the truck and into a wet clingy fog.

"Where's the house?" We were parked by the side of the road; there was nothing but trees all around.

"This way," Gabriel said, and started walking. Less enthusiastically, I trailed along behind. Tree branches caught at my hair, my clothes. There wasn't really a path; it was more a series of breaks among the close-set trees. Browning leaves layered the ground in great drifts, soggy and unpleasant, and the air hung heavy, so damp and thick that it felt hard to breathe. My face felt clammy; I put a hand to my hair and found it wet. My old people were wandering though woods like these, possibly through weather like this.

"It's fortunate you were sick," Gabriel said, in a tone clearly meant to be conciliatory. "Your father wanted to confront the midwife days ago."

"Yeah. What luck."

"Don't be a smart aleck." He spoke without heat, but it was still annoying. Rain was right—he treated us like children. "Eric Alleyn wouldn't leave you while you were sick, and that allowed him time to cool off and listen to reason, which is fortunate. We need to approach her in such a way as will elicit information. It would have done no good for him to show up here shouting and angry, putting her on the defensive."

"She probably doesn't know anything anyway." I stepped over a rotting log covered with lichen. "The Dream Recorder is the one in charge, like the Watchers in Optica. All the midwife did was hand over babies and lie about it. And anyway, Farrell Dean has already talked to her."

"Perhaps Farrell Dean's methods of persuasion are inferior to mine."

I wasn't sure that was anything to be proud of, or exactly what he meant by it, since he'd made it clear he was going to try a soft approach, and I had trouble imagining Gabriel as a virtuoso of friendly persuasion. But I said nothing, settling for a glare of disapproval. He didn't see it. He was striding along ahead of me, oblivious to everything but his own agenda for the day, whatever it was. For a moment I tried to keep up, but when I slid on a muddy patch I decided to take my own sweet time.

What an unpleasant day for a walk in the woods—gray sky, the kind of wet chilliness that went straight to your bones, and the trees in that pitiful half-state, clinging to a few withering leaves as if desperately trying to shield themselves from the winter to come. And then there was the fog. Generally I liked foggy days; they turned ordinary landscapes into beguiling mysteries. But this fog didn't drift or beckon; it sat, dull and heavy.

The midwife didn't know anything useful. This was a waste of time.

And it had been bad enough, listening over Tristan's radio as Farrell Dean talked to the woman, hearing myself discussed as a *transaction*. I knew I'd done nothing wrong; the things that had been done by the midwife and Tristan had been done *to* me. Still, being bought and sold made me feel ashamed, as if there were a weakness in me, some vulnerability that begged to be exploited. I didn't want to see this woman face to face.

Gabriel slowed to wait for me. "You realize it just as easily could have been Fiona," he said, and this time when he pushed a tree limb back, he held it out of my way. He was trying to be conciliatory, yet again.

I ducked past the branch and looked up at him. "How did you know what I was thinking?"

He threw a quick sideways glance my way. "I didn't," he said. "The topic has been on my mind ever since I learned what happened to my brother. Why did the midwife choose him rather than me? That one moment determined my entire life, and his. But there is no answer; she had no reason. There were two babies. One was taken, one was left. That's as far as the answer goes."

Maybe. I still didn't want to see the midwife.

"It's not much further," he said.

I was glad; the foggy woods were disorienting. Though we'd come only a short distance I wasn't sure I could find my way out, if I had to make my way back alone. But we weren't too far from town, as the crow flew. I could even hear the distant sound of someone spading up ground. It was muffled and distorted by the mist, but maybe I could follow it back to Ionia, if I had to.

We came to the edge of a small clearing with a small house in its center. It wasn't an inviting house. The stones it was built from were green with moss. The roof was green with moss. The whole thing blended in with its surroundings—the forest behind it, the undergrowth that grew almost to its door. Why would anyone choose to live closed in like this, in a hovel damp and dark and overgrown, with barely a glimpse of the sky?

A huge pile of firewood, neatly stacked, ran along the edge of the clearing, under an open-sided shelter. It looked like way too much wood for one house.

"Evan's work," Gabriel said, nodding at it. "He sells it."

He walked up to the door and raised his hand to knock, then stopped short. The door was ajar.

"Rowena?" he called. "Are you home?"

No one answered.

He pounded on the doorframe. When there still was no answer, he nudged the door. It swung inward, creaking softly. As far as I could see, the house was dark inside.

"Rowena? Evan?" Gabriel gave up and turned to me. "Come on," he said. "I'm not leaving you out here alone. Stay right behind me."

We passed through a narrow entryway and into a dark chilly kitchen, neat but faintly musty. The sink was empty of dishes, and two cups stood draining on a folded dishtowel.

No lights were on and the windows, hung with thick yellowy-green curtains, let in only the halfhearted light of a foggy morning deep in the woods.

"Rowena?" Gabriel called again. I knew no one would answer; the house was cold and empty. It felt as empty as Rafe's house, the night I'd gone there alone after he died.

Gabriel started into the next room and then stopped so suddenly that I ran into him.

"We're too late," he said over his shoulder. "She's dead."

"You mean—she—" Images of blood and bodies crowded in on me: Tristan drifting in the sea tide, blood blooming red and oily in the gray water; people burning, bleeding, falling in the artificial light of Optica's city circle; and Rafe, my memories of the city meeting always came back to Rafe, fighting and calling out and dying, his blood on the soles of my feet.

Gabriel was watching me narrowly. "Perhaps you'd better wait here," he said.

I shook the memories away. "I'm all right," I said, but before I could move another thought struck me. "Was it Eric Alleyn?"

Gabriel didn't answer; his dark eyes were unreadable.

"He killed Tristan," I said.

"Tristan was drowning you." Gabriel turned away from me, and when he went into the next room I followed.

It was a living room, with a sagging couch and too many chairs. Like the kitchen it was dark, heavily curtained, but the gloom didn't hide the woman lying on the floor, her long white hair scattered in a spray around her head.

She was very thin, almost skeletal, and very old. But her eyes were open and her expression was both pained and startled, as if she hadn't expected death just yet, despite her age and condition. I didn't see any blood, or any sign of violence.

"Did she just happen to die of natural causes?"

Gabriel didn't answer. He knelt beside the woman and touched her hand, then leaned closer still and sniffed at her sagging mouth. "Do you smell that?" he said, turning to me.

I leaned a little closer—not nearly as close as he was—and sniffed. "I don't smell anything in particular," I said.

Gabriel sat back on his heels. "She was poisoned."

"How do you know?"

He gave me a long look and I tried to keep my face expressionless.

"You're determined to think the worst of your relatives." He sounded tired instead of angry. "I may not be your noble Rafe, but I don't go around murdering people. Nor does your father. But there's an odd odor I don't recognize, and this." Opening his hand he showed me a small glass vial that had been snapped in two.

"Maybe you shouldn't be touching that," I said. "If it's poison."

Gabriel set it back down. "Maybe you're right."

I tried to imagine this woman tending an infant, handing a helpless baby over to Angel. She looked too frail to hold even a baby, far too frail to be in league with vital, vigorous Angel.

"She looks so fragile," I said.

Gabriel snorted. "Physically, yes." He got to his feet. "But she knew how to get her own way. And she had a mean streak that came out when she was thwarted." He looked away from me. "There was no reason to set the whole island against your father, for instance. We all thought he was losing his grip on reality; that was more than sufficient to cover what she'd done. She had no need to start the rumors that he'd sold you."

Edging further away from the body, I asked, "Who do you think killed her?"

Gabriel shrugged.

"Do you think they killed her because she knew something important?"

"It's certainly possible. And if that's the case, whatever she knew died with her, unless she left some hint of it in writing."

Stepping over the woman's body, he squeezed past two overstuffed chairs and made his way to a small desk against the wall. It was piled high with books and papers, all tumbled this way and that. Some had even fallen to the floor and been stepped on.

Gabriel riffled through the mess. "We won't find anything here," he said, turning back toward me. "Someone has already searched her things."

"How do you know?"

Gabriel nodded toward the kitchen. "Everything else is neatly kept. I suspect that's more Evan's doing than hers, but in any case I've never seen anything out of place here until today."

A clock had been ticking quietly; now it seemed suddenly too loud in the small house.

"Where is Evan?" I said. "What if he's dead, too?"

"Evan doesn't have anything to do with the experiment. He's an ordinary hardworking man, and so far as I know he's never in his life agreed with his mother about anything of significance. He takes care of her, but he's not in cahoots with her, of that I'm certain."

"But still," I said, looking toward a dark hallway that led, no doubt, to the bedrooms. The only thing worse than standing beside a dead body was thinking there might be another somewhere nearby.

Gabriel nodded. "All right," he said. "I'll check."

As he started for the hallway, however, the outside door creaked. In two strides Gabriel was at the kitchen door, blocking the room from view with his body.

"Evan," he said. "I'm sorry to surprise you like this."

I couldn't see the man who answered. "Good morning, Gabriel," he said. "You're late for the Dream Recorder meeting."

For a heartbeat Gabriel was silent. Then, "What do you mean?" he said.

"Not much. Just that the Doria Dream Recorder was here earlier. I was in the woods and caught sight of her leaving."

As he spoke he shifted into view. He was a muscular man in his mid-thirties, and he stood very straight. His hair and beard were short and neatly trimmed and his clothes were carefully pressed, and he was wearing only socks on his feet; he must have taken muddy boots off when he came inside.

When he saw me, he raised his eyebrows. "Fiona Alleyn?" he said. "You've had half the island out looking for you, or so I hear."

"I'm not Fiona. I'm her sister, the one who was sold and sent away."

Interest kindled in Evan Marchrest's face and he began to move toward me, but Gabriel raised an arm and blocked his way.

"Wait," he said. "I don't know if you're aware, but—"

Evan Marchrest didn't make him say it. "I'm aware that my mother is dead, yes. I came in and found her like that. I've been out digging her grave."

He sounded perfectly calm and untroubled.

"Is the Doria Dream Recorder responsible?" Gabriel asked.

"I would assume so. I also assume it wouldn't be prudent to look into the matter too closely."

He was an odd sort of woodcutter; he sounded more like an instructor.

Before Gabriel could reply, the man went on. "Not that I don't appreciate your company, Gabriel, but I have work to do. If you weren't planning to meet the Doria Dream Recorder, why are you here?"

"I wanted to talk to your mother about Eric Alleyn," Gabriel said. "About the many variations on the story of his daughters' birth."

"That seems to be a popular topic these days," the other man said. "Last week we had a visitor from Locria who wouldn't leave us be until Mother spoke with him about it. Your daughter was with him on one of his visits here, in fact."

"He wasn't from Locria," Gabriel said, and he turned and gestured toward me. "He came with her. Perhaps we should go out front to talk."

Evan didn't seem to notice the suggestion. He looked at me, never so much as glancing at his mother's body on the floor. "You've been to the other island?" he said. "You and the young man have seen it?"

I blinked. Maybe whatever the midwife knew hadn't died with her after all.

"I grew up there," I said. "So did Farrell Dean. How did you know about it? Did your mother tell you?"

"Not exactly, no." He hesitated, smoothing his short beard with his fingers. "But I think I must have come from there."

"Why is that?"

He gestured vaguely at the body, still not looking at it.

"She isn't my biological mother," he said. "I had wondered, given her age. I found out for certain last spring when my ax slipped and I needed a blood transfusion. Hers didn't match, and I asked whether she knew what my father's blood type had been."

He grimaced. "She laughed at me. She said she knew nothing about my father, nor about my mother either."

It had never occurred to me that twins might be born in Optica, and one sent over here.

"Did she explain what she meant?"

"Not intentionally. But she's been growing forgetful of late. She doesn't always remember to keep her secrets entirely secret."

He paused, but only to collect his thoughts. Apparently now that she was dead, he was willing to talk. "As best as I can figure," he said, "people used to buy and sell children between the two islands. They don't anymore—at least, Mother isn't involved if they do. It seems to have been a trade like any other. Those with a surplus of children sold them, and those with a deficit bought them. But as I said, Mother never spoke openly of it. Buying and selling humans was considered shameful, I expect."

"I expect," Gabriel echoed, his voice as sardonic as Evan's.

Evan turned his head and looked at him speculatively. "You had a brother who was said to have died," he said. "It's possible he was one of the surplus children."

Gabriel nodded. "He was. Valentina knew him, over on the other island."

"Is that so?" Evan studied me. There was a question in his eyes, and I wished I could give a different answer.

"I'm sorry," I said. "I've never met anyone who looked like you."

"Do you know everyone there?"

"At least by sight," I said, edging a little further from the body on the floor and hoping he'd take the hint that it was time for us to move outside. "It's a much smaller place than Aislin. Have you ever taken Dream Drops?"

He didn't seem startled by the change in subject. Then again, not much seemed to disconcert Evan Marchrest. "I haven't taken Dream Drops lately," he said. "I've never been into chemical substances. But I was given them regularly as a child, until I got too big for Mother to force me."

"Why didn't you like them?"

Evan Marchrest looked at me narrowly for a moment, crossing his arms over his chest. "They gave me bad dreams," he said. "Was there more to the baby trade than simple economics?"

I nodded. "Some sort of experiment," I said. "And it's still going on over there. My friends are in danger. Do you know anything else that might help us?"

Evan seemed to be considering whether to press me for more. He didn't, though. "You might want to watch out for the intermediary," he said. "Apparently he's a fairly ruthless sort. Handsome, but ruthless. Mother wasn't easily cowed, but even she took care not to displease him."

Something about that sounded odd. It took a second for me to put my finger on it.

"Was he more than an intermediary?" I asked. "Was he somehow in charge?"

Evan's eyebrows went up. "You know, I think I've always assumed so. I don't know why. Except that I can't imagine Mother caring what anyone thought, unless he had some sort of power over her."

Then something flickered in his eyes. "I wonder—" he said, and broke off.

"What is it?" Gabriel said.

Evan turned to him. "Once, when I was ten or so, I heard Mother talking to the Dream Recorder. They were assuring each other that they were very good at their jobs, but it was apparent that someone thought they weren't, and that was why they were discussing it. Then Mother said something about a watchmaker sent to teach them a lesson. I thought she was changing the subject, because in fact our clock at the time always ran slow. But our clock was never repaired and of course watchmakers don't give lessons. Perhaps they were using code words so I wouldn't understand."

Gabriel was nodding slowly.

"Perhaps they were referring to the intermediary," Evan said. "They were afraid, both of them. That's why the incident stuck in my mind, no doubt. I rarely ever saw Mother afraid."

Gabriel said something in response, but I wasn't listening. It wasn't Angel. Sir Tom hadn't been speaking of Angel when he said the watchmaker had walked away and left the experiment ticking itself out, because Angel was still around.

And besides, Angel was far too young; he'd have been only a small child fifty years ago, when the experiment started. The watchmaker had to be old enough to have built the watch in the first place.

Then another thought struck me—this was the first time I'd heard someone besides Sir Tom speak of a watchmaker. I'd assumed that was the old Guardian's poetic term for the man who began the experiment; but apparently other people called him that, as well.

And anyway Evan's anecdote was confusing on another level, too. If the watchmaker was the one who'd set up the whole experiment, surely he wasn't an enforcer, like a warden. Surely he'd be above that sort of thing.

Evan Marchrest was watching me think. "I don't know what it means," he said. "As I said, I was very young."

Then he pushed away from the wall. "If I think of anything more I'll let you know, but now I must get busy. Once the odor of death begins, there's no getting it out of your nose."

Chapter 20

Eric Alleyn sat in one of the rocking chairs by the fire, listening silently to Gabriel's long recitation of everything that had happened since I'd climbed out of my sickbed in order to go break into the Dream Recorder's house.

Papa had heard some of it from Angus, but Gabriel went through it all again anyway, just to be sure my brother hadn't left something out or told it wrong. To give him his due, Gabriel laid everything out matter-of-factly, without shading anything with his own opinions. Maybe he thought criticizing Eric Alleyn's daughter wouldn't be diplomatic, given the newness of their truce.

And Eric Alleyn didn't chastise me, either; he didn't even glare at me. In fact once, when Gabriel described how I'd squeezed into the dog door of Edgeling's barn, while the Devil's Night dancers cavorted by the nearby fire, I distinctly saw the corner of his mouth twitch.

"I'd have been scared witless," Fiona said, setting down the dish she'd been drying and then turning to face me. "That was very brave of you."

"And very stupid," Tor put in. "Mick shouldn't have asked you to do it."

Fiona ignored him. "You lead an exciting life," she said to me. "Mine seems quite boring by comparison. I wouldn't have wanted to trade places with you, of course, but I have to say that now and then I'm a little envious of your adventures."

"That's only because they've turned out all right," Tor said. "You wouldn't feel at all envious if she'd been killed during one of her exciting adventures."

Fiona responded with a quelling look.

"Seriously," Tor said. "Adventures are only exciting afterwards. They're terrifying while they're happening. Am I right, Valentina?"

"Yes," I admitted. "But being scared is better than sitting around feeling trapped and helpless."

"See," Fiona said.

Tor shook his head at her. "You don't feel trapped and helpless."

"May I continue?" Gabriel said, and waited until Fiona and Tor, both looking a bit embarrassed, nodded.

So Gabriel continued.

And all the while, Papa said nothing. When Gabriel handed him the handkerchief that had been wrapped around the camera, he took it and spread it out over his leg. Then he gazed into the fire, rocking gently in the rocking chair, his expression growing increasingly remote the longer Gabriel talked.

Fiona left the sink and went to stand beside him.

"It's hers," she said, and Eric Alleyn nodded. He smoothed the beautiful handkerchief, stroked the embroidered edges.

"Yes," he said. "It's hers." Looking up at the rest of us, he explained. "Mother had a different design for each of us. We used to say we ought to frame them and hang them on the walls, not blow our noses on them."

He wasn't going to say a single word about the midwife's death, I realized. And I couldn't read his expression. Was he glad Rowena Marchrest had been killed? Did he wish he'd had time to confront her himself, after all the suffering she'd inflicted on him? My father was remarkably indecipherable at that moment.

He opened his other hand and studied the camera. "I wonder where this was hidden," he said, looking around the room.

Gabriel turned away from the fireplace. "Don't get ahead of yourself. The fact that the camera was wrapped in Michael's handkerchief might be nothing but a coincidence. People lose handkerchiefs, loan them out."

"Not us. Not those. We weren't careless with my mother's gifts."

He looked at Tor as if for confirmation, but Fiona was the one who spoke up.

"Papa's right," she said. She had returned to the sink and was sliding another dish into the soapy water. "Grandpa wouldn't have lost that. Even Angus never lost one of Granny's handkerchiefs. They were special."

"All the same, that camera might have nothing to do with Michael."

"Don't be a fool," Eric Alleyn said. "That camera has everything to do with my father."

"How can you be so sure?"

Eric Alleyn looked impatient. "Because it explains why he left us."

He stood up and dropped the camera and handkerchief on the table. Then he paced to the middle of the big room, where he turned in a slow circle, glaring at his four walls.

"They were watching," he said. "They were watching my father, and we all thought he was losing his mind. And then he left us for good, and he built that new house from the ground up. Built it, and never left it. If we wanted his grand-children to see him, we took them there."

"He felt safe there," Tor said, nodding. "If he'd left that house, someone could come in while he was gone and plant another camera."

"Like Tristan did at Nana and Grandfather's." Fiona turned away from the sink, a bright angry blush rising on her cheeks. "In the pot with her jade plant. Except Tristan was only a Listener, not a Watcher."

Eric Alleyn stood leaning on his cane.

"My father had proof," he said. "He could have shown us that camera. He could have demonstrated objectively that he wasn't paranoid, that someone was in fact watching him. But he didn't. He let me think he was losing his mind, and he ran away and left me living in this house."

For a long moment he stood there in silence. Then Eric Alleyn looked at me. "Why didn't he tell me?" he said, sounding very young.

I didn't know what to say, but when Fiona went and stood beside him, putting an arm around his waist, I got up and did the same thing.

Gabriel shook his head and sat down beside the fire, turning his chair so that his face was away from us. Tor, however, got up and began pacing around the room, studying the walls with his sleepy blue gaze.

"I can see why Michael would leave this place," he said. "Once he'd found one camera, he'd always be looking. He could never be sure he'd found them all."

Eric Alleyn made an angry noise deep in his throat. "Is that what you're doing? Looking for another one?"

Tor shrugged.

"You can stop right now. I will not be afraid in my own house. I will say what I please, just as I have always done. And if anyone is listening, may my words burn through their eardrums and eat like maggots into their depraved brains."

I blinked. "But, Papa—"

"Don't *but Papa* me!" he roared, slamming the tip of his cane against the floor. "I saw what it did to my father, there at the last. He barely spoke to me. If he had to speak—if he had to say so much as 'pass the salt'—he whispered. And he took every opportunity to be gone, sometimes without a word, vanishing for days. Or else he'd head out to the sea and swim, straight out toward the horizon, so long and so far we'd think he was never coming back." His voice dropped. "Whatever love he had for us was nothing compared to his desire to get away."

His eyes were dry but tears were streaming down my cheeks. Fiona stood silently by. My father looked at me, and his face softened and he put a hand on my shoulder.

"They will not do that to me," he said, looking me straight in the eye. "I will be who I am, regardless of who is watching."

If anyone could do that, it would be Eric Alleyn. Still, being yourself when eyes were on you was harder than he seemed to think.

The thought made me remember something Sir Tom had said.

"Some doors, once opened, can never be shut again," I quoted. "Maybe that's why Michael Alleyn didn't tell you, Papa. So it wouldn't change you like it changed him."

Over by the fire Gabriel turned and looked at me with surprised approval. "That's very perceptive," he said. "Sometimes it's better not to know."

Eric Alleyn harrumphed skeptically.

"What I didn't know couldn't hurt me? Is that it? And yet you see what happened." His hand tightened protectively on my shoulder.

Fiona nodded. "Grandpa must have thought they only watched. He couldn't know they'd come. He didn't know they'd steal his grandchild."

A shudder ran through me. It wasn't like that, was it? I was randomly stolen because I was a twin, and the experiment needed twins.

But the experiment was over by the time I was born, and Angel knew it. He knew the experimenters over on the mainland were dead, yet he still came to get me. Why? To please the Watchers, who didn't know the experiment was over?

Not likely. They had called me a bad practical joke.

Maybe he'd intended to deceive them, to make them think the experiment was still on.

You belong to me, he'd said. Rain wanted to know what he wanted. An interesting question, and maybe the more practical one. But I wanted to know something more basic. Who was he? Who was Angel?

Now I was shivering in earnest.

My father looked down at me, his face concerned. "Fiona," he said. "Put the kettle on."

"I'm fine," I said, but my voice came out faint and thin.

My sister put the kettle on, and Eric Alleyn guided me over to sit by the fire. Gabriel put another log on, and Tor stopped examining the walls and came and sat down with the rest of us, and silently, while Fiona bustled around the kitchen, we watched the flames and studied the handkerchief and the camera lying on the table. I stared at the handkerchief so long that my imagination began to play tricks on me, the beautiful scrolling embroidery becoming familiar, as it would have been if I had been raised in this house.

It was Fiona who broke the thoughtful silence.

"Could there be cameras in other houses?" she said, handing around mugs of chamomile tea. "Maybe other people were being watched as well."

Tor shook his head. "Not everyone is as secretive as Michael Alleyn. If anyone else had found something as peculiar as a camera, someone on the Council would know."

Over by the fire, Gabriel nodded in agreement. "Someone would have heard," he said. "And I find it unlikely that cameras have been hidden all these years—probably from the very beginning—and never found."

"Michael lived here from the very beginning?" I said. "Since the plague, I mean?"

Everyone nodded.

I looked at Tor. "But you said everyone started over in Ionia."

He raised a curious eyebrow. "Most everyone," he said. "The Alleyns were the exception that proves the rule."

I couldn't see how exceptions actually did prove rules, necessarily, and Tor was irritating me again, but before I could say anything my father spoke.

"We were the only ones on this side of the island until the Van Staverns came," he said. "We needed room for the cattle. And of course my father was never what you'd call sociable."

Gabriel's eyes met mine. It was yet another way Michael Alleyn was different from everyone else on Aislin—the camera, his own Dream Recorder book, his paranoia, and now this.

"Michael got along fine with my grandfather," Tor said.

Eric Alleyn nodded. "Your grandfather was just about the only person my father could bear to be around for any length of time. Family included."

Tor frowned. "I've never thought it right—" he began, but my father cut him short.

"It was what he wanted."

"But—"

"It was their agreement, not ours."

"But Grandpa Jack never liked it—"

"But he agreed. They both agreed. We've no business going against them just because they're dead."

They were driving me crazy. "What are you talking about?" I said.

Tor turned to me. "Everyone on the island thinks my grandfather invented all sorts of wonderful things, but he didn't."

"He had the ideas," Eric Alleyn said with finality.

Tor looked at him warily, but went on nevertheless. "Grandpa Jack dreamed. That's all he did. Michael was the one who got the dreams out of Grandpa's head and into his hands. But Michael didn't like for us to talk about that. He was a very humble man, your grandfather."

Eric Alleyn snorted. "Very afraid, more likely," he said, nudging the camera. "He didn't want to call attention to himself. He knew he was being watched."

He knew he was being watched, and apparently Tor's grandpa was his closest friend.

"Tor," I said, wrapping my cold hands around my mug. "Did your Grandpa Jack ever talk about Michael Alleyn? Did he say anything about why Michael was the way he was?"

Tor shrugged. "Nothing but the offhand remark now and then. He didn't pass on any deep dark secrets, if that's what you're hoping." Then a strange expression crossed his face.

"What is it?"

"Nothing important," Tor said. "But it was strange." He looked at Fiona. "You remember when Grandpa Jack was sick that last time, when he was dying? He seemed to be completely in his right mind, except for the fact that he wasn't always sure who I was."

"I remember," Fiona said.

"Well, one night, very late, I was sitting up with him and he started talking about Michael Alleyn. Some of the things he intentionally was telling me—me, Tor—but other things I think he was saying to your grandfather."

The light was fading; heavier clouds must have been rolling in outside. Fiona got up without a word and began to light the gas sconces.

"He spoke of you, Fiona," Tor said. "About how long our families had known each other, and so forth. About our intentions for the future. And then he asked me if you ever had bad dreams."

Fiona glanced back at him, one arm raised to light a gas lamp. A sick feeling began in the pit of my stomach.

"No more than most people, I told him." In the firelight Tor's face was shadowed, stark. "Then my grandpa began to tell me about the dreams your grandpa had. Dreams in which he was following someone, watching someone, betraying someone. The inverse of his waking life, if you will."

Tor paused, and when he went on his cadences were not his own. We were hearing Grandpa Jack's voice, or perhaps even Michael's. We were hearing the story the way Tor had heard it himself, and for the first time I caught a glimpse of Tor's artistry, saw how he could be someone who made stained glass windows.

"Often Michael dreamed he was looking into a mirror," Tor said. "He could see his own face in the glass but he also saw, in the darkness on the other side, someone else looking back at him. He couldn't make out individual features, but he knew the man was there. And he'd study that mirror, Michael would, looking for a way through it, a way around it, a way into it. He wanted to reach the man in the mirror; he wanted to make him stop. At the very least he wanted to meet the man's eyes, face to face, so that the man would know that he'd been seen. But the glass was flawless, smooth and impenetrable, and all Michael ever could do was catch glimpses, shadows, hints of what lay beneath. And Michael knew that no matter how well he hid, no matter how far he ran, he would never escape the man in the mirror, the man he was always watching, and who was always watching him. He could never be truly alone."

Tor's voice shifted, became his own once again. "Then Grandpa Jack spoke to me as if I were Michael Alleyn."

"What did he say?" I whispered.

Tor looked at me. "You helped make my dreams a reality, and I wanted to do the same for you. But your dreams weren't anything you'd want to meet face to face in the daylight. Your dreams were better left to the darkness, to the night.'"

I could have sworn the room grew suddenly darker.

Tor added, almost under his breath, "Jack's dreams were so much kinder to him."

Chapter 21

O ut of five brothers, there was bound to be one I didn't much like.

"Revenge won't taste as sweet if one of us gets killed," Sean said.

"It's not revenge," I said.

"Not for you, perhaps. But for Papa? It's vengeance, plain and simple."

He'd raised his voice over the clinking of serving spoons, but my father pretended not to hear. Instead he nudged Rory. "Pass the salt," he said.

Sean watched Eric Alleyn sprinkle salt on his potatoes, and I watched Sean, trying not to glare balefully at him. He was my brother, after all.

Like Mick he fell in somewhere in the middle, as far as family resemblances went—he didn't look as much like Papa as Rufus and Angus did, and he didn't look as much like Mama as Rory and Fiona and I did. Sean's eyes were blue and his hair was a sort of light sandy brown, and he was bigger than Rory but not nearly as big as Rufus.

"If something went wrong, it would only give you something else to be bitter about," Sean said, though Papa was ignoring him. "You'd come back without Mick, or Rory, or heaven forbid Valentina, and have only yourself to blame."

"Now that's a load of rubbish," Mick said pleasantly, turning toward Sean. His shoulder jostled mine, and I sloshed the apple juice I was holding onto my plate.

"Sorry, love," Mick said, trading our just-filled plates. "I've always been a clumsy oaf."

A silver-tongued charmer was more like it.

He caught my skeptical look and grinned. "Play nice," he said. He studied the plate he'd claimed, and added one more piece of fried chicken.

Sean adjusted his wire-rimmed eyeglasses and moved his cup a little further from the edge of the table. "It's not rubbish," he said. "No one does guilt as well as our father. Self-flagellation is his middle name."

"Sure. But you said he'd have *only himself* to blame." Mick set down his fork and leaned back, draping one arm around the back of my chair. "Last I checked, I was a grown man. Papa has no control over what I do or don't do."

"As well I know," Eric Alleyn muttered.

Mick grinned. "There, you see? Even he admits he'd have to share the blame with me. Though for myself, I'd be blaming no one but the person who killed me." He reached for the gravy, pouring another small lake onto his plate. "This is the best dinner I've had in months, Fiona. Thank you."

"Show your gratitude by moving that plate," Fiona said, edging a platter of biscuits onto the crowded table. All my brothers were present except for Rufus—he and Farrell Dean were still up in Locria, working on the engine—and all of them were eating as if they'd never get another meal. Gabriel was there, too, but was keeping studiously silent.

"Don't be naïve, Mick," Sean said. "You know quite well that the person pulling the trigger is only the last link in a causal chain."

Mick shrugged. "I take responsibility for what I do, so why shouldn't he? Angus, send the butter this way."

Sean plowed ahead with his lecture. "I'm simply saying that revenge doesn't right injustices. Revenge doesn't alleviate pain—it compounds the evils it seeks to address. It's a weapon that wounds the one who wields it."

Angus sighed heavily. "This is supposed to be a celebration," he said. "Valentina's home, and she's not currently abducted, and she's not even sick. Can't you at least say hey, Valentina, we're glad you're home?"

"Of course we're glad she's home." Sean turned to me and smiled, but it was only for show, and I didn't smile back. "And if we're truly glad she has returned, we'll keep her safe. We'll put this unfortunate incident behind us and move on."

I almost dropped my glass of juice. *This unfortunate incident?* That was a bizarre way to refer to my entire life.

"What about my friends?" I said. "They can't move on. *I* can't move on when they're about to be killed."

"Friends are not the same as family," Sean began, but I cut him off.

"I wasn't raised with a family. Friends were all I had." I had a lot to learn about families, I supposed, but surely they weren't meant to be an excuse to blow off the rest of the world.

Sean smiled again, and this time it was a pitying smile. "There's nothing wrong with having friends," he said. "I'm glad you did. But consider how many wrongs are done in the world every single day. If we were to try to right every one of them, where would it end? We can't always fight other people's battles."

"Other people's battles," I echoed, and now I was so angry my voice was faint. "I was kidnapped, Sean. I was taken over there where people are being killed, where I was going to be killed. That's not exactly someone else's battle."

Sean smiled benignly at me. "It is now that you're safely out if it," he said. "Look here, Valentina. It's commendable that you're willing to risk yourself to help those people. But let's look at the matter logically. Set your emotions aside and ask yourself whether you can actually help anyone by going back, or whether you'd merely endanger still more of your loved ones."

My face flamed. If this was how he taught school, the kids probably hated him. Rafe never spoke to us like that. He never patronized. And Sean had a child of his own—was he raising that boy to be a pretentious prig?

Under the table Mick bumped my leg with his. "I don't know if you've heard, Sean," he said. "But Valentina prefers to go by Red."

Sean nodded. "I've heard," he said. "And I'd like to discuss that with you, Valentina." He leaned forward, careful to keep his elbows off the table. It gave him the look of a pecking hen.

"Calling yourself by the name the oppressors gave you sends a message," he said. "It sends a message to yourself and to others. That message says, 'I once was enslaved against my will, and now I am choosing to remain inside the framework established by my oppressors.' A healthier response would be to reclaim the name your family bestowed on you, the name that was given to you in love rather than in domination."

Perplexed silence met this statement.

Then Angus spoke up. "Papa," he said. "Who named her? You or Mama?"

Eric Alleyn looked at Angus warily, unsure where his son was going.

"I named her," he said. "She was a tiny frail thing, so I thought she needed a strong name. That's what valiant means. Strong. Brave. Determined."

"Oh, Papa, that's so beautiful," Fiona said, stopping beside the table and clasping her hands over her heart. Mick looked at me and winked.

"Valent-ina," Rory said. "The little valiant one. I never thought of it that way before. I like it."

"Right," Angus said. "Great. Good job, Papa. But moving right along, is there any rule that says parents can only name children when they're first born?"

He held up a hand in Sean's direction. "I'm not asking you," he said. "I'm asking our father. Your opinion is not solicited."

Now Eric Alleyn seemed to be trying not to smile. "I know of no such rule," he said. "Gabriel?"

Gabriel shook his head. "Parents can name children whenever they wish, as far as I know." He shifted in his chair and gave Angus a look that was almost approving. "Generally it's done at birth as a matter of convenience, that's all. The Council certainly has no rules regarding the parameters of name-giving."

"Well, then," Angus said, beaming. "Papa, I hereby suggest that you give your youngest child an extra name. Some people have more than one. Why can't she?"

Eric Alleyn looked at me. "Would you like a second given name?" he said.

I nodded. "Yes, please," I said. "I do like the name you gave me, but it doesn't feel like mine, except when you say it. When other people say it, I feel like they think I'm someone I'm not."

"That's only because it's new, Valentina," Sean said. "In time you'll grow accustomed to it. You'll see."

"And it makes me feel like they're trying to boss me around," I added.

Rory and Angus laughed, and Mick stifled a grin. Even my father looked amused as he got to his feet and began clomping around the table toward me.

Sean made an exasperated sound. "I see no need for this farce," he said.

"That's because nobody's suddenly trying to make you answer to Rumplestiltskin instead of Sean," Rory said, in a good imitation of Sean's overly patient tone. "If they were, then you might see Red's point a bit more clearly."

Eric Alleyn stood behind me and put one hand on my head. "In the presence of these witnesses," he said, "and by the power of my paternity, I officially name this woman Valentina Red Alleyn. I decree that she may go by any variation thereof, or by any other name that she of her own will chooses."

The table broke into applause and approving yells. Angus and Rory lifted their water glasses and clinked them together.

Sean shook his head and crossed his arms over his chest. "All this silliness doesn't change things," he said. "And besides, if she needs permission to choose her own name, then she isn't truly free to choose one."

"We don't care," Fiona told him, pulling out a chair and sitting down. "Stop picking on Red."

"Yeah, you big bully," Angus said. "Leave off."

Sean tossed his napkin onto the table. "Go ahead," he said to the table at large. "Make me the bad guy. That's obviously the game of the day. But if you go against my advice and end up losing a child—if you have another grave to dig, another person to mourn—don't say I didn't tell you so."

"I wouldn't dream of it," Eric Alleyn said.

That was the last thing I clearly remembered, come morning.

Chapter 22

Someone was pounding on the door.

I scrambled out from beneath the heavy quilt, disoriented, not sure how I'd ended up in bed. Had someone carried me? I vaguely remembered sitting by the fire with my siblings after supper, limp-limbed with drowsiness, but I couldn't remember anything after that.

And now was it morning?

It was still so dark, I couldn't say. It could be anywhere from thirty minutes after I'd drifted off, to the last few minutes before dawn, and now someone was banging on the door and a female voice was shouting.

I made my way out of the dark bedroom, whacking my shin against the nightstand in the process, and entered the living room in time to see Fiona swing the front door open, letting in a gust of wind and rain. Her nightgown billowed around her legs and she shivered and stepped back, holding her flickering candle aloft, as Rain and Will Bright hurried inside.

"What is it?" Fiona said, her eyes wide.

"No need to be alarmed," Will said. "I had a dream, and Rain drove me over here so I could tell Red about it."

Fiona stared blankly at him; she looked as disoriented as I felt.

Rain waved a hand in Fiona's face. "Hello?" she said. "Anyone in there?"

"Stop it." Fiona moved out of range.

"They were all dressed in white," Will Bright said, coming to stand in front of me. "And they were sitting behind this table, and they put me—Louie, I mean—across the room from them, against the wall. And a guard was standing on either side of me, and those guards were angry and pointing guns at my head. And I was trying to think of the best way to cause more trouble."

He grinned at me.

I blinked. Why on earth was Will Bright excited that his brother was in trouble? I looked at Fiona, hoping she had some idea, but she looked as baffled as I felt.

"I don't understand," I said finally.

Will spread his hands. "He's not a traitor."

"Louie—a traitor?" I couldn't keep the incredulity out of my voice. "Of course he's not. How could you think that?"

"I didn't know him," Will said. "All I knew was that I was having these dreams where Louie was talking to a Watcher, all friendly-like, and the Watcher was suggesting he stage an escape for the old'uns."

That was more than I could absorb. That escape had gotten people killed. *Mariella* had been killed. Louie would never intentionally have injured his friends—I was sure of that. But if the Watcher had been using him, playing him ...

"You see?" Will said, nodding. "I kept hoping I was wrong, and as it turns out I was, because last night I saw Louie in a room with Watchers and guards, and those guards were pointing guns at him, and there was nothing friendly about it. They were talking about killing me."

"So Louie didn't escape with the others."

"Apparently not." Will frowned. "I didn't see much of what happened in that incident—at least, not much I could

AMANDA WITT

make sense of. It was all kinds of chaos. Mostly I watched Margo bleed to death. Mariella, I mean. We were trying to help her but we knew all along there was no hope."

I swallowed hard.

Fiona threw me a compassionate look and then turned away—giving me privacy, I thought. She began moving around the room, lighting gas lamps with the flame of her candle, and after she gave Rain a pointed look our cousin followed her, pausing to pretend to examine a photograph here, a book there.

"So what else happened last night?" I said.

"A lot of talk, mostly," Will said. "The Watchers asked me all sorts of questions, one right after another. Asked Louie, I mean. I got the feeling they were testing our memory. They asked about our parents, our childhood. And I didn't remember over much, but I did remember some. Told them about a dog I'd had, how he'd slept on the foot of my bed, how he scared a burglar away one night when he was just a pup."

Will stopped, scratching his head. "I'm eighty-five years old," he said. "And I've only now remembered the dog Louie and I got for our fifth birthday. Where's that dog been all these years? What did they do to me, that I couldn't remember that dog, much less my own brother?"

I sure didn't have an answer for that.

"But Louie remembered it?" I said.

Will nodded. "He remembered a fair bit," he said. "He didn't want to talk to the Watchers, but the more I talked the more uneasy the Watchers seemed to be getting, so I started to enjoy it."

That made me smile. It sounded like old Louie.

"I told them everything I could dredge up. And the farther back, the better. I told them about that dog, and about the old windmill clattering in the wind, and about the storm

212

cellar with the jam jars all in rows. All the earliest things. And all the things I told them—all the things Louie told them—I remembered, too. When he remembered, I remembered. I remembered our folks, our house. I remembered school. I remembered a whole lot of things from when I was a boy."

He stopped abruptly, running a hand over his face. "Then one of those Watchers spoke up—the one Louie had been conspiring with before. She said that it was interesting, how much Louie had remembered, and that if they could understand how memories resurfaced, that might help them keep troublesome memories down. She said maybe they ought to keep Louie around for awhile."

Suddenly it all made better sense.

"Did she have shoulder-length gray hair, really thick?"

Will nodded. "That she did," he said. "She was the youngest Watcher, by a fair bit, and the most reasonable sounding."

"That's Marta. She's okay. She helped me remember what Rafe had been trying to tell me when he died. And when Meritt and I spied on the Watchers, she was the one trying to stop the city meetings."

Will grimaced. "They didn't seem inclined to heed her advice," he said. "Some old twig said they'd always had trouble with keeping memories buried in people older than forty, and then a man in love with his own voice said unless Louie could remember a way to make a couple of loaves feed a crowd, I'd run through my usefulness and might as well be pruned. And then I woke up."

He looked around the room at each of us. "I've never in my life been so unhappy to see morning. Felt like I was running off and leaving my brother all alone."

"You couldn't have helped Louie, even if you'd stayed asleep longer," Fiona said, and her voice was very gentle.

Will's face tightened. "I know it," he said. "Thing is, I keep trying to think of some way to get a message to him." He gave a humorless laugh. "It's crazy to imagine I could. But then, this whole thing is crazy."

"And Meritt wasn't with the Watchers?" I said.

Rain gave an exasperated sigh. "You have a one-track mind, do you know that?"

I ignored her, and Will did too.

"There was a young man in the room, sitting with the Watchers, a tall good-looking kid with dark hair. He was wearing gray, not white like the others, and he never said anything. Didn't look real happy when they talked about killing Louie, though."

"That's him," I said. "That's Meritt."

Relief must have been apparent in my voice, because Will held out a hand warningly.

"I saw him," he said. "But that's all. Worst case scenario, he still doesn't know he's been betrayed by that friend of yours, and the Watchers are biding their time."

Still, Meritt was alive. My heart felt lighter than it had for days. "I'll get Gabriel," I said. "He'll want to hear this too."

As I started down the dark hallway, I could hear the others talking.

"Sorry to wake you," Will said. "Rain thought sure you'd be up by now."

"Why, it's after eight o'clock." Fiona sounded surprised. "I never sleep this late."

The doors to all the bedrooms except Fiona's were closed. Papa had probably taken his sleeping pills, but I was surprised Gabriel hadn't heard us talking and come out.

I knocked at his door, but quietly, so as not to disturb Eric Alleyn. After a moment, when Gabriel didn't answer, I knocked again, more loudly. Fiona came up behind me, still carrying the candle. It made flickering shadows along the narrow hall. Her eyes met mine, and something in her expression made me aware of the unnatural silence around us.

Fiona reached for Gabriel's door and turned the knob. The door swung open on an empty room. The bed was neatly made, as smooth as if it had never been slept in.

Quickly Fiona turned and went to Eric Alleyn's door.

"Papa?" she called, rapping hard. Without waiting for a reply she opened the door.

That room, too, was empty.

"They're gone," Fiona said, looking at me. "They're both gone."

Together we hurried back to the living room. Rain was standing at the window, pulling the curtains aside, and now I could tell that yes, it truly was daybreak on a gloomy, darkly overcast day.

"Gabriel isn't here," Fiona said. "Neither is Papa."

Will looked perplexed. Rain's face darkened, but she didn't speak.

"Were you still awake when the boys went home?" Fiona said to me, rubbing at her eyes with her free hand.

I shook my head. "You weren't either?"

"I don't remember much of anything after supper." For a long moment we stared at each other. Then Fiona turned and hurried across the living room, toward the kitchen. "If Papa left a message it will be in here," she said over her shoulder.

When I reached the threshold she was lifting a piece of paper from the kitchen table, automatically holding her candle over it though the gas lights gave plenty of reading light.

"What is it?" I said, watching my sister's face grow curiously blank. Behind me Rain and Will drew close.

Fiona handed me the paper.

My dear daughters, Fiona and Valentina,
Angus and Rory have made arrangements for the live-

stock, and Sean is willing for you to stay with him while I am away. You should have no trouble—the Council has put out a warning, so no one will dare claim the Dream Recorder's reward for you, and your Uncle Gabriel visited both the doctor and Edgeling and negotiated satisfactory understandings with each of them, though the best strategy is avoidance. Better safe than sorry, which is why I'll be easier in my mind knowing you're with Sean and Sonia. Use good sense, I beg of you both, and stay together. Do not go wandering around alone.

I hope to return soon with good news, Valentina—Red— about your friends. I am grateful to them for doing what they could to take care of you in my absence, and I am glad to be able to do something for them in return.

Please understand that I could not protect you before; I must do so now.

Your loving father

Droplets of rain spattered hard against the windows.

"They left me," I said, not quite believing it. The floor felt suddenly cold beneath my bare feet.

Fiona looked as stunned as I felt. "Papa drugged me."

Rain gave a harsh laugh. "Don't act so surprised. Uncle Eric has always had a ruthless streak."

Outside thunder rumbled, and the sharp loud rain changed to a sheeting deluge.

Will Bright cleared his throat uncomfortably. "I imagine it was perfectly safe," he said. "Eric took herbal sleeping remedies because of his leg, didn't he? Probably just gave the two of you a little dab of those."

Fiona rubbed again at her puffy eyes. "But how can they go?" she said. "Did they get the engine to work?"

"Must have," Rain said. "Dad sent Earl up to check on Rufus and Farrell Dean yesterday. I guess he came back with good news."

Farrell Dean.

Relief flooded me. "He won't let them leave without me," I said. "I can go after them, catch up to them. Farrell Dean won't leave me behind."

"Don't be so sure of that."

We turned; it was Sean, fully dressed and apparently wide awake. "You heard them last night, Valentina. They were determined to go regardless of what anyone said. And they were just as determined that you weren't going. If your friend disagreed, they will have left him behind as well."

Something hollow opened up in my chest.

"He's gone," Rain said. "You'd do the same in his shoes, Red. He was outnumbered six-to-one."

"Eight to one," Sean corrected.

Rain's eyebrows came together. "My father, Eric Alleyn, four Alleyn brothers. That's six."

"Plus Tor—"

"*Tor?*" Fiona looked scandalized.

Sean nodded. "I know," he said. "I thought Tor had better sense. But it seems he considers himself practically a part of the family, so if the family throws themselves off a cliff, he's leaping off it as well."

Fiona frowned at him. "That's not fair," she said. "They're doing a good thing."

"And who's the eighth?" Rain wanted to know. She had an air of detached interest that rankled.

Sean nodded at me. "Your friend Ezzie," he said. "He oughtn't be traveling, not so soon after surgery, but they insisted that they needed someone to show them the way to a stockade. And apparently he was as eager to go as they were to have him."

I was speechless. They took Ezzie—injured, weak, contaminated Ezzie—and they left me behind?

Rain nodded knowingly. "He rode up there with Earl

yesterday, to check on the engine progress. He said he was stir crazy, he's been cooped up so long. He said he wanted some fresh air." She smirked. "I guess that's not all he wanted."

So I was alone. Farrell Dean was gone, and Ezzie was gone, and it was just me left here on this island.

"What was the plan?" Rain said. "When were they to leave?"

"At midnight, to make best use of the departing tide." Sean looked at the clock. "They wanted to stress the engine as little as possible, given that it's untried over such a distance. I suppose they might have arrived at the other island by now."

I could picture them arriving, dragging the boat up on the sand, making their way through the woods to the stockade. What would my father do if the wild men came after him? He couldn't climb a tree, not with his leg. He could be killed and I'd never see him again, the father I had only just begun to know. He might die, or one of the boys—Mick's ankle couldn't be well already, and Angus had hair like a beacon.

Sean interrupted my thoughts. "I must be going, or I'll be late to school," he said.

I stared at him blankly. School?

Oh yes. He was an instructor. So my other brothers were crossing the sea and facing who knew what danger, and Sean was going to school.

He turned to Rain. "How did you get here?" he said.

"In my truck."

"You have a truck?"

"I do now. Tristan doesn't need it any longer, that's for sure."

Will gave a short bark of laughter. "You won't need it much longer yourself, the way you drive."

Rain ignored him. "Why do you ask?" she said to Sean.

"Can you run my sisters to my house? I'd prefer they not set off on foot, alone."

"Sure," Rain said, a glint in her eye. "I'll protect the little dears."

I wasn't sure if she was baiting me or Sean.

Sean didn't react. Instead he turned to Fiona. "Don't forget to bring your birthday present," he said. "Papa specifically wanted me to remind you not to leave it behind when you come to town."

"I won't," Fiona said, and smiled sweetly at Rain.

Before I could ask what that was all about, Sean looked at me. "Try not to worry," he said, surprising me. "It's an unnecessary, dangerous expedition, but they are competent men. You could even say Papa and Gabriel have been practicing for this battle for a long time. Only now they're on the same side, and they don't have to pull their punches."

Then he came forward and gave Fiona and me each a peck on the forehead. "Be good," he said. "And have a nice day. I'll let Sonia know to be expecting you."

He grabbed a waterproof coat from the hooks near the door and went out into the pouring rain. The door closed behind him with a solid final-sounding click.

I was stuck here on Aislin. I was stuck here, with Sean and his wife babysitting me. I might not find out for weeks, or even months, what was happening in Optica. All I could do was wait, and wonder how long it would take to receive news, and in the meantime anything could be happening to my father, my family, my old people, my friends; to Meritt and Farrell Dean.

And I hadn't even said goodbye.

Chapter 23

I wheeled away from the others, toward the living area. If it hadn't been pouring rain I'd have gone outside. I needed space to think, to try to figure out my next step. Because I wasn't going to sit here doing nothing, while my father and brothers and Farrell Dean risked their lives, while Meritt was over there in danger. I wasn't going to stay with Sean and do nothing. I couldn't stand that.

Frantically I paced around the living room, trying to come up with a plan. But nothing came to me—I couldn't think what to do. I was still groggy from Eric Alleyn's sleeping drugs, that was the problem. Groggy and frantic both, and that combination couldn't possibly be conducive to clear thinking. I had to calm down and I had to wake up— maybe I should go splash cold water on my face. I had to think. I had to find some way to help or I'd go crazy, just like poor Michael Alleyn—

My gaze fell on his handkerchief, lying neatly folded on the arm of the couch, where Eric Alleyn had left it. I saw it there and something important flickered in my mind, then was gone. I stood very still, hoping no one would speak to me, hoping the glimmer would return.

It did. It came, and when it did I couldn't believe what I was thinking.

Going to the couch I sank down on my knees in front of the handkerchief, opening it, smoothing it out against the cushions. It was true; I was sure of it. But what did it mean?

"Red?" Fiona's voice was concerned. "Are you all right?"

I didn't turn around. "Have you ever been up to Locria?"

"No."

"I need to go back up there," I said, getting to my feet, the handkerchief in my hands. "Rain, can you take me? Or let me borrow the truck?"

It wouldn't untangle the right problem, this thread I was pulling. It wouldn't get me to Optica. But it was something—it was an oddity—and chasing it down was better than sitting around doing nothing.

But Rain was shaking her head. "They're gone," she said. "You can't catch up to them by rushing off to Locria, if that's what you're thinking."

"No, it's not that." I didn't want to slow down and explain, but I was going to have to. "There's a man named Mal there. The man who gave us a boat, who was helping Rufus and Farrell Dean with the engine."

The others watched me, their faces perplexed.

"Oh," Fiona said, and turned one hand over helplessly.

"You've never seen him, Fiona, or you'd know."

I held Michael Alleyn's handkerchief out to her. "Mal has this design painted on his skin."

Silently they came and grouped around me, studying the handkerchief in my hands.

"He's not much older than we are—nineteen or twenty, maybe. So he'd have only been two or three when Michael Alleyn died. And he was still living with his parents then. He lived with them until he was five, and then he was or-phaned—" I left out the gory details—"And someone else raised him, and painted those designs on his skin to hide a birthmark. I think that someone was Michael Alleyn."

"After he was dead." Rain's voice was flat.

"No! That's the point. I don't think he died when everyone thought he did. And so I want to go ask Mal—"

"That can't be true," Fiona said.

"I'm not saying Michael Alleyn's still alive now—Mal said he isn't—but I think maybe he was alive back then."

"It can't be," Fiona said, looking unhappy.

I tried again. "Look, I know it sounds bad that Michael Alleyn lied to the family and faked his death. But he was afraid—he knew about the cameras. He needed to hide, and what better way to hide than to pretend you're dead?"

"No—I meant it really can't be true." Fiona was being uncharacteristically awkward. "Or at least, I always took it to mean that—I don't think he would lie to himself, would he?"

"Fiona," Rain said, flinging herself down on the couch, "what are you talking about?"

Fiona looked embarrassed. "Well," she said, not quite meeting my eyes, "There's a diary."

"Whose?"

"When Granny Rose came to live with us, she and Papa packed away Grandpa's things."

"And he had a diary?"

Fiona nodded. She still wasn't looking at me. "You know how Papa is about privacy," she said. "He'd never read someone else's diary."

"But you did."

She nodded. "I was looking through the chest after Granny Rose died, packing her things away with his. And I'd never known him, and I was so curious, and, well—I read it." She hesitated, giving me a quick sideways glance. "Grandpa Michael didn't go away to hide. I really don't think he did. I think he died."

"But somebody painted those designs on Mal."

"It wasn't Grandpa Michael."

"Here's a thought." Rain's voice was sardonic. "Stop talking and go get the diary."

I blinked. "It's still here?"

Fiona nodded and, without another word, turned and left the room.

"It'll be up in the attic," Rain said, examining her fingernails. "The Alleyns never throw anything away. Sit down, Will. Fiona and Red are both too addled to play hostess."

Will Bright sat down on the couch, a little gingerly, and on the far end from Rain. I stood in the middle of the room, too antsy to sit.

"Mal said the man who raised him was a good man," I said, just to be talking. "He took him in when nobody else would."

"Michael was a good man, sure enough," Will said. "One of the best."

I wheeled around. "You knew him?"

An odd expression crossed Will's face. "I must have done," he said. "But at the moment I can't quite recall. I heard tell of him, of course. The anti-social dairyman way over here on the far side of the island."

His gaze drifted off to the corner of the ceiling. My eyes met Rain's and she put a finger to her lips.

Silently, we listened to the patter of the raindrops against the windows, and to the sounds marking Fiona's progress. Hinges creaked loudly, followed by a solid thump. Then came footsteps overhead, and sounds like heavy boxes being shifted. There was a brief silence, then footsteps going the other way. Will was still staring up at the corner of the ceiling, waiting for whatever elusive thoughts might come.

And then Fiona was back, her white nightdress smeared with dust, cobwebs in her hair. In her hands she held a book with a brown leather cover. It was smaller than the dream record books.

"You found it," I said unnecessarily, going to her.

Fiona nodded. She started to hand the book to me, but stopped midway. "It isn't pleasant reading," she said. "He might not have been as crazy as we thought, but he wasn't exactly sane either."

And then the book was in my hands. It looked like someone had been careless with it. I'd seen problems in some of the Dream Recorder's books—pages stained with tea or other drinks, covers bent or broken—but this book was practically ruined. The cover was salt-stained and cracked down the middle as if the book had been folded right in half, and the first few pages were stuck together, the ink smeared and unreadable. Maybe at some point the book had been dropped in the sea.

"Come sit down so we can see too." Rain was being bossy, but it wasn't worth arguing about. Sinking down between her and Will on the couch, I tried to open the diary at the beginning, carefully prying the pages apart, but one tore, shredding the words on the page beneath it.

"I only read the parts that weren't stuck," Fiona said.

I let the book fall open where it liked. Rain and Will leaned in, and Fiona bent over Rain's shoulder.

I do not know whether to be glad or sorry that more people are moving to this side of the island. Will their presence drive the secret watchers away, or will the newcomers draw this unseen danger upon themselves as well? Yesterday I tried to warn three men who are building houses in Doria, but they seemed to attribute my words to misanthropy rather than to sincere concern for their welfare.

I glanced up and met Fiona's eyes. Poor Michael. He had been right, and everyone had thought he'd been paranoid.

Gently I turned back, as close to the beginning as I

could. The first few pages were stuck, and then came a few that were smeared and discolored beyond reading, but after that came a page that was perfectly clear, except for a discolored strip of damp in the top margin.

I do not trust her; she has a sly look about her, as if she knows something about me that I do not. I will not put myself in her hands, not my thoughts, my dreams, the half-waking musings that are mysteries even to me. It goes against my nature, and I would do so, I believe, even if I did not feel someone's eyes upon me.

For I do. I cannot talk myself out of it.

But who would be watching me? I would like to blame the Dream Recorder, for she is the one who picks at me, pursues me, tries to persuade me to "share" that which is mine alone. Why do we even need a Dream Recorder on our side of the island, with so few of us here? There are hundreds of people in Ionia; let her join her colleagues in pestering them, and leave me alone!

And yet I do not see how she can be to blame. I cannot fathom how anyone could see me all the times that I feel seen. Always, every moment of the day, every time I wake at night, I feel someone watching. The only time I ever feel free is when I am out in the distant woods or in the water, and sometimes even then the sense of being watched lingers, like the afterimage one sees after looking at too bright a light.

Rose says I make too much of it.

Then came more stuck pages, and then the page we had begun with. The next few pages after that section were unreadable, the inky words all run together into an uneven puddle. I could only pick out short phrases here and there—

Rosie enjoys the company, and *I grant that it is convenient*, and *distracts me from my thoughts*. Maybe this section recorded the time when the Van Staverns moved nearby.

Then came another portion that had been spared.

She has come back. For two weeks she left me in peace, and her addicts murmured in discontent, and scoured the island and couldn't find her, and I hoped—God forgive me—that she was dead. Every time she vanishes, I hope never to see her again.

Sometimes I think I am losing my mind and no one is watching me but myself.

I dream that I am looking in a window at myself, seeing myself do things that I have never done, that I hope I would never do. Sometimes I dream that I am watching other people, as the Dream Recorder does, but she watches through their words and I—I am like God. I can see all, their thoughts, their hopes, their deepest and most private secrets.

I am an abomination. I am a horror to myself.

Yet despite this, the man of my dreams—the man of my nightmares—is still me. And who can tear out his own heart?

Goosebumps rose on my arms. Fiona was right—this wasn't pleasant reading.

Why do I dream of another woman when I love Rosie with all my heart? She is strong and good, my Rose, and the woman in my dreams is not strong. I do not know whether she is good. She is sweet. She has pet names for everyone, and she clings to me fondly, and I love her but more than that I pity her, and most of all I desperately fear for her, for she is not strong and I know that I cannot protect her. And then I wake up and I am with Rose, and my heart is relieved because Rosie is strong and does not rely on me to protect her, and yet all the time I am with her, and relieved, I am also seeing in my mind a faint reflection of the dream woman, and she is breaking into pieces, shattering like glass falling deadly and glittering and my son walks across the floor, stepping on the shards, bleeding.

No wonder I dare not sleep.

I must do something to protect my son.

I had no idea what to make of that.

Rain was leaning hard against my shoulder, trying to see. I elbowed her, but she didn't budge. Will was leaning close, too, not touching me, giving off that faint musty old-man smell.

Rose is a good woman, far better than I deserve.

For I am dark and broken. I have done things that I would give my life to retract—I know this as surely as I know that the sun is shining now on Eric's bright hair as he plays in the garden outside my window. But I do not know what it is that I so regret, and so I cannot even attempt to make amends. This plague, this thief who takes my memory but leaves behind its shape, its shadows, is a cruelty I would not have expected of a universe that also gave me Rosie and my son.

My son.

Those words carry my greatest joy, and yet they strike chill into my bones. I see the boy playing here in front of me, and at the same time I feel myself turning away from him, knowing he is crying for me, knowing we will all be punished for whatever it is I have done.

I think that I am going mad.

I tried to turn the page, but I'd come to another ruined section where the pages were melded together in one solid blurry chunk. Then there were several jagged edges, where pages had been torn out. After that there were three more legible pages.

It is not a dream. It is a memory. It must be a memory, for why would I dream such an outlandish, egotistical, evil thing?

If it is true, I must make amends. But how? I am trapped in a nightmare of my own making. I walk as far as my legs will carry me, I swim until my body cramps with exhaustion, and then I drag myself back to shore, back to the prison that is both punishment and refuge, cruelty and mercy. And yet I must find a way to undo what I have done.

Rosie and Eric, Rachel, all my dear grandchildren, my flesh and blood—they are real, they are not a dream, they are my here and now. But this is cold comfort. They are a luxury I do not even remotely deserve, and by clinging to them I endanger them. For I have been made a lesson, a living testament to the futility and danger of swimming against the ruthless tide of progress and ambition.

How I wish I could explain to Eric. He would understand, I think. But I cannot explain, for that which would be a comfort to me would be trouble and danger to him.

And now the danger is redoubled, for Rachel is with child again, carrying this time not one but two babes—children to whom I owe profound apology, children whom I by my very presence continue to endanger.

If I am sane.

What a choice that is! And yet I know I would choose insanity in a heartbeat if it meant my children were safe, if it meant that the only demons were in my dark confused mind. What is real, what is nightmare? Much of the time I simply cannot know. Certainly most people think I am a lunatic. The only exceptions are Jack and my wife, and even they must make excuses for me. Jack comes up here to visit me and tries to persuade me to move back to Doria. They need me, he says; he says I am a genius, capable of creating entire worlds out of dreams and visions, and that genius is always called madness by the workaday world. Rose listens to my clouded stories and says I am a mystic, born into a fold of time, touching other ages, other places; it is not lunacy, she says, but an extra type of vision.

I say they are all wrong. I am not genius, mystic, or madman, but a seafarer swallowed whole and spit up on a beach, a cursed mariner with an albatross decaying around my neck.

And therein lies my hope. It is a feeble hope, but it is at least a chance, and because it is a chance I must take it. To say goodbye forever to those I love so dearly—to deliberately and ruthlessly sever the ties that bind us—this will be by far the hardest thing I have ever done.

But do it I must, if I would free my children of this curse. I will not pull my lovely ones down with me into the depths.

I will go alone.

My heart was pounding. Gently I tried once more to separate the ruined pages, but they were melded into one solid mass. After that last passage nothing else was written in the book; there were only two or three water-stained pages.

But I didn't need them. I had the handkerchief, and the pattern on Mal's skin, and the carefully chosen words of the final pages of the diary, begging the reader to assume suicide by drowning but never quite saying it directly, never quite telling the lie.

Rain was thinking along similar lines.

"He drowned himself," she said, making quotation marks in the air around the word *drowned*. "This diary is perfect—he knew it made him sound unstable, so he left it to persuade anyone who asked questions after the fact. The pages that are torn out might have said something that would have given away his plan, or given away how much he was remembering."

Fiona looked unhappy. "I truly thought he had killed himself," she said. "And I was glad that Papa respected privacy too much to read this diary and find out. But reading it again, knowing what we know now—maybe you're right. Maybe he really did fake his death."

She moved away from the couch as if distancing herself from the idea, and perched on the edge of a chair. I wasn't sure why she was so unhappy about this; Michael had raised Mal, after all, and that was a good thing. It was something worth living for, something much nobler than committing suicide.

Will leaned forward, his elbows on his bony knees, and spoke to Fiona. "Why's that book in such bad shape?"

"It was in his pocket when he drowned," she said. "He always carried it around with him, wrapped in a piece of oilcloth."

Ah. That was what was troubling her.

Will connected the dots, too. "And your Granny found his body?"

Fiona pushed her hair out of her face. "She found it and buried it."

"That means if Michael faked his death, Rosie knew it." Will's voice was gentle, but he spelled everything out. "She didn't find his body—she dunked this diary in the sea and presented it as evidence of a death that never happened."

"Unless—" Rain began, and Fiona turned hopefully toward her. "Unless there was another body."

Fiona's face fell.

Rain went on. "Unless there was a body that had been in the water awhile, that was dressed in Michael's clothes, with his journal in its pocket. A body anybody might have found.

But Rose was the one scouring the beach, looking for her missing husband, so she was the one who found it."

Fiona was shaking her head. "He wouldn't do such a thing," she said, but her tone was uncertain.

"You didn't know him," Rain said. "You never even met him. So how do you know what he'd do or not do? And anyway I'm not saying he killed the other person, necessarily— just that there could have been a handy body lying around."

Fiona gave another stubborn shake of her head, and Rain threw out her hands. "If he didn't substitute a body, then your Granny was in on it, and she kept up the deception for years and years. Those are your only choices, Fiona. Either Michael fooled everyone, including his wife, and that requires a body. Or else sainted Rosie Alleyn lied to Uncle Eric and everyone else."

Fiona didn't answer.

The rain outside had slowed to a steady thrumming, and in the glow of the gas lights the room felt secretive. I wondered if any secrets truly had been kept here, or if all my family's private moments had been seen. Despite myself I glanced around the walls, as if I might see another camera eye winking at us. Fiona watched me without comment, her face sad. Her past wasn't what it had seemed, her family not as honest with each other as she'd believed.

And if I was right, there was worse to come.

There was no tactful way to say it, so I simply blurted it out. "I think Michael Alleyn was the watchmaker."

Chapter 24

Fiona found her voice first. "The watchmaker? *Grandpa?*"
"That's what they call the person who set up the whole experiment," Rain said to Will, aside.

Fiona was shaking her head. "Not Grandpa," she said.

"It makes sense," I told her. "We have to go talk to Mal."

"No, it doesn't make sense at all," my sister objected. "Granny Rose would never have let him experiment on people. And besides, Sir Tom told you the watchmaker died over on the mainland. This isn't the mainland. This is an island."

"Sir Tom *thought* the watchmaker died on the mainland, but think about what Michael says." I waved the journal. "He felt horribly guilty, and he talks about creating worlds from dreams and visions, and he can't figure out how to make amends. And he says you and I were in danger because of him, Fiona. *Twins* were in danger because of him. That's because he was the one who started it—he was the one testing Dream Drops on identical twins."

"He was a dairy farmer!"

"He wasn't exactly your usual cattle hand. Didn't you listen to Tor? And besides, he had his own Dream Record book. The Dream Recorder really did watch him more than she watched anybody else. And there was the camera—"

"None of that makes him the watchmaker!"

Rain broke in. "Why would the watchmaker end up inside his own experiment?"

She'd put her finger on the only hole in my theory. Scientists didn't usually climb into their own petri dishes. Still, so many other things fit I was sure there had to be a logical answer to Rain's question.

I threw out a guess. "Maybe he wanted to see what it was like."

"No," Will said, finality in his tone. "It was because he tried to stop it."

We all froze, staring at the old man. "Maybe I shouldn't say *stop* it," Will said. "Because Michael started the experiment, sure enough. But then he tried to stop the experiment from *expanding*, and that's where he ran into trouble."

With that frustratingly tantalizing bit of news, he stopped. He didn't say anything else. Instead his gaze drifted away, up to the corner of the ceiling. I cast a warning glance at Rain and Fiona, but I saw they already knew to stay quiet. The only noise was the ticking of the clock.

Finally Will spoke again, still gazing off into the middle distance. "I remember when it happened," he said. "I remember I was sitting at a little table with Louie. We were laughing about something when Michael came in, and what he told us was so unexpected and so dire that it took me a minute to realize I was still smiling. It was like part of me didn't want to hear what Michael was saying, like I was pretending I could stay forever in the warm café that smelled like sugar and cinnamon, laughing with my brother."

Abruptly Will broke off and turned toward me. "I don't have much more," he said, grimacing. "And nothing as specific as that one moment. The rest is like pieces of broken glass.

"But this much I can fit together: Louie and I had been helping Michael. And not just the two of us—there were lots of us, identical twins from all over the place. We got together now and then for a week, maybe two. We were volunteers, and it was interesting and exciting, being a part of ground-breaking research. We thought it was great fun. We felt important.

"But then Michael came in, all angry and upset, telling us they wanted to take it further. They wanted to stop piddling around and do it up right. Michael told us, that day in the café. Meritt wanted to wipe our memories."

"Meritt?" Rain said, sounding strangely triumphant.

Fiona looked at her. "Not Red's Meritt. This Meritt would have to be really old by now."

Will nodded. "That's right. Michael's brother Meritt. His twin."

I shut my eyes. Of course Michael had a twin.

I should have realized—all those dreams about the man in the mirror, about drowning a man whose face was Michael's own. It was perfectly obvious.

And maybe that was why they were interested in identical twins to begin with—because they were identical twins themselves. They were twins, and they were brilliant scientists, and Michael had an idea and then Meritt took that idea too far, and—

Rain elbowed me. "Why does your Meritt have the same name as some old evil scientist?"

"I don't know," I said, my eyes still closed. "Maybe it's just a coincidence."

Rain snorted.

I opened my eyes. "No," I said, as the answer came to me. "It's because this other Meritt was in Optica. He had to have been. The Watchers mentioned him, as if he'd been around but wasn't any longer. I bet he was the Watcher who left, and then Marta came and took his place. So Angel must have known him over there."

"Sometimes people name their children after people they admire," Fiona said dubiously. "But why would Angel admire someone who experimented on people?"

Rain rolled her eyes. "Angel kidnapped your sister," she said. "Have you forgotten? He's not exactly averse to experimenting on people. Maybe ruthlessness is the pinnacle of wonderfulness, as far as Angel is concerned."

"Evil be thou my good," Will muttered.

"Yeah. Like that."

"No," Fiona said, her voice rising. "How about this? Those Watchers are dangerous, and Angel's son was in the city with them. So Angel named his son after the leader to *protect* his son. Not magically or anything—" she waved a hand at me, as if expecting me to protest—"but just by association."

"In any case," Rain said, clearly tiring of speculation, "the upshot is that this evil twin decided to take the experiment further than Michael had ever planned, and Michael tried to stop him. But it was too late."

"I'd say that's a safe conclusion," Will said dryly.

Rain nodded. "And Michael got caught along with the rest of you and stuck here. He got caught in his own trap."

"It doesn't sound like it was a *trap*," I said. "Not until his brother expanded it."

"That's right." Fiona glared repressively at Rain and nodded with satisfaction at my comment. "This is our Grandpa we're talking about, Rain. Please don't refer to him as setting traps for people."

"Trap, petri dish, experiment," Rain said, waving an impatient hand, "whatever. The point is, your grandfather didn't come here willingly. He was tricked by his brother."

"And another thing," Will said, squinting, trying to gather together the broken shards of memory. "We were put here to be studied. But not Michael. He was put here as a lesson." He reached over and tapped the journal. "That's what he says here. Meritt made a lesson of him."

And the midwife had said the same thing, though Evan Marchrest had misunderstood. The Dream Recorder and midwife weren't afraid the watchmaker would be sent to teach them a lesson; they were thinking of what had been done to the watchmaker. Michael was a living example to the other experimenters: If the watchmaker could be stuffed into his own experiment against his will—the one who set it all up to begin with—it could happen to anyone.

No wonder the Watchers were wary about what the other Meritt would want or not want. He must have been a completely ruthless man.

"And grandfather's brother watched him." Fiona tactfully avoided saying Meritt's name. "He watched Grandpa with the cameras, and with the Dream Drops."

Rain nodded. "No wonder he could never shake the feeling he was being watched." She looked at each of us in turn. "What does it feel like, when someone is spying in your head?"

Will was the only one who answered her. "I've no idea," he said. "But I hope Louie knows I'm cheering him on."

Chapter 25

R ain was a terrible driver.

"Go easy on the clutch," Will said.

He was sitting in the passenger seat beside her, and Fiona and I were crammed into the back, along with our bundles of clothes. It was chilly and I was wrapped in one of Fiona's cloaks and wearing, once again, my own black cap, which Angus had found in some bushes near our grandparents' house, where Tristan had grabbed me.

The truck lurched.

"Don't stomp," Will said.

The engine whined loudly.

"Shift up," Will said. "But don't stomp. Ease down the clutch to the sweet spot, shift up, then ease up on the clutch."

The truck lurched again, but then the engine noise quieted. I just hoped we wouldn't meet any oncoming vehicles. Though the windshield wipers swept back and forth frenetically, they couldn't keep up with the downpour. Rain was driving blind—if you could call it driving.

"Shift down," Will advised. "This hill is fairly steep, so put it in second."

"I can't." Rain was wrestling with the gear shift. "Something keeps sticking." The gears ground with a terrible noise. "It's not my fault!" Rain said.

The wind rose, whistling, and the pounding of the rain on the roof grew suddenly deafening. I put my hands over my ears just as Will called out a warning and we hit a bump that threw me hard against Fiona.

"Sorry," Rain said as I righted myself. "That *was* my fault."

We were never going to get to Doria at this rate, much less Locria—at least, not in one piece.

Although, honestly, I didn't know why I was so anxious to get there. Figuring out Michael Alleyn's role would be interesting, but it wasn't exactly urgent. He was dead; the experiment was over; and Mal wasn't going anywhere. He'd be right there in Locria whenever I managed to get there.

And as for me—well, I might as well admit it. I had many long days to fill before I could even begin to hope for news from Optica. Days, or even weeks.

So what was my hurry?

Maybe I just wanted to go stand on the empty beach. Maybe I wouldn't really believe Farrell Dean had left me until I saw the bare sand, the empty sea.

The thought was depressing.

My sister was watching me. "They shouldn't have left you," she said, putting a hand on my knee. "It isn't right."

Rain called an answer over her shoulder. "You realize that's why Eric Alleyn drugged you as well, Fee. Because you're so predictable. They knew you'd take her side."

Fiona eyed the back of our cousin's head coldly. "Of course I would," she said. "It isn't right for them to leave her, without even discussing it with her. Not even if they're trying to protect her."

Rain steered around a low spot in the road.

"They're protecting themselves as well," she said. "That's more important than Red's hurt feelings."

I stared at the back of her head, uncomprehending.

Then I glanced at Will for help, but the inside of the windows had fogged up and he was busy wiping them clear with his sleeve.

"All right," I said. "I'll bite. What's that supposed to mean? Why would I endanger them if I went back to Optica with them?"

Rain was directly in front of me, so while I could see Will's profile, I couldn't see any of her face. "I would think it should be obvious," she said. "A girl consorting with the enemy is likely to get her allies killed."

Gabriel had said something similar back on the beach at Locria, when he was angry that I'd answered Angel's transmitter call.

"You sound just like your father," I muttered, knowing that would irritate Rain.

It did. "No, my father sounds just like me," she retorted. "I told him what I thought, and he agreed with me. If love is blind, you must be madly in love."

It took me a moment, but then I got it.

Shaking off Fiona's arm, I leaned forward in my seat. "You told Gabriel what Sir Tom said about Meritt?"

"Told him what?" Fiona said anxiously, but neither of us answered her. Will Bright shifted, looking from one face to another.

"That transmitter conversation was private," I told Rain. "You shouldn't have even been listening. Sir Tom was talking to me, not you, and you had no right to repeat anything he said."

"I had every right," she said calmly. "My father is going across the sea into the unknown. I had an obligation to tell him that your precious Meritt is dangerous."

"He is not!"

"Tell that to Uncle Rafe. *Dead* Uncle Rafe."

"Meritt didn't—"

Rain went inexorably on. "Yes, he did. You know he did. Sir Tom said so."

"Sir Tom is confused—and he didn't say that exactly—"

"Sharla said the same thing. Dad told me so. Sharla said that her sister, your friend Cynda, didn't feel bad for betraying Meritt because Meritt was the one who betrayed Rafe."

"She didn't say that! Cynda *thought* Meritt had betrayed *me*."

"Ah," Rain said. "Well, in that case."

This was maddening—I was trapped in the back of the truck, behind her. I couldn't even see her face. It felt like she was ignoring me.

"Meritt didn't betray me—that was just a rumor—the Watchers wanted him to turn me in, but he didn't." I looked at Fiona for support. "He didn't."

Fiona was looking alarmed. "But if he'd had the opportunity," she began apologetically, and broke off. "Isn't that why Farrell Dean brought you here?"

"It isn't true!" I said.

"So you think Sir Tom's a liar," Rain said. "And Cline, and Cynda, and Farrell Dean. Everyone who isn't utterly blinded by Meritt's charms must be lying about him."

"It was *your father* who betrayed Rafe. He's the one who's been tattling to the Dream Recorder all these years."

Rain grabbed the rearview mirror and tilted it so she could see me. Her eyes were narrowed to green slits. "Oh really?" she said. "And who betrayed Farrell Dean?"

It was an unexpected blow, and I was struck momentarily speechless.

Rain nodded meaningfully. "I had a little chat with Ezzie, and he told me all sorts of interesting facts you've never mentioned." She looked over at Will. "Farrell Dean punched Meritt out, and some other guys had to break it up before he did real damage. And not twenty-four hours later,

Farrell Dean got arrested and flogged and then put in a city meeting."

"Watch the road!" Will said.

I was shaking my head, but despite myself I was remembering the day when Farrell Dean told me at breakfast he was going to come to my field and talk to me about Meritt, but he never came. He never came, because he got arrested.

Was he going to tell me then that Meritt had taken Cline's place, that Meritt should never have been out there with Rafe? Was he going to tell me that Meritt might be crooked? But he'd had plenty of time to tell me later, when we were in the boat, and he hadn't said anything about Rafe. He'd said he was afraid Meritt might turn me in, but he never said Meritt might have gotten Rafe killed.

"Ezzie didn't know why Farrell Dean hit Meritt," Rain said. "But I can guess."

"Ezzie would never—he's Meritt's friend—we're all friends, Meritt and Farrell Dean and Ezzie and me—" I was babbling.

"Which is exactly why the rest of you have no perspective," Rain said. "Ezzie told me the facts, and I had enough distance to see what they mean."

"Meritt *saved* Farrell Dean," I said, getting control of myself. "He saved him, even though he could have been killed for interfering in the city meeting."

In the rearview mirror I could see Rain roll her eyes. "Sir Tom already explained that," she said. "It wasn't dangerous for Meritt. And just think what a great set up it was— Meritt secretly gets Farrell Dean arrested, then rescues him publicly and heroically. How could any of you doubt him after that? He scammed you. You're reacting exactly the way he wanted you to react."

No. It wasn't true. It couldn't be true.

I turned to Fiona, pleading. "Meritt was surprised when

we found out Farrell Dean was in prison. He was surprised and he was worried, because he thought that if they tortured Farrell Dean, he might tell them that Meritt was up in the watchtower. Why would Meritt be worried about that, if he and the Watchers were in it together?"

Fiona, put on the spot, made a helpless gesture.

"He was faking it for your benefit," Rain said.

"He was not!"

"Then he didn't know when exactly Farrell Dean was going to get arrested, and it was the timing that surprised him."

Will Bright spoke up. "Or else Meritt didn't turn the boy in after all," he said.

His intervention was so unexpected that before I could take it in, Rain was already speaking.

"Who'd have taken you for an old softie?" she said, throwing him an impatient look.

Will returned her gaze stoically. "Louie looked guilty to me, at first blush," he said. "It's a complicated situation over there. I for one won't rush to judgment on Meritt."

"Well, good for you," Rain said, her expression cold. "But I didn't have the luxury of waiting."

The other shoe dropped. "You knew they were leaving," I said, incredulous, half-standing, almost coming over the seat at her. "You knew they were planning to sneak away."

Rain shrugged.

"I didn't know," she said. "I guessed. It's my father's standard operating procedure."

"Watch the road," Will said again, just as Fiona said, "Red, sit down!"

"Why didn't you warn us?"

"Why would I? Like I said, you're a danger to yourself and others."

We had reached the outskirts of Doria. Buildings

loomed up in the rain, lights flickering in windows. One or two people hurried along the wet street.

"Don't run over anybody," Will said.

I shoved at the back of Rain's seat. "Let me out," I said.

"Don't be stupid. I did what was best, and now I'll take you to Locria so you can figure out what your grandfather did—that's my peace offering, even though I didn't do anything wrong."

She downshifted and the gears made an ominous grinding noise.

"It wasn't doing that when we were idling," Will said. "It could be the shift lever, but with that noise, I'm thinking not. Could be you need grease in the CV joints. Or it could be a bad bearing. With luck, nothing worse than the axle flange shaft roller bearings. Otherwise you're looking at a fairly complicated disassembly. Not something I want to tackle."

Rain shot a look at him. "Are you speaking English?"

"Let me out!" I said again. I was furious at her, and I wasn't going to let them change the subject or placate me with so-called peace offerings. Rain could have warned me; I could have been on my way to Optica right that minute.

I kicked the back of the seat hard.

"Stop it!"

"*Let me out.*"

Rain stopped the truck.

"You want to walk to Sean's in the rain?" she said, swinging open her door. "You want to walk all the way to Locria? Fine with me."

As she climbed out, Will leaned toward me. "We need to get this truck looked at anyway," he said. "We'll find a mechanic, and once everybody's cooled off we'll pick you up at your brother's and go on up to Locria."

I didn't answer him; I was too angry to say anything even marginally polite, and Will didn't deserve to be snarled at. I squeezed between the seats and shoved past Rain and out onto the road.

Then Fiona was standing on the street beside me.

Then Rain got in the truck, slammed the door, and pulled away. She drove through a puddle too fast, splashing a man on the sidewalk. He shouted something at her and pushed open a shop door, sending the aroma of cooking meat drifting through the cold wet air.

"You didn't have to get out too," I said curtly, turning to my sister, not quite looking at her. I wasn't as mad at her as I was at Rain, but Fiona hadn't exactly defended Meritt.

"No wandering around alone. Papa said so."

"Papa isn't here."

Fiona gave a little shrug. "I know. He would be, if he thought we were in any danger."

"So … therefore, what? You could have let me wander around alone?"

"I could. But I wouldn't want to. I'd rather be with you than with Rain." Her tone was conciliatory and even a little apologetic, but I couldn't see much of her face, thanks to her hood and the rain that kept getting in my eyes. "You don't know the way to Sean's," she said. "Come on. It's not far."

She started walking, and after a moment or two—feeling angry, feeling sorry for myself—I followed.

The streets were mostly deserted. The few people we saw were hurrying along, heads down, shielding their faces from the rain with cloaks or hats. Not a single person gave any indication of noticing that there were two of us. But our hair was hidden, of course, and like everyone else we kept our faces down. And even if someone spotted us, we weren't in any danger. Gabriel and the Isle Council had taken care of all that. No one would try to claim the Dream Recorder's reward.

That was actually a bit of a letdown, oddly enough. It

made me feel even more useless, even more removed from all the trouble in Optica. Over there, they had Watchers and wardens to cope with, and wild men and rogue Guardians. Over here all I had to cope with was a Dream Recorder whose claws had been clipped.

I stopped in my tracks.

The Dream Recorder wasn't always here.

Once she'd been gone two weeks, and the people addicted to Dream Drops, or to talking about their dreams or whatever—they hadn't been able to find her anywhere. Michael Alleyn had said so in his dairy.

Fiona noticed I wasn't with her and turned around. "What's wrong?" she said, retracing her steps. She still sounded deferential.

"The Dream Recorder wrote those books for the experimenters," I said. "To compare your dreams with our actions. So how did they get the data from her?"

"Maybe Angel took the books back and forth to them."

"Maybe … but Grandpa Michael said the Dream Recorder vanished sometimes."

The rain had eased just a little. Fiona pushed her hood back and stared at me.

"That's right," she said. "He did. Do you think she left the island? Maybe she took the books to the mainland, or to Optica. Do you think she has a boat?"

The words hung in the air. *A boat.*

A boat that surely had a good engine. A boat that must be hidden somewhere nearby, somewhere convenient. A boat that could make it to Optica.

For a long moment we stood there staring at each other.

"Nobody's helping her anymore," Fiona said slowly. "And she's only one old woman."

It was true, but I didn't immediately answer.

I knew what was happening; Fiona felt bad for me

because I'd been left behind, and she felt bad for herself because I was a little mad at her. She didn't like strife. She wanted to make things up to me.

And I was tempted to take advantage of her niceness, I truly was. I was desperate to get to Optica, and I felt humiliated by Rain's scorn, and by Gabriel's assessment of me.

They were wrong—I wasn't a liability. I wasn't blind. I had important new information, and those were my friends, over there. My friends and Meritt, with all the world against him.

"No," I said, hearing regret in my voice. "It could be dangerous."

"Even before the Isle Council stepped in, the Dream Recorder never wanted to hurt you," Fiona said. "She told the men out looking for you to make sure you weren't harmed."

I looked at my sister in surprise.

"All we want to do is talk to her," she went on. I couldn't believe my ears—she was actually arguing for this. "And there are two of us and one of her, and she's old and sick."

Well, that was true. "If we had someone else with us," I said. "Or a gun …"

Fiona smiled. "But I do," she said. "I have my birthday present." Reaching under her cloak, behind her back, she pulled out a small handgun.

It was very dainty and feminine looking, nothing at all like the guns I'd helped steal from Edgeling's barn. It even had a decorative inlay on the handle, smooth and pretty like the inside of a seashell. It changed colors as Fiona tilted it toward me.

"Papa gave it to me last year," she said. "The boys like to tease me about it."

"Does it work?" I said. "Do you know how to use it?"

She laughed. "The weasel that got into the henhouse thinks so."

"So you're a good shot?"

"I'm an Alleyn."

I looked at the gun, and I looked at my sister. And I asked myself, what was the worst that could happen?

Chapter 26

The shop had lights on inside, but they were feeble and few and didn't make the place seem cheery. Instead the windows looked like dim disheartened eyes, as if the building were barely clinging to life. The outside gave the same impression; the paint on the siding was peeling, and the front steps were beginning to rot.

Carefully I climbed up them, avoiding the parts that looked downright unsafe. I wondered whether the window around back had been replaced.

At the door I hesitated. "Remember to stay out of reach," I said, turning to face my sister. A gust of wind blew rain into my face and I held up a hand to shield my eyes. "If she lets us in, don't go into the room with the books. It has grates on the doors, so she could trap us."

Fiona nodded but didn't reply. She was looking down the street, and I started to turn and follow her gaze, but before I could move the door behind me opened.

"What have we here?" said a voice, unusually low and resonant for a woman. "Two Alleyn girls, as like as peas in a pod. What an absolutely delightful surprise."

The Dream Recorder was as I remembered—short and broad, with eyes that were mere slits in the slab that was her face. Her lips were very thin and seemed longer than was right, running almost from ear to ear even when she wasn't smiling unpleasantly, as she was at that moment. Her hair was thin and pulled tightly back from her face, her scalp showing in patches.

I expected her to immediately chastise me for breaking into her shop and stealing her books and her transmitter. She had to know I was the one who had done it; Cobb surely would have told her. But she didn't say a word about that. She didn't even give me a dirty look.

"Come in," she said instead, and her tone was pleasant. "Take off your wet cloaks. Warm yourselves."

So she didn't want to have this conversation on the street. That was good. Maybe my rather sketchy plan would work and she'd be willing to buy our continued silence—for after all, what would the people of Aislin do to her, once they knew the truth?

Taking one last deep breath of fresh air, I followed her inside. Behind me I heard Fiona shut the door, and then felt a tiny draft as she silently eased it back open a crack. Good for her—we absolutely didn't want to get trapped in this house.

We were in the shabby and poorly lit room where the Dream Recorder interviewed people. I'd seen it before, when Farrell Dean and I broke in. Then there had been only two threadbare armchairs and a small table; now, however, a straight-backed chair had been brought in to join the others.

The Dream Recorder saw me notice it.

"I have been expecting you," she said. "Hoping, rather, that you would come. Do please have a seat." She moved heavily away from us, toward the kitchen. Cautiously Fiona and I came further into the room, but we didn't sit down.

"Take the comfortable chairs," the Dream Recorder called, out of sight. "I will be with you shortly."

I scanned the room again, but nothing I saw made me any more wary than I already was. It looked like it had looked before, cluttered and dusty and dim, and the straight-backed chair wasn't in between the other chairs and the door. As best as I could judge, there was no immediate threat.

Fiona looked at me; I shrugged, and together we went over to the group of chairs. I took off my wet cloak and hung it on a hook on the wall, then pulled one of the armchairs a little further from the straight chair. I didn't sit down, though, and neither did Fiona. She followed my lead in everything, which was both reassuring and a little unnerving. It made me feel like it was entirely up to me to keep us out of trouble. At least Fiona was in charge of the gun; she had it tucked in the back of her pants, hidden by her shirt.

The little table was strewn with books and papers. Two or three small bottles rolled amongst the clutter—Dream Drops, I knew. I picked one up and tipped it this way and that, watching the thick golden liquid shift and flow. Fiona did the same.

Hastily I set the little bottle down as the Dream Recorder came trundling back into the room, carrying a tray with a teapot and three mugs. Ignoring the piles of papers, she set the tray on top of them, nudging at the bottles until they rolled away and the tray sat smooth. Then she smiled her broad ugly smile at each of us in turn.

"Please, sit down," she said, and began lowering herself heavily into the remaining chair. It seemed to take quite an effort. "I am getting old," she said, and chuckled. "Let us be honest. I *am* old."

It was true that she was breathing hard, as if fetching the tea had stretched her resources. I knew, though, that she'd been perfectly capable of trailing Tor and me through town that day we'd come through looking for Farrell Dean. Either she was exaggerating now, or she'd been ill since then, as I had been. Or maybe she had a chronic illness that flared up now and then. That would explain her bloated, sallow face.

Or maybe she was breathing hard because she'd done something to exert herself when she was out of our sight.

Quickly I shot a glance at the doorway. No one was there, and I saw no shadow or flicker of movement, heard no sound. We truly were alone, I thought. Whatever she had done—if she had done anything at all—it hadn't involved hurriedly fetching another person.

The Dream Recorder reached for the teapot, straining to lean forward over her stout belly. A long mottled stain ran down the bosom of her dingy white dress. It didn't seem very scientific, to be so grubby. The midwife's house had been very clean. Then again, maybe the Dream Recorder had never had to follow sanitary habits like a midwife would.

"You will not recognize this," she said. She was pouring a stream of brown liquid into the mugs. "It is proper black tea. I saved the last of it for a special occasion, and I can imagine no occasion more special than this one. Here you are."

She pushed a sugar bowl toward Fiona, along with one of the mugs. "Try it with a little sugar and milk. You will be most impressed, I assure you. Chamomile cannot compare." She actually bounced a little in her seat.

With a quick glance at me Fiona took the sugar bowl and added a tiny bit to her mug. I was pretty sure her glance meant she wouldn't drink, but I watched her closely to be sure. She stirred in the sugar, and then pushed the bowl away. Only when she clasped her hands behind her back did I dare to look away.

Meanwhile the Dream Recorder had busied herself with her own tea. She added sugar and milk, and then without hesitation raised her mug and took a long drink. Her throat moved, and when she set the mug down, her lips were wet. A few drops ran down her chin, joining the older stain on her front. She picked up a napkin and blotted at herself, then turned toward me.

"Would it be a terrible imposition to ask you to remove your head covering?" she said. "I have never seen any participants together as adults, and I admit to a strong curiosity."

"Participants? That's a funny way to put it." I did, however, pull off my cap, shaking out my hair so that it fell over my shoulders in a fiery curtain.

The Dream Recorder stared. "Quite remarkable," she said, looking back and forth between Fiona and me. She didn't ask which one of us was which, but then, I wasn't bothering to try to sound like an Aislin person.

"Thank you for indulging an old woman," the old woman said, picking up her mug of tea. Fiona and I were still standing, but she didn't press us again to sit down.

"I do understand your reservation regarding my terminology. The official word is *subjects,* of course, but I have never felt comfortable referring to any of you that way. You and your colleagues have contributed enormously to our base of scientific knowledge, as well as to national security. You should be honored. You should be held in the utmost respect for what you have done."

As ugly as she was, she had a truly beautiful voice. No wonder so many people were willing to come talk with her. They probably just shut their eyes and listened.

The Dream Recorder leaned forward, looking up at me, her broad face twisting earnestly.

"I do apologize for any disrespect shown to you by my colleagues in Optica. I am aware that they are heavy handed, over there. They forget that it is *we* who are indebted to *you.*"

I couldn't believe she was talking about Optica and the experiment, openly talking about it with no pretense or evasion. She was playing some game I didn't understand. All the same I felt increasingly awkward, towering over her, refusing to sit down, refusing to drink her tea. She was wrong-footing me with her courtesy. She was gaining some crucial edge.

In an attempt to minimize her advantage I sat down, though only on the edge of my chair, and out of the corner of my eye I saw Fiona do the same.

"We know a lot of your secrets now," I said, sounding more truculent than I intended. "We know you wiped everyone's memories. We know you separated twins and gave one set Dream Drops so they'd read the minds of the others."

The Dream Recorder nodded. "Do you have any remaining questions?" she said. "It would be my pleasure to answer them."

I managed not to gape at her, but just barely. "You wouldn't answer Gabriel," I said. "He came to see you, and you wouldn't even let him into the shop. And he's a twin, too."

The Dream Recorder nodded, the thick folds of her chin and neck quivering with the movement. "You are quite right," she said. "But Gabriel Drewblood didn't come to ask me questions about the experiment. He didn't know about the experiment at the time, though I daresay he knows now. He came to read my books, and I was concerned that he might be looking for information to use against various people—against your father, for one. Gabriel Drewblood is a businessman, after all, and a ruthless one."

"And now that we know, you'll talk to us? Just like that?"

She smiled at me. "Why should I not? The experiment is over. We have heard nothing from the mainland for some eighteen years, nothing from Optica in almost as long. Clearly something went awry, and no one saw fit to notify us. Now that you are here, sterile conditions have been unalterably compromised." She shrugged. "Some of my colleagues might disapprove of my decision, but I do not care. I am too old and tired to fight a futile battle, and besides, I would like to hear news of Optica."

"Then why did you give orders for Farrell Dean and

Ezzie to be killed?" I said, pulling my cap back over my hair. I felt safer that way.

The Dream Recorder blinked at me with her tiny eyes. "Killed? I never gave such an order. I never gave any order at all regarding you people from Optica."

She could play innocent all she liked, but I knew it was only an act. "Edgeling's men said you did. They were tracking us down, and they said they were acting under your orders. They were to bring me to you, and do as they liked with Farrell Dean and Ezzie. They said you were offering a reward."

The Dream Recorder looked down at her tea, her long lips curving down in a frown. "I wish this came as a surprise to me," she murmured. "But I fear it does not."

She looked up again, at me. "You have heard, I assume, of Rowena Marchrest?"

I nodded. "She's the midwife who sold me to Angel."

The Dream Recorder winced slightly. "Rowena did not sell you," she began, but I cut her off.

"She let Tristan sell me. It's the same thing. She stole me from my family so Angel could take me over to Optica."

The Dream Recorder nodded. "I will try to help you understand," she said. "But first, please allow me to explain about Edgeling and the young men."

Politely, she waited until I nodded before she went on.

"Rowena was for many years a good friend of mine, and a good colleague. But alas, age does as it will with our minds as well as our bodies, and of late she has grown confused. She forgets to eat, or forgets that she has already eaten. Worse, she is paranoid and suspicious. It is a tendency inherent to certain forms of senility. Old people misplace items, and their response is to accuse others of stealing them."

Her expression grew apologetic. "You can see, can you not, how it happens? We must blame others, because we cannot believe our own minds could so betray us."

She glanced at Fiona, and my sister nodded. "Tor's grandmother got like that, before she died."

"Just so. Well. Much as it pains me to say so, Rowena is no longer in her right mind. She makes decisions that are unconscionable, and, I fear, may at times present them as my own. For we did act together, for many years. I had final say, but generally I took Rowena's advice. Sometimes I authorized her to make our arrangements." She gestured at her body. "Rowena finds it easier to get around than I."

"What exactly is your point?"

Beside me Fiona flinched, probably at my tone.

The Dream Recorder, however, didn't react. "My point is that Edgeling and his men might well assume we act together still. I will have to speak with them so that such misunderstandings will occur no more."

I snorted. "They can't very well occur now that she's dead."

The Dream Recorder inhaled sharply and one hand went to her bosom. "Rowena?" she croaked. I could swear that her sallow face had grown a shade paler. "But—it was only yesterday that I saw her. Was it her heart?"

"You should know," I said mercilessly. "You killed her."

The Dream Recorder's mouth opened, moving as if she were trying to form words, but only a strangled noise came out. Her hand went to her throat, and beads of sweat popped out on her forehead.

Fiona got to her feet.

"She didn't know," she said to me, pushing the mug of tea toward the old woman.

The Dream Recorder made no attempt to drink. Her face quivered, and tears began rolling down her cheeks.

"Here," Fiona said. "Let me help you." She lifted the mug to the old woman's mouth.

"Fiona—" I said warningly, not wanting her to get too

close to the woman, but my sister threw me a reproving look.

"She didn't know," she said again.

The old woman stayed as she was for another long moment, while Fiona pressed the mug against her lips. Then she blinked and opened her mouth for the tea, raising one fat hand to steady Fiona's.

"Better," she said, gasping, and Fiona set the mug down on the table. "Rowena. Oh, poor Rowena."

I watched her, but she never broke character, not by the tiniest flicker of an eyelash. She was exactly like an old woman grieving a friend.

"Someone poisoned her," I said, and Fiona shot me a look of admonishment.

"Well, someone did!" I protested. "If it wasn't her, we need to know who did it."

I looked at the Dream Recorder. "You want to find out who did it, don't you? You want to know who killed your friend."

The Dream Recorder mopped at her wet cheeks with the back of her hand. "I already know," she said, and took a long shuddering breath. "Rowena and I were given suicide ampoules. Long ago, back when the experiment first began. They were intended to protect us."

"*Protect* you?"

She nodded. "Yes. If our nation's enemies got wind of what we were doing, they would want access to our methods. Their methods of persuasion were widely known to be very unpleasant indeed."

With a trembling hand she reached for her mug and took another drink before continuing. "Rather than enduring such torment and possibly betraying ourselves in the agony of the moment, and then facing execution at the hands of an enemy nation, we were told to simply crack our ampoules. A drop or two, that was all it would take, and a heartbeat later we would be safe from our torturers, and our nation's secrets would be safe as well. And Rowena ... when I spoke to her yesterday, Rowena was in full paranoia mode. She thought you would come after her, or that Gabriel would come after her, or Eric Alleyn, any number of the others. She was worried about betraying the cause." Again she wiped away tears. "I shouldn't have left her alone. I should have stayed with her until her son returned home."

Her mug was empty now, and she seemed to notice our untouched drinks for the first time. "Please," she said, gesturing. "It is very good tea, and it is the last I have."

Fiona picked up her mug and drank before I could stop her. The tea was probably fine—the Dream Recorder was still fine after drinking all of hers—but I knew Fiona was doing it as a reprimand to me, for being rude.

That didn't inspire me to be nicer; if anything it had the opposite effect. "Do you still have your suicide ampoule?" I said.

The Dream Recorder nodded. "Yes," she said, but then an expression of uncertainty crossed her face. "I believe so, in any case. It has been many years since I carried it with me at all times, as we were supposed to do."

"So if someone showed up and tortured you, you couldn't do anything about it," I said. "Maybe that's just as well. Maybe you deserve to be tortured. You and the other experimenters stole so many lives, so many memories. You drugged us, and you stole us from our families, and you watched us, and treated us like rats in a lab. How could you do such a thing?"

The Dream Recorder sighed tremulously. She looked smaller now, shrunk into herself.

"That question requires a fairly lengthy answer," she said apologetically.

"Go ahead."

From the corner of my eye I saw Fiona glare at me. Maybe she was right; maybe the Dream Recorder was innocent of setting Edgeling's men after Farrell Dean, and innocent of killing the midwife. But the fact remained that she was one of the experimenters. She had pried into people's most private thoughts. She had harassed poor Michael Alleyn for years, until he felt he had to fake his own death in order for his family to be safe. Did Fiona think the old woman's grief over the midwife erased all that?

The Dream Recorder poured herself more tea.

"Back before all this began," she said slowly, sounding very tired, "our spies risked their lives infiltrating enemy territory. They tried to find out when and how the enemy intended to attack us, so that lives could be saved. It was terribly dangerous work. If our spies were captured, they were tortured and killed in ways too horrible to repeat.

"Then your grandfather—Michael Alleyn, that is—had a brilliant idea. What if we could spy with complete impunity? Then our spies would never be captured or tortured. They would never be made to reveal our secrets. It would be a great boon, not only to our country, but to all humanity. We could prevent wars before they ever began. We would all be safe from one another. Where there are no secrets, there can be no secret attacks."

She poured milk into her tea and drank.

"I don't understand," I said. "Twins can only spy on their own twins. What good would that do, spying on someone who lived in your house with you?"

The Dream Recorder blotted at her forehead with the sleeve of her dress. "That was the brilliance of Michael's plan," she said. "Many of our enemies' twins were not raised together. That was because our enemies thought they had too many people—they were worried about running out of food, oil, even water. So they forbade parents to have more than one child. This rule applied to everyone, including important government officials. One child, and one child only. If parents broke that law, then the government took the extra children away and warehoused them.

"It was meant to be a deterrent, a way to convince parents to voluntarily limit their family size. But of course all the care in the world can't prevent twins from occurring. So families continued to accidentally have extra children, and the extras were impounded by the government. And of course the government did not want to feed those extra children—that was the point, that the country thought it couldn't support extra people—so conditions ... deteriorated.

"The women in our country heard about the situation and were appalled. Babies, left to lie in their own excrement. Babies, left to starve in their own cribs. Babies crying, their cries growing feebler and feebler, until they cried no more. So we began taking in those babes."

"The enemy's babies."

The Dream Recorder nodded, a faint smile touching her lips. "It was a truly beautiful plan on Michael Alleyn's part, do you see? And fitting. For our generosity toward the children of our enemies, we would be rewarded with safety. All we had to do was find a way for the extra twins, the exiled twins, to read their siblings' minds. Then we could prevent bloodshed, war, all manner of pain and suffering.

"And so the Alleyn brothers began quietly contacting identical twins in our country, asking them to help with this patriotic and entirely humanitarian effort. Asking them to help the Alleyn brothers perfect the method, you see, so that eventually we could begin to employ it internationally for the good of the human race."

No wonder Will and Louie had been excited about helping with the experiment. It did sound like a good idea, on the face of it. When they were still volunteers.

"It was entirely secret, of course," the old woman went on. "If our enemies caught even a whisper of our plan they would kill all the children in the orphanages, and all the twins they could find elsewhere. So the volunteers were made to understand how critical it was that they never breathe a word of the experiments, not to anyone. Fortuitously, this secrecy allowed us to expand the experiment later on, with no one in the country being the wiser."

"But why did the experiment have to be expanded?" I said. "Why did you think you needed to wipe away everyone's memories?

She shook her head regretfully. "The Dream Drops worked beautifully," she said. "Unfortunately, in our preliminary experiments it became clear that the siblings who watched had a tendency to fall prey to scruples." She looked away from me, at Fiona. "They couldn't control what they saw and what they didn't see."

My sister began blushing, and the Dream Recorder nodded.

"You understand. Only natural voyeurs made good spies. And as it turned out, there are fewer of those than one might expect, especially when it comes to spying on one's own flesh and blood."

I thought about seeing Fiona's life from the inside, experiencing her arguing with Angus, weeping when Granny Rose died, kissing Tor. Just thinking about watching all that made me uncomfortable.

The Dream Recorder turned back toward me.

"When our watchers fell prey to scruples, they closed their eyes, metaphorically speaking. Although they could not completely block out what their minds saw while under the influence of the serum, they distorted events, misunderstood them, misconstrued them." She gave a weak smile. "They were next to useless, in other words. So then of course the watchers had to be made to watch without knowing they were watching."

Fiona was nodding as if it all made perfect sense. Picking up her tea, she drank again.

Without thinking I picked up my tea, too, and lifted it to my lips. I would have drunk, then, but something else occurred to me.

"What about Optica?" I said, setting the tea down untasted. "We weren't taking Dream Drops, so why did we have to be made to forget?"

The Dream Recorder's fat face was compassionate. "Optica was not a pleasant place," she said.

"No."

"If those of you in Optica remembered your origins, there would have been constant uprisings. We had to have a heavily controlled group who both knew they were constantly watched, and who more or less accepted their circumstances."

Tears came to my eyes. "But why did we have to live in those circumstances? We're told who to marry, what jobs to do, where to live, what to eat and when. Everything is decided for us. We don't have a say in anything."

The Dream Recorder's face was creased with pain.

"It was a terrible necessity," she said. "Our enemies made their people live like that. And we knew, from defectors who had come to our country, that if someone knows he is constantly watched and controlled, he learns to hide. It is a survival mechanism. He learns to hide his actions, his words, his opinions, anything that might call attention to him or mark him as a threat to the authorities. We needed to know if, as a corollary, he even learned to hide his thoughts."

She paused, blowing her nose on her napkin.

"As it turned out, most people do let their twins into their minds, at the very least in moments of intense emotion or distress. But not all do. Some people apparently have a stronger or more effective sense of self-preservation than others."

I wondered where I fell in that category. If Fiona had taken Dream Drops, would she have been able to read my mind, or would I have kept her out?

I thought about the night I had gone alone to Rafe's, the night I realized that warden Zee could be ignoring the monitors, playing cards and drinking his warm milk and whiskey, but that I had to act as if he were watching me. Even if he wasn't at his station, he was always in my mind.

Suddenly chilled, I wrapped my hands around my mug and lifted it toward my face, feeling the warmth of the steam.

The Dream Recorder nodded approvingly at me. "It's from the mainland," she said. "Imported there, from China." She looked at Fiona. "Would you care for more?"

I didn't know what China was and I didn't like the smell of the tea. I was setting my mug back down as the Dream Recorder turned to Fiona, and instead of completing the movement, on a whim I quickly poured half my mug back into the pot. I still didn't quite trust the old woman, but this way Fiona couldn't scold me for being rude and refusing hospitality. Fiona was big on hospitality.

While the Dream Recorder fussed over Fiona, pouring more tea and passing her the sugar bowl and little pitcher of milk, I decided it was high time I broached our purpose in coming here.

"We need to go to Optica," I said bluntly. "And we won't tell everyone here what you've been doing to them, if you'll help us. Do you have a boat?"

The Dream Recorder shook her head. "No, not I," she said. "We did have regular meetings on the mainland, where we compared data from our respective sides of the experiment. But we were fetched. It was too risky, storing a boat here where someone might run across it. Not like in Optica, where subjects generally were confined far from the shore."

She leaned forward and peered into my mug, then reached for the teapot and refilled it. Great. Well, I would just have to be rude, because the smell of that tea made me want to gag, and suddenly now for some reason I was suspicious of the old woman again, more than I had been before.

Subjects. That was why. She had just called us subjects.

Beside me Fiona made a faint sound and slumped against the arm of her chair.

Chapter 27

In a split second a million thoughts ran through my mind. Was it the suicide ampoule, was Fiona dying? I didn't think so—her color was good, and she was breathing, and didn't the old woman say the ampoule worked instantly?

So it was some other drug—and she had tricked us, how had she managed to drug us and not herself?

It didn't matter, not now, now I had to go get help, as fast as I could—but no, I couldn't go, because I couldn't carry Fiona and I sure couldn't leave her behind, not even for the few minutes it would take to find help.

That old woman had been lying to us all along, faking friendliness, acting a part, and Fiona had fallen for it and I almost had— and what was I going to do now? The gun was trapped beneath Fiona's body.

Before the thought was fully articulated in my mind, my body was reacting, imitating Fiona, slumping in the chair.

I would beat the old woman at her own game.

"Now we'll see who ought to be tortured," the Dream Recorder said, and her beautiful smooth voice made her words doubly chilling. She got up from her chair—with less effort that it had supposedly taken her to sit down—and circled the table, peering first at me, and then Fiona.

"Can you hear me, you silly girls? How dare you

suppose that you could manipulate me, threaten me, use me for your own ends. You break into my home, you steal classified documents, you put me at risk of Meritt Alleyn's wrath, and then you have the arrogance to think I would meekly lie down and take it."

Fiona's eyes were not quite shut, so I kept mine partly open as well and tried to see what the Dream Recorder was doing. She pulled something out of her pocket and bent over the table, fiddling with it. Whatever the item was, it was small enough to be hidden by the teapot.

"This experiment is not over," she went on, clearly enjoying venting her pent-up annoyance at us. "Rowena thought it was, but Rowena has always been short-sighted, as evidenced by her decision to let Tristan become involved in our work after our original tech expert had the stupidity to dive into shallow water and break his own neck.

"And was he replaced in a timely fashion? No, because administration never does anything in a timely manner, the bureaucrats. They take their sweet time and we are forced to make do with inferior transmitters and loose cannons like Tristan Oldfamily and whatnot." She waved one fat hand. "As if science should bow to anything as mundane as a budget."

Leaving the table, she went to Fiona and lifted one eyelid. Fiona didn't move.

"I, however, am not shortsighted," the Dream Recorder went on, turning to me. "I am quite aware that one set of subjects are often used for multiple experiments, and that the ones who monitor experiments are often part of an experiment themselves, unbeknownst to them. Moreover it is quite possible that this is a test, that Meritt Alleyn is about to return to reward or punish those of us who have been for so long abandoned."

She turned toward me, moving so close that I could smell her sour breath. "And so what shall I do with you? I believe I shall follow his example. Meritt Alleyn allowed his own brother to suffer the consequences of impeding scientific progress. Why should his great-nieces be exempt?"

She reached for my eyelid. I tried not to flinch—I really did—but I couldn't help myself. I squinched my eyes shut.

The Dream Recorder laughed and stepped back. "Yes, you delayed in drinking your tea. Perhaps you thought it might be drugged, until you saw me drinking mine. But it was not in the tea, silly girl. It was in the bottom of your mug. And now you will have the joy of being acutely aware of what is about to happen."

She shifted and then I could see what she was doing. She was holding a syringe up in the air, thumping it.

"I am going to wipe your memory, and your sister's."

It took everything I had not to jerk away from her that instant. But she was standing poised between Fiona and me. If I moved, she'd simply turn around and plunge that needle into my sister. I had to wait until she was committed in my direction; I had to wait until she reached for me, and then I'd—

I wasn't sure what I'd do, but whatever it was, I'd better make it count.

"Once your past is gone," the Dream Recorder said, "I will make pets of you both. No one will ever find you, and I will play with you and teach you tricks, and you will be my own personal experiment. My reward, if you will, for waiting so patiently for a single word of explanation from the mainland, for maintaining my end of the bargain until the end of time."

Her bloated face was downright merry. "Now you understand, do you not, why I was willing to answer all your questions? I can tell you anything at all, and in thirty minutes you'll remember nothing. It all drains away, gradually, like water down the sink. And then you'll be quite ill for a time, and while you are out of your head I will plant new memories. I shall tell you stories about your family, about your past. I shall show you pictures and moving pictures. And everything I say, you will believe. You will remember it as if it actually occurred."

Her voice was low and hypnotic. I hadn't drunk any tea—surely breathing the steam couldn't be affecting me— but I felt the pull of her words, the power of them.

She leaned over me, still holding the needle up in the air. I kept a close eye on it, but she wasn't ready to wipe my mind just yet. She hadn't finished boasting.

"That's how we set up this entire island, one mind at a time. One family at a time. Everything you see around you, I made. I and my colleagues, rest their souls. This world is our creation." She gestured, spreading her arms wide, the syringe still held high. "Only identical twins were of any use to us, obviously, and we did not want to waste resources feeding and housing extraneous people. So we set up new families, composed only of identical twins."

The last piece fell into place—that was why Michael Alleyn dreamed of another woman. He'd been married to someone else, and then put here and made to believe he'd always been married to Rosie. No wonder the poor man had been so confused.

The Dream Recorder hovered over me, peering into my eyes. It was hard to stay still, but I did.

"I can tell that you are thinking hard about something," she said. "Are you wondering why the families back home did not object?"

Now that she mentioned it, that was a good question.

In an annoying falsetto she answered herself. "Yes, dear Dream Recorder, why didn't the families object?"

"I will tell you why." She had dropped back into her own voice. "The families didn't know. A virus *supposedly* emerged to which identical twins *supposedly* were peculiarly suscepti-ble, thanks to *supposed* irregularities in your genetic makeup. A few twins were killed, enough to make it plausible that all other twins should be quarantined. For their own safety, nat-urally. And some of those twins made it home afterwards, but many, sadly, did not. The virus supposedly found them, even in our sterile facility."

She cocked her head, at least as much as her thick neck would let her. "Do you find that ruthless? Heartless? No doubt you do. Your grandfather did, the more fool him. He simply could not see that science is the only truth, and the pursuit of truth justifies everything." She winked at me. "And what the pursuit of truth does not justify, national security does."

Then, with no warning, she brought down the syringe.

I almost wasn't fast enough. I reached up and caught her wrist in both of my hands, flinching away, the point of the needle only a couple of inches away from my shoulder.

The Dream Recorder gave one quick gasp of surprise, but then she was grabbing my right wrist with her free hand, her fat fingers digging hard into the nerves between my bones. Pain shot through me like an electric shock and my fingers opened.

Before she could do the same to my other hand I twisted in the chair and raised my legs, shoving against her fat belly with both feet. The air went out of her but she didn't let go of my wrist, jerking me out of the chair as she staggered back-wards. Now I was on my feet, struggling for some advantage, but she was so heavy and she wouldn't let go of me and I couldn't let go of her because she'd turn on Fiona.

"Help!" I screamed at the top of my lungs. Fiona had left the door cracked—maybe someone outside would hear.

We struggled awkwardly, desperately, each with only one free hand. Her other held the syringe, and I kept hold of that wrist. I clawed at her face but she blocked me; she reached for my neck, her thumb extended, but I shoved her hand away. I wasn't getting anywhere and she had the advantage—one slip and that needle would plunge into me, erasing me.

Then she jerked back hard with the hand that held the syringe, throwing me off balance, and I remembered watching Farrell Dean fight and I stopped resisting the tug and went with it, tumbling against the old woman, making her stagger heavily backwards. She lurched against Fiona's chair and I kicked mine away, coming down on top of her, forcing her to the floor.

Then the Dream Recorder was flat on her back and I was on top of her, pushing the hand with the needle away from me, trying to force it all the way back to the floor by her head, trying to make her let go of it.

Her other hand came up and twisted in my hair, yanking my head back. I clawed at her hand but I couldn't get free, and I couldn't keep shoving the needle away while my head was being pulled the other direction.

"What's going on here?" a voice asked, and my heart stopped. I knew that voice. It was Edgeling.

"Let go of her and get up," he said, sounding closer. "You hired me to deal with her, so let me deal with her."

She'd hired him—we were doomed—he'd hold us down and she'd inject us both and we'd never know our father again, I'd never know Farrell Dean, Meritt—

I felt Edgeling coming toward me, reaching for me, and fear made me desperate. I stopped pushing the needle away and went limp, letting myself be yanked half off of the old woman by her grip on my hair. The needle shot down, toward me. I let it.

At the last second I shoved with both hands, deflecting the needle, angling it toward the Dream Recorder's thigh. She

269

shrieked, struggling to untangle her fingers from my hair, her other hand holding the syringe.

I was holding it too, my hands on top of hers. I pushed it down toward her leg and then, with one sharp shove, I forced the needle into her flesh.

Then I found the plunger and thrust it in.

Chapter 28

Strong arms yanked me up, propelled me away. Then Edgeling let go of me and bent over the old woman who lay twitching on the floor.

I staggered to my sister. "Fiona," I hissed urgently, shaking her. "Get up—we have to go—*get up!*" Her eyes were open. She blinked at me and moved, but spastically, her arms shooting out at awkward angles, her legs splaying. I grabbed one arm and tugged, trying to reach behind her for the gun.

"Get up! I can't carry you—we have to get out of here!"

Edgeling stood up abruptly and turned toward us, and I flinched back, startled. *This* was Edgeling? He was a compact, hard-looking man in his mid fifties, with pale assessing eyes, and if I had seen him that night at the barn—

"What was in that syringe?" he said.

He was the Dream Recorder's enforcer. I wasn't going to tell him what I'd done—he'd kill me for sure if he knew.

"Fiona," I said loudly, putting myself between her and the new threat. "Time to go."

Edgeling crossed his arms over his chest. "She's not going anywhere anytime soon," he said, and suddenly it was all too much for me and I turned toward the door—I had to get help—and then I turned back to my sister because I couldn't leave her alone, not with him. And black spots were rising before my eyes, and the room gave a sort of shiver—but I hadn't drunk any tea, had I, unless I had forgotten, and what would he do to us if we both were vulnerable, unable to move—

"Please let us go," I said, my voice catching on a sob. "Please. I didn't mean to do it. She was going to use it on us."

Edgeling's eyebrows came together. "You seem to mistake me," he said. "You can go wherever and whenever you please, so far as I'm concerned."

I stared at him, trying to focus.

He gazed steadily back at me. "You might try cupping your hands over your nose and mouth," he said, and demonstrated. "You're hyperventilating."

I did as he said, and he stood there and watched me, and after a bit the room began to come back into focus.

Just as it did, Edgeling pointed. "She's about to end up on the floor." I looked down and sure enough, Fiona was trying to sit up, sliding precariously toward the edge of the chair. I helped her, putting an arm around her shoulders, steadying her. Then I clamped a hand back over my face and tried to breathe slowly.

"What did you give Jean?" Edgeling said again, nudging the Dream Recorder with his foot.

This time I answered him automatically, without meaning to. "I'm not sure. She said the injection would wipe out our memories, and that we'd be sick for awhile."

He flashed a sudden grin that vanished as quickly as it came. "Well then. This is the easiest money I ever made, I'll tell you that."

Suddenly, belatedly, I remembered the note Papa had left on the table—Gabriel had negotiated with Edgeling, Papa had said. Did that involve money?

"What did you mean, before?" I said.

"What do you mean, now?" Edgeling's face was deadpan; I couldn't tell whether he was messing with me or not.

"Something about someone hiring you?"

"That's right." A thoughtful expression crossed his face. "But I was told you were aware of it. How is it that you're not?"

I didn't answer.

Edgeling picked up the chair that had been overturned during the struggle and sat down in it, leaning back and propping one ankle on the knee of the other leg.

"So Drewblood didn't get back to you regarding our terms," he said. "It sounds to me as if you people are running around this island like chickens with your heads cut off."

I had never seen chickens with their heads cut off, but it was a vivid image, I'd give him that.

He gave a cursory glance around the room, then shrugged as if to himself, and looked at me. "Drewblood came to see me yesterday. He said he was going to be busy for the foreseeable future and asked if, during that time, I would make sure the Dream Recorder stayed well away from you two. He paid me quite well for the favor."

For a moment he examined me, his face expressionless. "He did not, however, give me to understand that you would be actively seeking her out."

I looked away.

"Good thing I was down the street and caught a glimpse of you coming in. I didn't know it was you, of course, or I'd have dropped by sooner. Your hair was covered. I do have to say I'm curious as to what you expected to accomplish, coming here."

I didn't answer.

"I'd also like to know why Drewblood and the Alleyns are suddenly cozy enough for him to spend a fair amount of his hard-earned wealth to ensure their well-being."

I couldn't help myself; I answered him. "Papa wasn't to

blame for me being stolen. It was the midwife's fault. So now Gabriel's sorry for being so hard on Eric Alleyn for pretty much their whole lives."

Edgeling thought about this. "That makes perfect sense," he said presently. "And you explained clearly and with no wasted words. Well done."

I decided to ignore that. "I knew Gabriel was going to talk to you," I said. "I didn't know he'd *hired* you, that's all."

"Of course he did." Edgeling's pale eyes were unreadable. "My services are never free."

Fiona was sitting up on her own now. She raised her hands carefully, as if unsure whether they'd obey orders properly, and pressed them to her temples.

"Does your head hurt?"

She gave a tiny nod. "I'm so sorry," she whispered. "My fault."

I hugged her. "Could you hear what she was saying?"

Fiona gave another small nod. "She was going to destroy our memories," she said, still in a whisper.

"Your uncle told me about the plague." Edgeling jerked his chin at the syringe still quivering in the old woman's leg. "Is that what caused it?"

"I think so." If Gabriel had told him that much, I might as well tell him the rest. "How old are you?" I asked him.

He laughed, surprising me. "You're definitely the one from the other place."

"I told you I was."

"Yes, but I never believe anyone's say-so. I require verification. You speak differently than we do, and you clearly don't know that it's rude to inquire as to someone's age."

I looked at Fiona; she nodded confirmation. "More so with women," she said. "Men generally don't care."

Edgeling gave another sharp laugh. "She's right. I don't care. I'm fifty-four. Why do you want to know?"

"The Dream Recorder said they wiped everyone's memories and built families here out of only identical twins. That happened fifty years ago, which means that everyone older than fifty was deliberately put here. It means you were brought here as a four-year-old."

I waited a moment, letting that sink in. When he rolled his hand, telling me to go on, I did.

"So the people who raised you weren't your parents. Your real parents were told you died of a virus. You and your identical twin. They put you here, and put your twin on the other island."

Edgeling didn't look surprised; but then, I thought he prided himself on not ever showing surprise.

"I don't have a twin," he said, putting both feet flat on the floor and leaning forward, his elbows on his knees. "Drewblood told me about the experiment. He asked whether I'd ever seen that city—your place—in dreams. And I haven't. Not ever. Not once. Not even back when I occasionally took Dream Drops."

"But—"

"I don't know why they wanted me here, given that I'm not a twin. Maybe they didn't." He gestured at the old woman lying on the floor. "Maybe she lied to you. She's fairly free with lies, you know."

"I don't think she lied about that."

He leaned back in his chair, looking at me. "Get to the point," he said.

"On the other island I worked in the fields," I said. "There was a farmer who supervised. He's your brother."

For a long moment Edgeling looked at me. He didn't blink, and his expression didn't change.

"He's a good farmer," I offered. "I think he's probably very good, given the circumstances. But all the same they're in trouble, over there. They're going to starve, if they aren't killed first by the Watchers. They're the experimenters over there. So we're going back to help."

"Exactly who is going *back*, as you put it? More than you and the two boys, presumably, or you wouldn't have bothered to come to this island in the first place."

At his casual mention of Farrell Dean and Ezzie, a chill ran through me. He had been perfectly willing to let his men kill them. Did he really do anything people wanted, as long as he got paid?

"Most of my brothers are going," I said, feeling weary. "And my father, and Gabriel."

"And Tor," Fiona said faintly.

Edgeling looked, for the first time, a little off balance. "They're going away? Off the island? All of them?"

"All but Sean are going." Then I corrected myself. "Actually, they're already gone. They left without me. Do you have a boat? I need a boat."

"No, I don't. And I wouldn't give it to you if I did. It's a poor risk."

"But you could come with us." The words surprised me even as I said them. I was inviting *Edgeling*?

I was. "You could protect your investment," I said. "You could come along and take care of your boat, and know you were doing a good deed."

"I told you I don't have a boat. And I don't do good deeds."

"Oh. Well, you can still come."

I was practically begging; and why? This was Edgeling, not my farmer.

Still, he was wily, able-bodied, experienced with conflict, and—since he'd almost shot Mick—I knew he could handle a gun.

For some reason Edgeling was beginning to look almost amused.

"What?" I said.

He looked at me, half smiling. "You don't have a boat," he said. "But you half think that if you want it badly enough, you'll find one."

"So?"

"So, good luck to you. But even if your boat materializes, I'm not going with you. Gabriel Drewblood gone, Eric Alleyn gone. Someone has to stay and help the Council Chief run this place. That'll be worth a fair penny, I reckon, stepping in to help the Council. No, I'm not going anywhere."

Then his expression changed. "But at a guess, my guns are."

Chapter 29

By the time Fiona was able to walk and we made it to Sean's house, the rain had stopped and the air had that autumn smell, wood smoke and wet dirt, and a hint of cold coming fast.

Rain was waiting for us, pacing up and down beside her banged-up truck.

"Where have you been?" she said, coming toward us. "Sonia said she hadn't seen you. She's off to run errands."

I didn't want to tell her what we'd done. "We're here now," I said. "Did you tell her we're going to Locria?"

Rain nodded.

"Sean won't like it," Fiona said, sounding subdued.

"Sean will be glad you're in good hands."

Fiona threw a skeptical glance at Rain, who laughed. "Not me," she said. "Him."

We looked where she pointed. Earl was coming around the corner, talking with Will.

"He won't let me go to Locria without him, and therefore you can't go to Locria without him."

Fiona looked relieved. "Sonia knows he's with us? And she'll tell Sean?"

"Yes, and yes," Rain said. "And she packed a lunch for us, and Earl and Will have picked up a few things as well, just in case we have to stay the night, since we're getting off so late. And the truck's repaired."

She was acting as if everything was fine between us; I wasn't going to complain, given that I wanted to get to Locria—and I wanted to go right then—but I wasn't exactly feeling warm and loving toward her either.

Fortunately for the rest of us, Earl wouldn't let Rain drive. He drove us, smoothly and efficiently. Outside the rain spattered hard against the windshield, as if someone were flinging handfuls of gravel at us, before settling back into a light patter.

We were all crowded—Fiona and me in the back seat with all our supplies, and Earl, Rain and Will in the front. But I didn't care. I was thinking about what Edgeling had said.

Gabriel Drewblood was gone. Eric Alleyn was gone.

So it was unlikely, but surely possible—

"Here's something I don't understand," Will said, turning as best as he could to look at me. "If this Meritt is a Guardian's son, then how did he end up inside the city?"

"His mother lived in the city," I said. "He was born there. We didn't even know his father was a Guardian until we were leaving the island."

"He knew," Rain said. "Surely he knew before you did."

"Why? None of us knew our parents. Meritt grew up in the city, just like the rest of us—he's one of us, he's our friend."

"Yeah, right," Rain began, and I said, "Don't start," but Will spoke over both of us.

"Fiona's not feeling well," he said. Sure enough, she was looking a little green.

Earl glanced over his shoulder. "Do you need to stop?"

"No," she said. "I'll be okay."

"Be quiet and let Fiona rest." Earl's tone brooked no argument, and for once Rain didn't argue.

When we finally reached Locria, the clearing in front of the trading post was empty. Earl pulled to a stop and we all piled out, stiff-legged, glad to be free from the cramped truck.

Leaving the others still stretching by the truck, I walked to the edge of the clearing, to the place where the ground sloped down toward the water. I knew the men really were long gone; Sean had said so, and the absolute silence of the place told me he was right. Still, I wanted to see for myself.

Ahead of me the pale sand rolled smooth and unmarred right down to the sea, murmuring quietly far back in its bed. It had looked so different when Rufus and Farrell Dean and Mal had been working on the engines—cluttered with tools, streaked with footprints, gouged by heavy boat parts. Now no boat was in sight, and not a single footprint remained to show all the activity that had taken place. What the sea hadn't covered, the wind had wiped smooth.

An unexpected lump rose in my throat. They really had left me. Farrell Dean had left me.

Without a word to the others, I started down the slope toward the sea, struggling in the soft sand. The wind was cold and salty, but the tears on my cheeks were hot. Angrily I brushed them away; against all logic, I hadn't truly believed he'd leave. I'd half thought he'd be here waiting for me.

"Where are you going?" Rain called.

"To look for Mal," I said without turning around. "Wait here. He's shy."

The going was easier when I reached the smooth wet sand, and I headed in the direction of the inlet where Mal had stored his boat. I didn't particularly expect to find him there, but it was a place to start. Mostly, though, I needed a few minutes alone.

The tide was just thinking about coming back in, pushing toward shore. Above the whistle of the wind the water murmured knowingly, and I wondered whether the same whispers reached the shores of Optica.

When I reached the little cove—which was empty, of course—I checked to make sure I was completely out of sight of the others. Then I climbed up on a flat boulder and sat down, pulling my feet up and wrapping my arms around my knees. I sat there for several minutes feeling sorry for myself, looking out across the choppy gray water, more tears spilling down my cheeks.

Finally I decided it was time to get a grip. I couldn't do anything to help my friends in Optica, but I did have questions that needed answers.

I ducked my head to wipe my cheek on my shirt, and when I looked up again, Mal stood between me and the sea. He was wearing a scarlet shirt rolled to his elbows and looked scarcely less remarkable than the last time I'd seen him, though his designs were now mostly covered.

"You are sad," he said. Behind him the sea swept forward and backward, going about its business.

"They left without me," I said. "Of course I'm sad."

I climbed down from the rock, feeling stiff and cold, scraping my wrist on the rough edge.

"The most frustrating part," I said, "is that we have a friend over there who's in danger, and nobody wants to help him."

It seemed important that I make someone understand, and perhaps explaining about Meritt would inspire Mal to be unusually forthcoming. "He's trying to help us, but his father is a bad person, so nobody believes the son could possibly be good."

Mal's expression didn't change, but something in his eyes did.

"This friend—his name is Meritt—they won't give him the benefit of the doubt, and he could get killed. I really wanted to go back so I could warn him."

Mal seemed to be considering this carefully. His pale gold eyes were fixed on mine, but I couldn't read whatever thoughts were passing behind them.

"Sometimes a son is not like his father," he said after a moment. "Sometimes he is like the man who raised him instead."

He'd brought the conversation around to exactly where I wanted it to be. Come to think of it, the last time I was in Locria he'd also brought up the man who'd raised him.

"You wanted me to know," I said. "You didn't want to tell me, but you wanted us to know it was Michael Alleyn who raised you."

He shifted uneasily and didn't answer.

"He drew those designs on you," I said. "They match the handkerchiefs his wife used to make for him."

Mal threw a quick glance over his shoulder, as if making sure that we were still alone.

"Yes," he said, very softly. "It is true."

"Granny Rose knew." I wasn't at all sure, but I used the Locrian method.

He hesitated, and then nodded.

"Did she ever see him after that?" I said. "Did he ever go back and check on his family?"

Too many thoughts were coming at once, and I couldn't put them all into proper Locrian statements. And even if he'd wanted me to know Michael Alleyn had raised him, Mal didn't seem to want to be having this conversation. He had turned and was looking out toward the sea, facing half-away from me. I didn't want to scare him away.

"Michael Alleyn pretended to die in order to protect his family," I said carefully. "He remembered the experiment and the Watchers, and he pretended to die and ended up taking you in. Eventually he told you all about it. That's why you knew about the experiment. I should have wondered how you knew, that first day we came. I thought you'd overheard us talking, but you knew because Michael Alleyn had told you about the twins—" I broke off.

Mal looked around, as if to see why I'd stopped.

"Why would he think he could fake his death?" I said. "It doesn't make sense. They weren't just watching with cameras—they were watching his mind. He couldn't hide from them here. He couldn't hide from them anywhere. He knew that. It was his idea in the first place."

Reluctantly Mal turned toward me, more or less.

"Sometimes people believe things are a certain way, when they are not," he said. "Sometimes people remember, but not all at once."

I thought back over what the journal had said, and what it didn't say. "He thought hiding would work, and only realized later that it wouldn't. So what did he do, once he realized they could still see him?"

Mal shifted, scanned the rocks around us. He obviously wasn't going to answer me, so I kept talking, half to myself. I thought I was right; he was acting like I was right.

"When he realized they could read his mind, he knew that we were still in danger, and that you were in danger, too. Anyone he cared about would be in danger, he thought, because he was being punished for going against his brother. And so—" I sure hoped Mal wouldn't run off—"he died again. You said so."

Mal didn't look at me. "I said he was gone."

That was what I had realized, listening to Edgeling. Eric Alleyn was gone, he had said. Gabriel was gone.

The man who'd raised Mal was gone.

I took a deep breath.

"Michael Alleyn," I said, and Mal turned to face me, his pale gold eyes expectant. "The watchmaker. He's still alive."

Chapter 30

We waited impatiently on the beach, the waves creeping ever closer to our feet. Mal had been gone several hours now; we had eaten, rested, poked randomly around in the woods. Now it was long past dark, and I was tired, and the others were beginning to think Mal would not return.

"If Michael Alleyn has hidden from you all these years, why would he show himself now?" Rain said.

I let Fiona answer. "Because now we know he's still alive," she said. "And besides, it's all unraveling. There's no point in hiding any longer."

"Mal should have said something before," Rain said.

"He couldn't," I said. "Not outright. Locrians don't. But he tried."

And he had—he'd even flaunted his drawings, that chilly morning, waiting for Rufus or me to recognize them.

"He didn't try hard enough," Rain said.

She was in a strange mood, contrary and impatient—more contrary and impatient than usual, that is. I didn't know why—Fiona and I were the ones about to meet our long-dead grandfather, and Will his long lost friend. Rain and Earl were just along for the ride.

Maybe that was the source of her fidgets. She liked to be front and center, I was figuring out.

"How long are we going to stand around?" she said. "At some point we'll have to give up and find a place to sleep. *Not* in the bad house, thank you very much."

No one answered her. Like me, everyone else probably wished she'd just be quiet.

At least it wasn't raining, though the wind was still blustery and cold. High above us mackerel clouds scuttled across the moon.

"Someone's coming," Earl said, and we turned in the direction of his gaze. Sure enough, far down the beach were two figures, a tall one and a shorter one. They walked along the waterline, the rising tide curling white and foamy around their ankles, sinking back, returning. It must be almost midnight; the men had been gone from Aislin for twenty-four hours.

When the figures drew close I could see that the shorter one was in fact Mal, his twisted braids standing out around his head. The tall one moved easily, despite his age. He had straight shoulders and long pale hair that lifted in the sporadic gusts of wind.

When they were about a hundred feet away, Fiona started toward them. I followed her, and Rain started to as well, but Will and Earl each put a hand on her arm, stopping her.

"Give them a minute," Earl said.

Fiona didn't wait for me. She ran straight up to Michael Alleyn and stopped in front of him. She nodded politely at Mal, but spoke to our grandfather.

"Hello," she said, more breathlessly than the short run merited. "I'm Fiona."

I wanted to tell him my name, too, but I couldn't. I felt paralyzed; I was seeing my dead grandfather. The watchmaker. The one who had started it all.

He was quite old and his face was lined, but he stood straight and looked solid and strong. He was wearing dark pants rolled up around his ankles, and a white shirt rolled up to his elbows. His striking silver hair grew back from his forehead and fell past his shoulders. His eyes were light—in the moonlight I couldn't tell what color, but I thought either blue or gray.

Fiona gestured at me. "This is Valentina. She goes by Red because, well—" Suddenly, unexpectedly, she laughed. "You can't tell in the moonlight, but she has red hair. We both do. Like Papa and Granny Rose. We're your grand-daughters, of course. I should have said that before. Your youngest grandchildren. And you're Michael Alleyn."

My voice came back. "The watchmaker," I said.

Michael Alleyn looked at me sharply.

Fiona shifted, and vaguely I realized that she disap-proved, that I'd shorted the normal introductions and leaped straight into deep water.

But Michael Alleyn didn't seem to mind. "That's what he called me, yes."

His voice was deep and had a sort of authority to it, as if he had once been accustomed to being heeded. He paused for a heartbeat, studying our faces, and then went on.

"It was irreverent and inaccurate, that name, and I asked him to stop, but he merely laughed. I'm sure he thought it most humorous, later, to have the watchmaker bounded in the watch. A failed savior, and doomed to fail before the world began."

I wasn't sure I fully understood, but something in his eyes made me hesitant to ask. I wasn't afraid—he wasn't at all threatening—but there was so much distance behind his gaze, so much time. So many years of pain and confusion and loss and guilt.

Tentatively, I asked a different question. "Did you learn to hide your thoughts from him?"

"I haven't felt him for some time," he said evenly. "Did I

learn to block him out, or did he grow more adept at hiding his presence? I do not know. How can I say for certain?"

"I can say. He isn't watching you, not any longer."

My grandfather raised his eyebrows. "Is he not?"

"The time of the ashes—here it was a dark haze that lasted an unusual length of time—do you remember that?"

He nodded, never taking his gaze from my face.

"I think he was on the mainland then," I said. It occurred to me just in time that Michael Alleyn might actually be a little sorry to hear this news, and I gentled my tone. "I think he was on the mainland when it was destroyed, about twenty years ago. No one seems to have seen or heard from him since, not here, and not in Optica."

For a long moment my grandfather stood motionless.

"He's gone," I said again, and then, so there could be no misunderstanding, "Your brother, Meritt Alleyn, is dead."

The waves rushed around our feet, murmuring loudly. The moon shone on the shimmering waves. Michael Alleyn's chest rose as he took a long deep breath, then fell as he released it. He shut his eyes and seemed to be gathering himself. Then he opened them again, and his face grew wry.

"So for twenty years I've punished myself more effectively than anyone else has ever done," he said. "I separated myself from my family for no good reason."

It was a terrible thing. I couldn't think of anything comforting to say. All my life I'd been separated from my family, but not by choice; his situation was far worse.

Fiona pushed her hair back from her face; the wind was rising, cold and erratic. "You were trying to protect us," she said. "It was a noble thing to do."

Michael smiled at her, though his expression was still pained. "I hoped he would leave the rest of you be, if I wasn't there to watch you suffer. But it didn't work, did it?"

He looked at me, and I could tell he was seeing

specifically me, not a duplicate of my sister. "They went ahead and took you," he said, "even though I was gone."

I nodded. "I don't know why they did that," I said. "Angel knew the experiment was over before I was born, but he stole me anyway."

Michael Alleyn looked startled. "Angel?"

"The Guardian who stole me. That's his name. There must have been someone before, because he isn't old enough to have been involved right from the start. Maybe you knew the one who came before him."

My grandfather's face closed up.

"We know you tried to stop the experiment," Fiona hastened to tell him. "Will Bright—" she gestured back down the beach—"He told us you didn't want this to happen. And the Dream Recorder said you'd been punished for trying to intervene."

Michael Alleyn relaxed, just a little. "He has remembered?" he said, looking down the beach to where the others waited. "Will's memory has returned?"

"Not all of it. Just a little." Something struck me. "Why did your memory come back so soon? Everyone else is still mostly oblivious, but you started to remember years ago."

Michael Alleyn looked away from Will and at me. "I suspect that was part of my punishment," he said. "Most of my punishment, in fact. If I didn't know what I'd lost, what I'd done and failed to do, what I'd forgotten, then I wouldn't know to grieve. And I wouldn't know to be afraid. This Angel—is he still alive?"

I nodded. "He's alive, and so is Sir Tom. Thomas—" I tried to remember the rest of his name but couldn't. "There are other Guardians, too, but they're insane because of the time of the ashes. Because of whatever they got into, going to check on the mainland. And Sir Tom feels terrible for helping with the experiment. He wishes he hadn't."

Michael Alleyn's face was thoughtful. I wished the light were better—I was having the strangest feeling of déjà vu, and I thought if I could see him clearly I might be able to tell what echoes I was catching in his face—Mick or Rory, Angus, Rufus, Sean. And surely Eric Alleyn wore some trace of his father, even if he took more strongly after Granny Rose.

"The Watchers are still there," Fiona said. "That's why Red came to get help."

Michael nodded. "Mal says the situation there is very bad."

I tried to imagine that conversation. How on earth had Mal told him everything—so many things Michael didn't know—with the handicap of Locrian conversation? No wonder it had taken him hours and hours.

Naturally, Michael wanted more details. "What exactly are these Watchers doing?" he said.

I hated to tell him; he carried enough guilt already. But I didn't know how to evade the question. "The old people, the ones you knew—the volunteers who got sent to Optica instead of here—they're about to be killed. But Angel has a son named Meritt who's a good friend of mine, and he's trying to protect the old people until Eric Alleyn and the others can get there."

Fiona moved uneasily but didn't contradict me.

Michael glanced at Mal, then back at me. "And you are sure my brother is dead?"

"Pretty sure. The Watchers talk about your brother as if he's alive, but that's only because they're isolated, there in Optica. But Sir Tom sent people to the mainland, and all the places they went to had been destroyed. Your brother would have been, too."

Michael Alleyn nodded. "Good," he said, and then reached out and drew Fiona and me to him. "I am glad to see you both," he said. "More glad that you will ever know."

Fiona and I hugged him, and he felt solid and warm there on the cold beach, with the wind crying insistently and the shining waves washing around our feet. He smelled like pine needles and I wondered where he'd gone to live, once he felt he had to leave Mal, and whether he had spoken with Mal at all since then. He had exiled himself from everyone he loved in hopes that his brother wouldn't look through his eyes and see who else to torment, but surely he hadn't gone years and years without speaking to a single soul.

But that wasn't a question for now. It would wait, as would my other questions. Michael was an old man, and this had surely been a shock to him. I could give him time to adjust to us, and to the news that his brother was dead.

For, unfortunately, I had plenty of time. It wasn't what I wanted—I wanted to step into the tide right then, and be borne across the sea to my father, to Meritt and Farrell Dean and my brothers and friends. But at least it was something. I'd accomplished something. I'd found the watchmaker, and talking with him—piecing everything together, in the coming days—would at least give me something to help pass the time while I waited.

After a long moment Michael Alleyn put Fiona and me gently away from him. "The others have been gone a full day," he said. "My son. My grandsons."

We nodded.

"I can't undo the past." He turned to look out over the choppy moon-washed sea. "The moving finger writes," he said. "And having writ, moves on. Nor all thy piety nor wit shall lure it back to cancel half a line, nor all thy tears wash out a word of it."

He spoke half under his breath, and he wasn't speaking to us. His words made me want to hug him again, comfort him; and they made me want to run away. Most of all they made me feel young and strangely unscathed.

After a long moment he looked down at me. "What's done is done," he said. "I cannot unwrite the past or undo whatever harm befell those whom I forgot. But it's possible that you have given me the means to change the future."

Then he turned away from the sea and away from us, toward Mal, who was waiting patiently a few steps away. A look passed between them, long and thoughtful. The wind blustered, lifting Michael Alleyn's long pale hair, stirring the dry sand further up the beach.

I wasn't sure what was happening, but it felt portentous. I was a little afraid. Fiona reached out and took my hand, her fingers cold in mine.

"They are in danger," Michael Alleyn said to Mal, as if by way of explanation.

Mal nodded. "You are my father, and so they are my brothers," he said.

Michael Alleyn looked at him for another long moment. Then he turned back toward Fiona and me.

"Mal and I will leave tonight for Optica," he said. "Would you care to go with us?"

It was so unexpected that I was struck momentarily speechless.

Fiona wasn't.

"Yes," she said, glancing at me. "Yes, of course we want to go. But how?"

Mal gestured at the swelling sea. "They took my biggest boat," he said. "But not my best."

I found words. "But you said you didn't have another engine."

"Engines are for those who do not know how to sail," Mal said, and grinned. "But if we are to go, we must go soon. The tide will not wait."

Without another word he turned and began walking away. We followed him, collecting the others as we went, explaining to them, trailing behind Mal in an uneven line across the dark wet sand in the light of the gibbous moon.

Michael Alleyn and Will walked side by side, talking in low voices, two old men with one more battle to fight. Fiona stayed close to Michael's other side, slightly behind him, keeping him in sight as if he might vanish while her back was turned. I came next, alone and glad to be alone, thinking about where we were going, listening to Rain and Earl bringing up the rear, conferring with each other, taking up some self-appointed guard duty for us all.

The tide was almost full, muttering loudly against the shore, reaching for our feet. It was cold and secretive, but it knew the way home.

When it turned, I would go with it.

THE END, Book Three

The Red Series

The Watch (Book One)
The Stolen (Book Two)
The Watchmaker (Book Three)
The Forgotten (Book Four)

Visit the author's website
at www.amandawitt.com.

Acknowledgements

All four books in *The Red Series* were family endeavors:

My husband—a professional writer and editor, and former creative writing professor—provided invaluable editorial feedback, copy editing, and proofreading.

My mother—also an English professor—served as another proofreader. Any remaining errors are my fault, because I just kept fiddling around ...

My sister—yet another English professor—gave me a much-needed boost of enthusiasm at exactly the right moment, as did my sister-in-law Laura.

My father gave me a collection of Yeats poems for my nineteenth birthday, thus permanently fixing "The Stolen Child" in my psyche.

And my three (then-teenage) children not only talked me into writing these books to begin with, but also offered constant encouragement and insightful feedback every step of the way.

I am grateful to all of them for their help.

married and won't have to deal with you for the rest of our life."

"Ok, go on, Nisha, go be with whomever you want to and just be happy. I can't say anything beyond that."

Kabir shook his head and sighed. He held her shoulders, shook her in frustration and said.

"Nisha, don't you ever think you could also be wrong? You are actually acting immature. Don't ruin three lives because of your stubbornness."

She tries to be disaffected by his behaviour, shrugs his hands off her shoulders and screams.

"Kabir do you really think Kiran could influence me to break our relation? Do you think that the issue that you blew out of proportion was big enough for me to walk out of the world we created?"

He kept on listening to her.

"Kabir have you ever thought of the problems our relation faced because of you?"

Kabir was shocked at this question,"because of me Nisha??"

"Yes because of you. 'Samar' is your father's name Mr.Kabir S. Singh, but you hated that man all your life. I always tried to resolve the 'S' mystery but you took it so casually. After I forced, you once said it has come from your mother. Why this hypocrisy?"

"I never thought there was any need to mention that Nisha."

"Oh really Kabir!! It was not important for you to mention such an important part of your life to the girl whom you are about to get married. We were not fooling around.. Right!!"

"Ofcourse not." He says.

"You know what you are like one of those chauvinist men who would keep everything to self, let the situation spoil and then blame it on the girl for being to immature to understand love and life. We are two different people Kabir with not just different upbringing but also ideologies. I allowed you to know me and my life completely but you kept on silently living with your past until it spoilt our relation.

I tried every bit to make our relationship work. But you kept on thinking that you were the only one in charge of our life. Love and marriages don't work that way. They need a part of you and a part of me.

It's not my fault every time, even you could have been wrong to me, in your words, in your behaviour, in your decisions."

She could not control her emotions and tears begin to roll down her eyes.

"I am sorry for being wrong, Nisha. I am really sorry for being rude to you. I am sorry. I know you are not always wrong. That day I was wrong," he said in a soft, confessing voice.

She looks at him and cries even more.

"Why could you not say that before?"

"I wanted to apologize, Nisha, but you never allowed me. I love you a lot."

He says and she hugs him tight. This one moment is all she wanted, not to make him feel small, but to make him aware and acknowledge that she was not always wrong.

"I am sorry too Kabir, though I don't know for what," she says giving him a sheepish smile. Kabir looks at her astonished and they both begin to laugh.

"Nisha, on a serious note, you still have till tomorrow to decide whether we get married or not. I don't want you to ever complain that I did not give you the time to think. So, please think carefully and decide if you want to be my wife."

****

I spent the rest of the day alone in my room. My family and friends didn't bother me. All I had were my thoughts. I kept going over the conversations I had with Papa and Kabir, again and again.

I kept thinking about how every person in my life from my father to my boss who have come together to plot this drama for me.

I kept moving between anger and sadness. Am I such a selfish person that this was the only approach they could take? Am I so stubborn? Am I really responsible for ruining my relationship with my family?

Should I call up Vikram or should I just refuse to marry? Vikram is a gentleman and I am sure he will agree, but do

I really want to spend the rest of my life with him? Will I be ruining three lives?

If I refuse to get married at all, what would happen to my relationship with my family?

The day and night were long and restless. I couldn't decide what to do and I didn't have a sounding board to help me decide. Mom, Papa, Suraj, Shreyas and Preeti were all in favour of me marrying Kabir. I didn't know who else they had involved in this drama.

I have always wanted everything to work my way and things did work. Kabir Samar Singh loves me, he waited for me for so many years. He stood like a strong wall not letting anyone affect me when Kiran tried to implicate me in wrong doings at work. He did not let the gossip reach me. He loved me all through the time we were not talking. He tried to approach my family through a matrimony site. When that didn't work, he waited for me to grow in my career to the level I wanted. Bhai created this drama, but he never once tried to prove his point of view. Kabir quietly surrendered to everything — my temper, my immaturity, my insults and my ego all because he loves me. Who would have done so much?

Can I be luckier than this? Can anyone be more Right than him? No, no one can be. He has done so much for me, he was always my Mr Right but I failed to realise that. I too should have made an effort to understand him.

He has seen his mother struggle and so was over protective about me, but I failed to understand his behaviour. Had I known, I wouldn't have reacted the same way. How much I wish I had known.

****

Time to face Mr Right.

As I enter the ceremony hall, I see Shriya with her daughter. I guess even she is part of the game. She smiles at me.

"Hey, Nisha, look today I am in red, to show my happiness on your big day."

I don't know how to reply. I glance around the hall to avoid answering and I see my loved ones — my family, my friends. The ones who conspired against me.

Karishma is standing in the corner with her husband and child. She, who supported me during my heartbreak, has come to join me on my happiest day.

Sahu Uncle and his family are looking at me with smiles.

Preeti is also there. Preeti, my childhood best friend, the one who had not just seen Kabir's photo, but was also a part of the game. It was she, who pushed the game forward by forcing me to start the conversation and let him decide if I was his Mrs. Right or not.

All these people whom I love so dearly conspired to bring Kabir and me together. They conspired against me. Do they know if we really are right for each other?

Before I can talk to anyone, Kabir enters the hall. I need to state my decision. Do I continue with the ceremony or not? No, he will not argue even once, if I say 'no' but the entire community is here to view Prakash Chandra's daughter's ring ceremony followed by wedding the next day. Bhai has played this game extremely well.

I don't know what would he get by this? Happiness for everyone.

What would I get in return?

An opportunity to socially accept Kabir Samar Singh as my Mr Right, someone from whom I would never even think of running away. It's like a 'life' trap for me. He will take me to his sea-facing home, keep me happy for all my life. I would work with Bijal's as a VP and he will work as a Director. Our children would study in Bishops and grow up in Mumbai. We will make a happy, perfect couple. Mr. Wrongs would have their lessons learnt for dealing with me the wrong way as Mr. Right walks me into his life.

Kabir approaches me.

"Did you make up your mind?"

I hesitantly nod. I am aware that everyone is focused on the two of us.

"So, Nisha, will you marry me? I promise to keep you happy all my life, will you accept me as I am?"

I look around and see hope. I look into his eye and see love and sincerity. I nod.

"Yes."

That one 'YES' makes such a huge difference in the gathering. The drums start thumping and everybody starts to dance to the beats.

My family and friends cheer as Mr. Right and Mrs. Right finally get together.

Never thought it was so easy. My filmy family had already planned for the day. My friends for life had also come for the big day. It was so nice to see Vikram with his Ms. Right.

A day to remember, a journey walked, so many blessings, such a lovely family, such understanding friends. I can't ask for anything more. Suraj Bhai always lost in the games with me only because he wanted me to win, and this time he won only so that I could win forever.

As Nisha counts her blessings, the family celebrates the grand occasion with Dhara introducing Roma to everyone as her daughter-in-law. Yes, she does keep an eye on Shreyas, who was still surrounded by many girlfriends, invited as guests for the ceremony.

Roma gives him a naughty smile, indicating that Mom is watching him.